A PLACE IN HIS HEART

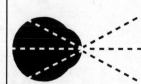

This Large Print Book carries the
Seal of Approval of N.A.V.H.

THE SOUTHOLD CHRONICLES, BOOK 1

A PLACE IN HIS HEART

REBECCA DEMARINO

THORNDIKE PRESS

A part of Gale, Cengage Learning

GALE
CENGAGE Learning·

Farmington Hills, Mich • San Francisco • New York • Waterville, Maine
Meriden, Conn • Mason, Ohio • Chicago

GALE
CENGAGE Learning®

LIBRARY OF CONGRESS CATALOGING-IN-PUBLICATION DATA

DeMarino, Rebecca.
   A place in his heart / by Rebecca DeMarino.
      pages ; cm. — (The Southold chronicles ; book 1) (Thorndike Press large print Christian romance)
   ISBN 978-1-4104-7315-8 (hardcover) — ISBN 1-4104-7315-5 (hardcover)
   1. Widowers—Fiction. 2. Large type books. I. Title.
PS3604.E4544P57 2014b
813'.6—dc23   2014026264

Published in 2014 by arrangement with Revell Books, a division of Baker Publishing Group

Printed in Mexico
1 2 3 4 5 6 7 18 17 16 15 14

In loving memory of
Helen Jean Horton Worley
1919 to 2005
my mother, and always my inspiration
and
dedicated to
Howard M. Worley
my dad, and always my champion

1

October 21, 1630
London, England

Wooden ships languished in the Thames, lolling to and fro, like oxen taking a mud bath. The murky water lapped at the blackened oak as Papa's words washed over her once more. Mary Langton leaned over the crumbled stone wall and buried her face in her arms. How long she wept she could only guess.

Someone moved beside her, but she could not bear to look — could not bear to face anyone. She turned her tearstained face eastward to the great port.

After an eternity, she pressed a handkerchief to her reddened nose and cast a sideward glance. "Papa." She straightened and turned from him. What use would a discussion be?

Her sister approached and hope rose in her heart. An ally, perhaps? No, Lizzie stepped aside, apology evident in her eyes.

Papa's voice was strained, with a sadness she'd not heard since her mother had died. "You shall come to know that I am right, my girl. You might not agree with me today, but you shall see."

"You are wrong about that, just as you are wrong about forcing me to marry Robert." She whirled to face him and raised her chin. "How could you? Please don't do this to me. Papa, the last thing I would want to do is to leave Mowsley and marry someone here in London. I could not bear to leave you and Lizzie. You know that."

Before he could answer, wind and tide came together. Sails snapped. With creaks and groans the ships moved in awkward unison toward the North Sea. The same gust of wind that billowed sails lifted her hat.

She grabbed the brim with both hands, firmly settled it on her brow, and watched the ships as they bumped about, leaving port. Fresh tears pressed from the corners of her swollen eyes to the inky water below. "You might as well be sending me off to the colonies." Her stomach clenched, causing the words to rush out in gasps, and she clutched her waist as she glanced at her father.

His cheeks reddened. "Hush. Do not say that. You know I love you dearly. I have always had your best interests at heart." His voice was rough and strained.

He hurt as much as she did, she knew that, but still the words tumbled out. "Do you, Papa? And Nathan? Was he best for me?"

"Do not speak to me in that tone. I agree. Marriage to him would have been a tragedy, indeed, but 'tis why you must let me take care of you."

It tore her heart to have words with Papa, but desperation urged her on. "I'm sorry, but how many tears must I shed? What must I do to make you see?" She was wailing now.

A second blast of wind caught her hat and sent it cartwheeling down the dock. She grasped her skirt as she raced after it. With her free hand she tried to hold her hair high on her head, but it tumbled down, swirling in the wind.

"Be careful. We shall buy you another," Lizzie called as Mary's boots flew over puddles in the chase.

The errant bonnet came to rest at the foot of the stone bridge spanning the Thames. With a sense of triumph, she scooped it from the mire, then stood to face her family. Her father, shoulders slumped, trudged up the cobbled path toward the shops as Lizzie came to her aid. Thank heavens. What took her so long?

"You should not run like that. You might have broken your ankle and then how would we get you home?" Lizzie's eyes rolled as she shook her head, but a gentle smile played on her lips. "Father says we should go to the milliner's. He has business to finish with Mistress Haskins." She eyed the muddied gray felt with its high crown and wide brim. "It looks worse for wear anyway. Perhaps you shall get a new hat out of all of this."

"Business to finish? I hope it has nothing to do with me and Robert. What shall I do? I do not love him. Not one whit. I shan't marry him."

Her sister's eyes filled with sympathetic tears and the corners of her mouth quivered. "Father is adamant. After what happened with Nathan, he feels there is no other solution. Certainly your prospects for marriage in Mowsley are naught. Perhaps here in London . . . Perhaps Robert . . ."

Mugginess draped her like a shawl. Her nose wrinkled at the acrid stench of the water below. Nathan. What shame he had brought to her family. She pushed her sadness aside. " 'Tis not as if I loved him, Lizzie."

"Whatever do you mean? Nathan? I thought surely after five years you had grown to care for him. You cannot tell me you have no pain, that you did not love him."

"I did not. Truly. I think I was more enamored with the idea of marriage than with Nathan." She folded the cuff of her sleeves back and fiddled with the lace. It looked much like the lace her sister had sewn into the gown for her wedding. She glanced at Lizzie sideways.

Did Lizzie believe her? She would never admit to another being, not even her sister, her love of Nathan. Not after he left her standing on the church steps. "I think by the time Nathan returned from university, he realized I lacked the skills he would need in a wife. Who needs a wife who rides horses and loves numbers? He feared I would rather be out riding than washing his clothes."

"But you loved him, yes?"

She closed her eyes for a moment, bracing herself for the whitish lie. "Lizzie, I only care about the disgrace he brought you and Papa — how the whole village must have laughed at us. But I do not give a fig about

Nathan or myself. I cried over the spoilt feast left on Papa's table much more than Nathan Cadwell. How could he have done that?"

"Disgrace to be sure, but 'tis why you must let Father take care of you. Everyone in Mowsley knows of your disgrace. It was not very manly for Nathan to just abandon you rather than admit to you he had a change of heart. Father truly wants you to be happy. Let him take care of you, Mary."

Lizzie wrapped her arm about her sister. "Tell him you shall marry Robert. Mistress Haskins will be a kind mother-in-law. She's a good businesswoman, and we know she is a good cook — we've supped with them many times. Indeed, you can keep the books for her, as you do Father's, and she'll treasure your help as well as your company."

They followed the narrow cobbled streets, and Mary covered her nose with her damp handkerchief. The perfume of the gardens mingled with the stench of garbage in the lane and underscored the capriciousness of the city. "I always look forward to our trips to London, but once I'm here I long for home."

Her sister took her hand, her voice gentle. "You should know, little sister, Father wants to find a husband for you quickly. And

London is the most likely place to find one. Mistress Haskins's son is a most eligible one."

"Do you not see, Lizzie? It cannot be Robert. I shall never love him." She'd played with Robert when they were little, but as they grew older he treated her in a most awkward fashion, staring at her without saying a word. And with her engagement to Nathan, he had become downright hateful. "You and Zeke love each other and I want that someday too. Besides, he looks rather like a pudgy pear."

An infectious giggle erupted and the two laughed until their sides ached. Lizzie smoothed her stomacher and tried to regain a degree of decorum. "You shall be a spinster if you stay in Mowsley. Father shan't be around forever. Besides, many women who marry for the social status fall in love later. It happens all the time."

"And the men? Do they fall in love?"

"A man would be a fool not to fall in love with you, little sister, but you are not getting any younger."

What could she say? Mary glanced up as the shops came into view and dabbed at the tears that still threatened.

Lizzie seized her arm, directing her into Haskins' Hats. "A wool hat or silk?"

"I — I am not up to looking at hats, Lizzie." She cast a look around, hoping to avoid Papa, Robert, and Mistress Haskins, as if that were possible.

"It will take your mind off your troubles. Come, this is always the favorite part of our trip. Please don't spoil it now. Please?"

Her look was more than Mary could bear, and soon the two buried themselves in feathers and lace. Lizzie tried on a pretty purple silk and Mary noted how it gave her crystal-blue eyes a hint of violet. Her sister's striking black hair, arranged in ringlets and piled high on her head, added to the pleasing appearance. "I always feel so plain when I am with you."

Lizzie doffed the hat and placed it on Mary. "You are so silly. I've always wished for your hair, so long and thick." She reached out to smooth the stray tangles that framed her sister's face. "And your eyes are so pretty. Watercolor eyes. 'Tis what Father calls them."

"Watercolor eyes." Mary fluttered her lashes as she twisted her long hair and tucked it under. "He does, but whatever does that mean?"

Her sister laughed. "It means they change, like they were washed in color with a brush. They reflect your mood. Father says they

14

are just like Mother's. I've always been a bit jealous, truth be told." She smiled. "Shall we try the blue? 'Tis your best color. That and green." She handed Mary the blue hat as she placed the purple back on her own head.

"Ahem."

Mary froze. There stood Papa and he did not look happy.

"You may each pick a hat, if you like. I need to show Mistress Haskins some samples of the felt I brought and speak to her about the wool order. After that we should be on our way. We need to make it to The Swan by nightfall. We shall sup there and stay the night."

Mary met Lizzie's smile with a wan attempt at joy. It looked like there was much more on Papa's mind than felt and wool. She turned to the window but caught her own reflection. Tears sprung, landing on her lashes like dewdrops on asters. What agony. If only her life could remain the same, her world the same comfortable existence she knew growing up.

She wiped at her eyes, picked a hat, and smiled at Lizzie as Papa concluded his business with Mistress Haskins. At least Papa had not mentioned Robert. Hope glimmered.

Stardust, Starbelle, and Starnight stood patiently as the boxed purchases were secured above the pommel of their saddles. Papa lifted both girls to their horses before he mounted his own. Lizzie rode with a ladies' sidesaddle, but Mary much preferred riding astride like the men. It was how Papa taught her and she felt much more in control. They urged the Old English Blacks into a smooth trot. As the sun began its descent, London fell behind. They rode toward Mowsley and home.

Hours passed. The dark clouds scuttled away like the ships in the harbor, while autumn's low sun turned the rolling hills of wheat to a burnished gold. The wind rustled through yellow heart-shaped leaves of the silver birch that punctuated the landscape and brought refreshment to the weary trio. At last, The Swan came into view.

Papa reined Starnight to a walk, and Mary left Lizzie to move alongside him.

He leaned in his saddle and touched her arm. "This is a difficult time for you."

She smiled at him. "Yes, Papa, but I'm all right."

"I am not one to beat about the bush, as you know, my girl. We shall not find a marriage prospect for you in Mowsley. Mistress Haskins's son, Robert, is a fine lad —"

16

"Papa, no."

"Daughter, quiet." With a wrinkled brow, he studied the road. "As I said, he is a fine lad, and his mother adores you. You can help her with her books, as you do for me. You shall always be well provided for. I shall come to London as often as I can and bring Elizabeth and the children. You may come home for visits. You know I love you dearly. I want the best for you, my girl. And may I remind you, there was a time when you were fond of Robert."

"We were six." She shifted in the saddle. "He rather turns my stomach now."

Her hands trembled and Starbelle lost her footing for a moment. "Papa, I will try very, very hard to learn all of the accomplishments of a good wife. Lizzie will teach me. I want to be in love when I marry. I want what Lizzie has."

"My dear girl, Elizabeth's marriage to Ezekiel was arranged long before they married. And they fell in love, did they not?"

"Yes, Lizzie and I spoke about that today."

"Believe me, it could be worse, and you will do as I say. This is my responsibility and for your own good. Your mother would have agreed."

Her voice was soft as she turned back to

her father. "Please, Papa, do not do this to me."

There was no answer and she turned to flash a look toward Lizzie. Had her sister known all along that Papa had made his decision? How could she say nothing in her defense? She took a firm grip on the reins and urged her beloved Starbelle into a gallop toward The Swan.

Night fell quickly, but not soon enough. She wanted nothing more than to hide away in darkness where she could let her tears fall unnoticed. How could she marry a man without the love and passion she thought she'd found with Nathan? How hollow life would be. If only Mother were still alive. Would she say London was her only chance of marriage? Robert her only chance of a husband? Was there no chance of ever finding love?

Barnabas Horton's eyelids fluttered, but the crusted salt of tears held them shut. For a moment he forgot the pain and willed himself to remain in that blissful state between sleep and full consciousness. That place before reality sets in. But the first rays of morning sun made it impossible. He rubbed the grit from his eyes and rolled to an elbow. His fingers gently touched the empty space beside him in the bed. His throat tightened, but he rose and pulled on his long white shirt and breeches. He trudged to the kitchen.

A shiver ran through him. He stirred the embers in the massive fireplace and arranged logs and dried moss in the center. The large cauldron of water in the corner of the hearth would simmer soon. He pressed at his eyes. It should be Ann ladling hot water from the pot. Ann preparing their porridge. Ann. The oppressive air, still thick with the smell of smoke from yesterday's fire, hung like a shroud. *Lord, be my strength.*

A breeze, warmed by the morning sun, drifted through the open casement window. He turned. For a moment he expected to see his dear wife, she felt so near. Clearing his thoughts, he scooped hot water and oats into a small iron pot and hung it from the trammel. Flames sprung up and licked at its blackened bottom. He knew to concentrate on each task, one by one. Get through the morning, then the day. But what to do about the long nights remained troublesome.

A knock on the door interrupted his thoughts. "One moment, if you will." He stumbled over the butter churn as he moved to pull the heavy door open.

19

Plump Lydia Cunningham, basket in hand, stood on the flagstone walk. Susan Howell, small and birdlike, hid behind her. He looked from one to the other. Neither spoke.

He forced a smile, but his face felt like day-old bread. "Good morrow to you. I've yet to open. Pray, might you come back later?"

"Mr. Horton, our apologies for bothering you so early. We are traveling today and wanted to leave our dough with you." Goody Cunningham held out her basket.

"How are your boys, Mr. Horton?" Goody Howell moved forward with her basket but stared at her feet.

"They do well." His shoulders sagged as he took the dough. "The shop closes at five o'clock."

"Aye, we shall be back early to pick up our bread. If it be helpful, we can stay and watch over your sons for you. Late afternoon is a busy time of day."

"It is. Pray thee, know that I do appreciate your offer. The ladies of the village have been most kind. But no. Thank you, but no." He shoved the door shut. The women's voices drifted through the window and he paused.

"He does not look well."

20

"Nay, he is not himself. I miss his cheerful smile. 'Tis only been three months, Susan. Not a wonder he still grieves, poor man."

"I visited Ann's grave yesterday. The blue slate is beautiful."

"The blue slate?"

"Aye, her gravestone. He carved it himself."

He set the baskets down and studied the fire. Ladies from all over the village would be at his door soon. He picked up the fire iron and poked at the logs. Ann appeared in his thoughts. Why could he not keep his mind on work? He forced himself to shift to the matters of the day as he ladled steaming porridge into the bowls. "Boys, come and sit."

They took their usual seats at the worn oak table. Benjamin sat too close to his brother, who immediately rolled his eyes and tried to push him away. Barnabas sent him a stern look, and Joseph, age five, and two years older than little Benjamin, obediently bowed his head and listened as his father led them in prayer and Scripture.

The three ate in silence.

Barnabas gave each boy a bit of bread to wipe their bowls and spoons clean. They popped the bread into their mouths, put their dishes on the shelf, and wiped the crumbs away with a kitchen rag.

"Before the ladies bring in their bread, we need to go to the shop for a loaf of sugar." He banked the fire and swept soot from the hearth. Pulling on his vest, he nodded to his youngest. "Come here, Benjamin, let me help you with your boots." He scooted the boys out the door, then stepped back inside to fetch a black handkerchief and tied it above his elbow.

They marched down the village green, a small hand clasped in each of his. Warm days and crisp, cold nights had dressed the line of old oaks in a splendor of yellow, orange, and red, but their glory was a blur as trickles of sweat wound their way down across his cheeks. Certainly, it was only sweat.

At the shop, he allowed the boys to amuse themselves with various balls of string from the display and went in search of his supplies. He wiped his brow with his sleeve and looked about for the proprietor, Mr. Webb. A young woman stood by the counter. Ah, yes. The new shopgirl.

"Good day, miss. If you please, I am not finding the sugar . . ."

She turned. Her wide hazel eyes reflected the green of her dress as she regarded him.

Fudge. He knew her but could not quite place her. The silk dress with the elegant lace was definitely not one of a shopgirl. She certainly looked pretty.

"Mr. Horton. 'Tis me . . . Mary Langton." A sweet smile spread across her lips. She quickly cast her look downward, a faint tinge of pink appearing on her cheeks.

"Miss Mary Langton? It cannot be. Why, Miss Langton, you were just a wee bit of a girl. Now, look at you — a — a young woman." His mouth felt full of gauze and he diverted his gaze.

"I know 'tis been a long time since you have seen me, perhaps not since my mother died? I remember coming to the bakeshop with her, and you would give me a ginger cake. She always enjoyed your stories. You know my sister, Lizzie — I mean Elizabeth — of course."

"Aye. Your mother was one of my favorite customers and certainly your sister still is."

"She makes all of the bread dough for Papa and me. Cook would rather make it, but Papa insists that Lizzie do it."

"Aye, I see. Our boys are the same age."

"Really? She never told me that. She has two girls as well. Rachel and Ruth."

He studied her closely. "I know." He tried a smile, but his face cracked. "How fortunate to see you today. It has obviously been too long."

A second blush of color sprang across her cheeks. "Forgive me, Mr. Horton, but I fear I prattle on. Pray give your wife my regards."

Long moments passed as he attempted to keep his grief in the private places of his heart. His throat tightened and he struggled to clear it. "My wife —"

"Give that back, Joseph!" Benjamin's forlorn wails filled all corners of the shop.

Barnabas winced and drew a deep breath. "I do believe that is my son. I hope we shall meet again. Now, I must go and see what the crying is about. Since their mother died, they seem to argue and fight constantly. Good day, Miss Langton." He bowed, turned, and hurried to the boys just in time to see Joseph seize Benjamin.

"Mother was right, Benjamin. You will always be the baby. A big baby."

"Stop this now, Joseph. What on this earth is happening here?" Barnabas viewed the string littered across the floor in a tangle of disarray.

"He was making a mess. I was just straightening it out. I told him he shouldn't be doing that, but he doesn't listen to me."

Tears streamed down Benjamin's cheeks. His blond curls and blue eyes reminded

Barnabas constantly of Ann. His heart melted as he stooped down. "Benjamin, let us see who can make the biggest ball. And, Joseph, you must come and tell me when you cannot control him. Do not fight with your brother. There are things that God expects us to fight for, true. But string is not one of them. Do you understand?"

Joseph stared sullenly at the string.

"Yes, or no, Joseph?"

"Yes, Father, but he was —"

"Do not argue. Listen to me." The agitation and tone of his voice gave him pause.

Miss Langton appeared with a sugar loaf. "Mr. Webb said he would add it to your account." Her smile was warm and sympathetic.

"Gracious. Thank you. No doubt I would have forgotten it." His eyes crinkled with a small smile of gratitude as she knelt near Joseph.

"I fear your father is in need of help here," she said. "Shall we pick up string too?"

She handed a strand to Joseph. The four worked at sorting and winding string, and with the last ball returned to the shelf, Barnabas took Joseph's hand. "Thank you, Miss Langton. It truly was a pleasure to meet you once again." He glanced at the scuff on his boots. "I do apologize for thinking you to be tending the shop." He studied her once more. Was she offended by his presumption or was that pity he saw in those lovely eyes?

Miss Langton curtseyed and looked him full in the face, her brow wrinkled, but a gentle look in her eyes. "I am so saddened to hear of your wife's death. You have fine boys, Mr. Horton. I must ask Lizzie if she might have them over to play with Joshua and the girls."

The sincerity in her voice struck him. His own words were not forthcoming — a rare predicament.

Joseph tugged at his hand.

"Thank you, again. You are most kind. I must take the boys home, it will be a busy day at the bakeshop." He bowed. "Good morrow, Miss Langton." Reaching for Benjamin's hand, he tightened his grip and led them out.

As they walked up the flagstone to their home and bakeshop, Barnabas paused. A wooden shutter hung askew. How long had it been like that?

Once inside, he pulled the door shut and sank into his chair. If only he could hide away from the world and allow his grief to consume him. Instead, he brought his sons into his arms and clung to them.

"Joseph." His words were jagged in his throat. "You are so much like me that I fear at times I am too strict with you. I look at your face, and it is like peering into a mirror. I expect much of myself and therefore I expect much of you. I know that is difficult for you to understand." He rested his chin on Joseph's head.

His gaze roamed the room as he took in every detail. The musket leaned against the wall. Ann liked to call it his quart pot, ever since he blew the end off of it. The tallow candle on the wooden beam high above the fireplace was squat and needed to be replaced soon. She never would have let the candle burn so low. Beside it lay the kitchen tongs. The memory of their wedding day, when she'd been presented with the tongs by his mother, caused his throat to constrict. Her pleasure at becoming keeper of the tongs — mistress of their hearth and home — he held close in his heart.

He pulled back and looked into Joseph's large, sad eyes. "Your mother thought I was too harsh with you. If that be true, I am sorry. I love you and Benjamin. You are all I have left of her. I will try to be a better father. I promised your mother I would always keep you safe and I will."

He sat for a while, his sons resting in his

arms. Ann did so many things to make their home comfortable and happy. She could reprimand with a gentle smile. A woman's touch, no doubt. He could never replace her, but did he not owe it to their boys to find a woman to raise them? Ann would want that.

The meeting with Miss Langton came to mind. Her father owned land a few miles north of Mowsley, on the road to Saddington, and did business in wool and felt. Her sister, Elizabeth, he knew to be an accomplished woman, skilled in all of the domestic arts. Mayhap Miss Langton shared some of her sister's domestic acumen. She was certainly lovely to look at.

Mary dawdled as she walked home. Why did her sister not tell her of the death of the baker's wife? Surely everyone in the hamlet knew. Her cheeks grew hot. The black scarf tied around his arm — she hadn't noticed it at first, but she should have. That Lizzie. Ever since their mother died, she always tried to protect her. Always thinking she knew better.

Her mind wandered to young Joseph. You certainly could tell they were father and son. Their hair — a mane, really — glossy and dark brown. And those green, penetrating eyes. She found herself smiling, a first since she'd returned from London. He certainly had his hands full with those two boys. Joseph wanted to be the big brother and take care of Benjamin. He tried to look tough when Mr. Horton reprimanded him.

She breathed in the fresh fall air as she passed a large manor on her right and fields of sheep on her left. Her sister liked living on the village green, but Mary enjoyed the short jaunt to and from the hamlet. As she turned up the lane to her house, she quickened her pace. She pushed open the heavy door and walked through the hall to the parlor. Her father sat next to the gateleg table, reviewing the figures she had given him earlier that morning. She listlessly sat and ran her hand over the green damask of the chair.

"Mary, I see you have returned."

"Papa, yes — yes, I'm back."

"And?" He lifted his eyes toward her expectantly.

"And what, Papa?"

"Did you not go to the shop? I thought you needed your . . . what was it? Soap?"

"Yes, Papa, I did go. I seem to be a bit light-minded today. I forgot my soap. Papa, do you know Mr. Horton, the baker?"

"Of course. His father owns the mill."

"What did Mother think of him?"

"She said he made her laugh. She liked him very much, but it is my impression all of the ladies do." His blue eyes twinkled as he ran fingers through his silvery hair.

"Papa, I have given a lot of thought to what I told you and Lizzie in London."

"What is that, my girl?"

"I need to apply myself to learning the skills every good wife should have."

"Such as?"

"Why, any of the domestic arts."

Her father returned to the list of numbers, then rubbed his eyes. "You will do well to learn from your sister, to be sure. Your mother taught her well. But know that Robert will take you as you are. He worships you, my girl."

Her heart wrenched. Why could he not see that Robert didn't worship her? That he was more a rascal than an admirer. "I think I shall wander now in the garden, Papa." She slipped out the door.

She followed the winding path where spent vines of clingy honeysuckle and sweet jasmine formed an arch. The gardener had been at work preparing to do an autumn planting of sweet peas. She knelt to the plucky herbs and haphazardly picked some thyme and the lemon balm that took over every bare inch. She needed to speak to her sister. And soon.

2

The sun sank from the sky, the last glint of light casting a golden glow across the wheat field. In a moment it would be gone and all would disappear in darkness. Ann's life had been like that — her golden countenance touched everyone she met. Barnabas clenched his hands. He'd been so blessed, but too soon the darkness descended and in an instant she was gone.

The air turned crisp and he walked back into the timber-framed home he built for her years ago. A big house with plenty of room for the many children they dreamt of having. For a moment, Mary slipped into his daydreams. How sweet. And so grown up. She was most likely around twenty, which put him ten years older. A sigh escaped. Or had he just moaned his beloved's name, Ann? He wasn't certain, but thoughts of her brought his attention back to his boys and the bedtime regimen awaiting him.

He wandered into the kitchen, picked up the two mugs he'd left to warm on the hearth beside the fire, and dipped a finger into each. Satisfied, he carried them to the bedroom. "Come, boys, sit and drink your milk."

His sons looked up from their play with hand-carved horses, treasures from Grandfather Horton. Joseph took his brother's horse and put it next to his on the small table, his face sullen. "I don't want to go to bed, Father. I hate going to bed."

He closed his eyes for a moment. How he needed Ann at moments like this.

He let out his breath in slow increments, at the same time reaching for his son. Joseph's wide eyes softened his heart. "Please, I know these times are hard for you. Mayhap we should put your brother to bed, and then you and I go out to the fire and read our Bible. Drink your milk. You too, Benjamin, and I will ready the washbowl for you."

The boys washed their faces and rinsed their teeth. Barnabas tucked Benjamin into bed and looked down at his small son, so much like Ann. His heart squeezed in his chest.

"Say your prayers, Benjamin." How strange his own low, ravaged voice sounded.

The soft words of his youngest drew him back.

"God bless Father, God bless Joseph, and God bless Mother, who is in heaven." Benjamin recited his prayer earnestly, and then as if he could feel the sadness and turmoil in his father, he added, "And God help us all."

Barnabas bent and kissed his son's forehead, blinking back the sting in his eyes. "Thank you." He tenderly tucked the quilt about Benjamin's shoulders. He closed his eyes and a vision of Ann flitted into his thoughts, bent over the quilt, carefully placing her stitches.

Joseph rolled his eyes and with a set jaw marched out to the front hall.

Barnabas followed from the bedroom and found him already settled in one of the two chairs, his head buried in his arms. The fire burned low. He picked up the iron poker and began to nudge the great charred logs. "Are you all right?"

His son looked up, eyes red and brimmed with tears. "No." His voice sounded so small, so sad. "Why did she die? I had the pox. Benjamin, too. It's not fair. I want her to come back."

"Aye, I do too. Joseph, I understand."

"No, no. She was my mother."

"True, Joseph, and she was my life." Air seeped out of his lungs. He eased himself into the chair and picked up the family Bible. He thumbed through the tattered pages. "Grandfather Horton gave me this Bible when I married your mother. He told me the best advice he could ever give me is all in this book. We need God's constant help and blessings. Both are in the pages of the Bible. Your grandfather and I never have agreed about the church, but on God's care we do."

He leafed through the book, searching for the help he needed now. He came to a verse Ann particularly loved, marked by her frayed, blue hair ribbon. He fingered the ribbon for a moment. "Joseph, listen. Philippians, chapter four, beginning with the sixth verse, 'Be nothing careful, but in all things let your requests be showed unto God in prayer and supplication with giving of thanks. And the peace of God which passeth all understanding shall preserve your hearts and minds in Christ Jesus.' "

He carefully returned the blue ribbon to the page as he closed the Bible and looked up at his son. "Do you understand what that means, Joseph? It means do not worry, but tell God your concerns. He will take care of you. He will take care of us. I know it is a very sad time, and I would want your mother back, if God be willing. But even though God has called her home, He has not forgotten us. He watches over us." He saw the intense loss and abandonment in his young son's eyes.

"Father, do you think Mother can see us? If she is in heaven with God, is she an angel too?"

He swallowed hard before he answered. He knew what the Bible said about angels, the heavenly hosts, but he also knew the Bible taught of giving milk to those who were not ready for meat. He regarded his young son. There would be time for him to grow in the Lord and the teachings of the Bible. He would give him the milk for now.

"Son, the Bible tells us that God has angels, beautiful angels. I believe your mother was an angel while she was here on earth. I see no reason why God would not want her to be an angel with Him in heaven. She is probably looking down right now and wondering why I am not putting you to bed."

For the first time in a long time, Joseph giggled. He stood up and turned toward the bedroom. "Good night, Father." He looked up and whispered, "Good night, Mother."

Barnabas breathed a sigh. "Good night,

Joseph, now go to bed." He rose and touched his son's shoulder, thankful that God gave him the opportunity to offer hope. "Let me carry the candle. It's burning low."

They carefully walked to the foot of the bed the boys shared and the flame flickered until it extinguished. Joseph grabbed for his father.

"Stay calm. There are more in the kitchen. Here now, son, let me tuck you in. Close your eyes and say your prayers."

He listened as Joseph began his prayers, then bumped his way to the front room. In the glow of the remaining embers he searched for the tallow candles. None. "Fudge! Is there no end? I cannot keep up with everything. Lord, why did You take her?" How many times would he ask that of God?

Whimpers from the bedroom brought him out of his sorrow and to the task at hand. He stumbled back through the dark and tried to soothe his boy. "I am so sorry. Look, son, out the window. Do you see the starry night? We are not in the dark. Do not be afraid. I am here and God has given us all of those twinkling lights."

He sat by the bed until slumber came to Joseph and then wandered back to the hearth, sank into his chair, and stared at the empty one. The enormity of his loss enveloped him again and smothered the hope he'd shared with his son. Silent wails erupted within his chest, causing it to heave with each wretched gasp.

He searched the depth of his soul. Was there anything he could have done to save her? Guilt engulfed him. Should he have been the caregiver when the boys first took ill? Why had he not called the doctor sooner? If he'd only known.

Exhausted, he leaned his head back. His hand dangled and a warm, fuzzy ball of fur soon rubbed against his fingers. He reached down and drew the small gray cat to his lap. "There, there, Miss Tilly, we will be all right." She looked at him with curious blue eyes.

He stroked her as she gently kneaded his leg with the pads of her paws. With great effort he rose and held her close as he banked the fire, drawing ashes over the few remaining embers. He needed to rise early and start the fires once again.

"Let me put you to bed, little cat." He tucked her between the sleeping boys, then tiptoed to his own bed. He paused and looked to the heavens. His voice was but a whisper. "Good night, Ann." Crawling under the quilt, he sought solace in sleep, but his eyes would not stay shut. *I cannot go on alone. Please, Lord, be with me.*

Mary spread a thick layer of butter over her crusty bread and savored a bite.

Her father walked across the elegant winter parlor to the long, polished table. "You look happy today, my girl. Perhaps only that the green of your dress brings out the emerald of your eyes, but I daresay it's been a long time since you looked this content. Have I ever told you how much you look like your mother? I always knew how she felt, just by her eyes."

"Yes, Papa, a thousand times." She grinned at him as she set her bread on the plate and dabbed at her mouth with the napkin she kept close by. "But you can tell me a thousand times more and I shan't tire. Sometimes I fear I shall forget her."

"Nay, only look in the silver looking glass she left you." His eyes crinkled as he smiled back.

She brushed the crumbs from her skirt, then rose to fetch her hat. She looked at her new felt but chose the simple muslin coif. "I'm going to visit Lizzie, Papa. I shall be home for supper." She stepped close to peck his cheek.

"Very well, my girl. I shall tell Cook. Tell

Elizabeth I send my love and to honor us with a visit sometime." He squeezed her hand.

Mary hurried down the lane but turned back to see Papa at the window, waving. She knew he would be. She gave a little wave and blew him a kiss.

Mostly she liked to linger on her walk to the village, but this morning she kept a brisk pace, with barely a glance at the fall color painting the landscape. Twenty minutes later she turned onto the main road into Mowsley.

To her left, the village smithy paused as she bustled by. "Good morrow to you, Miss Langton."

"Why, good morrow to you." She eyed the nails he tapered with his mallet on a broad anvil. "Four penny nails, Mister Long, or ten?"

He nodded approval. "They be the ten, Miss Langton."

A minute later she was in front of the Fannings' door. She tapped gently and Lizzie appeared, floured from head to toe. They embraced and the familiar scent of yeasty dough emanated from her sister.

"Mary, I didn't expect you. Come in. London was such fun, was it not?"

"Really, Lizzie? I think not."

"Cheer up and fetch a chair. I started my bread dough late last night. Usually, I'd have this to Mr. Horton by now, but of course it needs time and warmth."

Mary watched as Lizzie punched the dough down and worked to shape the mass into fat mounds. Her sister crisscrossed the tops with a sharp knife. "Why do you do that?"

"If you cut a little slit across the dough, the yeast will give one last burst in the hot oven."

"I know you have tried before, but would you teach me to cook? To embroider? I shall be miserable if Papa makes me marry Robert. Please, please, help me." She begged with her eyes as much as her words.

"Why, little sister, of course I will. But do not think for a minute it shall change Father's mind." She placed the loaves in a basket and covered them with a cloth. "Now, would you like to come with me to the bakeshop? Perhaps Mr. Horton would give you a ginger cake like he did when you were a child."

She smiled quickly at Lizzie. "Yes, by all means, I want to go. By the by, Lizzie, you failed to tell me Mr. Horton's wife died. Is that not odd that you would not tell me?"

"Nay, not that odd. You were so crushed

over Nathan you would not even leave your room. I went to her funeral, but Father did not. He stayed home to be close to you. We were both truly frightened for you. To add to your grief would be of no use. Nay, it was much better at the time not to tell you." She handed her the basket. "Now, shall we go? I am late and Mr. Horton will be in a state of ill humor."

The sisters walked arm in arm down the village green, passed the great elm, and turned to the shops. Mary dangled the basket from her arm.

The wind pushed through the bell-cote, raising a gentle peal, and caught their attention. The church, built in the shape of a cross and adorned with beautiful arched windows, was an ancient landmark in their tiny hamlet. The walls were made to endure for centuries with large pebbles and a limestone dressing.

They walked past the chandler and cobbler shops, admiring displays propped in open doorways to lure patrons in. The aroma of freshly baked bread drifted toward them. The bakeshop sat back from the road, just before the turn. Mary raised her nose and sniffed. "I smell ginger. Ginger cakes, do you think?"

"Mmm, yes. Would it not be lovely if I

could bake in my own oven and fill the house with such a heavenly scent? 'Twould cover the stuffy smell of smoke."

Mary filled her lungs with the mouth-watering aroma. Yes, she would love that too, but not with Robert. Oh no, it could not be with Robert.

Barnabas opened the oven door. The black ash had turned to white, but still he pushed his hand in to test the heat. Yes, it was hot enough. He wondered for a moment about Mistress Fanning. She was late this morning, but no matter — he had plenty of dough waiting to bake. He'd best get busy. The boys would be back from their outing with Goody Wentworth and then he'd have his hands full. He placed a fat loaf on the oven bottom. His thoughts drifted to Mistress Fanning's sweet sister, Miss Mary Langton. She had been so good with Joseph and Benjamin.

He knew the stories of her broken engagement — the gossip the ladies liked to share when they came to his shop seemed endless — but no matter. He had deeper concerns to deal with. His Ann was gone. Now Joseph and Benjamin needed to come first. He'd certainly discovered he was lost taking care of himself, and even more lost taking care of his sons. Miss Langton obviously noticed that as well, and stepped right in.

Why did he keep returning to Miss Langton? He had realized the night before, as he lay in his bed ready to give up, he needed to do something or he simply could not, would not go on. Thomas told him the solution was to marry again. Easy for his brother to say, though, with his own sweet-natured wife and darling little girl. Still, Miss Langton . . .

What would Ann think? He knew she would want him to do the right thing for their sons. She would always be the love of his life. He could never love again. Still, Miss Langton had been on his mind almost every moment since they met at the shop and could only be suppressed when he thought of Ann. Of course, the reverse was true. Ann was ever on his mind, unless he was thinking of Miss Mary Langton. What confusion.

The aroma from the oven reminded him how long he had been lost in reverie. He opened the oven door and hot air flushed his face. Carefully, he lifted the browned loaf with his long-handled peel. He gently set it on the table and stepped back to admire his work. As he took a deep breath and inhaled the fragrance of the loaf, the door swooshed open. He looked up and felt his cheeks flush anew. Before him was the object of his thoughts.

Miss Langton looked so pretty in her silk gown, her eyes greener than he remembered. Her white muslin cap did nothing to contain her auburn curls. He watched her walk toward him and as they came face-to-face, neither spoke.

Mistress Fanning took the basket from her sister and held it toward Barnabas. "Mr. Horton, I am sorry to be late today. You remember my sister, of course?"

Miss Langton did a slight curtsey. " 'Tis so nice to see you again, Mr. Horton. How are Joseph and Benjamin?"

"It is my pleasure to meet you once again. The boys do well. They are with Goody Wentworth today."

She stepped toward him, so close she seemed. "Her boys must enjoy playing with Joseph and Benjamin. How nice of her to watch them for you."

"Thank you." Why had he said thank you? She must think him a dolt. "Miss Langton, would you like a ginger cake?"

A blush crept across her cheeks as she nodded.

Mistress Fanning smiled. " 'Tis warm in your kitchen, Mr. Horton."

He turned to her and bowed. "Forgive me. My manners have been appalling of late. Aye, the fire keeps it very warm in here, but I am used to it. The rest of the rooms stay quite pleasant. May I offer you a sip of refreshment?"

"Oh, no thank you. We have sipped quite enough while we labored over this dough." She regarded her sister.

"Oh no, Lizzie, truly I barely touched mine. I feel a bit parched."

Lizzie graciously accepted and Mary noted his pleasure at having their company. He poured three small glasses at the great table, set a platter of thin, crisp ginger cakes down, and invited the ladies to sit.

Mary looked about the kitchen, her eyes growing wider. "I have never seen a kitchen such as this, Mr. Horton. Did you build this yourself?"

"Aye. Ann's father was a baker in London. He had a fine kitchen, a fine oven. When I was betrothed to Ann, I decided to apprentice with him and learn the trade. My own father had been a bit annoyed with me. I stood to inherit a large amount of land and the mill, but we had a bit of a falling out when I married. Not because I married Ann, but because Ann and I shared strong feelings about the church.

"Ah, but that is more than you asked, I am sure. Suffice it to say, after Joseph and Benjamin were born, we repaired our differences. But I do love baking — mixing the flour together with barm and water and watching it rise into a beautiful manchet. Or adding sugar and spices to make a tasty cake. Do you see the large fireplace? I can manage three fires all at once." His smile told her he sensed her awe, and she looked away quickly lest he laugh.

She looked at the red brick and various pots, kettles, and red ware. "What a fine meal that could be prepared with a hearth such as this. Do you cook your dinner here as well?"

"Aye, indeed. Some of my customers bring me a fat goose or turkey to roast, but I have plenty of room and can always manage a pot here or there for our own meals." He studied her for a moment. "Do you cook, then?"

A warmth blossomed on her cheeks. She chose her words carefully. "Papa has a cook, and she is very possessive of her kitchen. Indeed, she is miffed that Lizzie does all of our bread. But Papa wouldn't have it any other way. To answer your question, I do not have much opportunity."

Lizzie smiled. "When I was growing up Mother insisted Cook allow us in the kitchen. Mother wanted us to be accomplished in the womanly arts, all of them. Cook was very territorial in her kitchen, so when Mother died 'tis not surprising Mary's lessons did too." She reached out and patted Mary's hand. "You were still so young and I was married. I wanted to take you in, to teach you as Mother would have, but Father needed you." Her violet eyes puddled.

Mary squeezed her sister's hand as her throat tightened. A small fluff of soft gray fur rubbed against her skirt. Grateful to change the subject, she lifted the dainty cat to her lap. "Ah, and who is this little miss?"

"Tilly. Every baker needs a Miss Tilly." His smile was as warm as the room. He turned to her sister. "Mistress Fanning, would you like to take some ginger cakes to your children?" He stood up to find a sack to put them in.

"Why yes, they would like that very much. Ruth asked about them today."

"I will give you a dozen." He counted out twelve, then looked at Mary again and grinned as he added one more. "We shall make that a baker's dozen." He sent them on their way, insisting they were a gift, no payment necessary.

3

As the two sisters walked toward home, Lizzie was the first to break the silence. "Mr. Horton surprised me, to say the least."

"Why so?"

"He has been so somber, so much in grief. I wondered if he would ever recover. I have not heard him speak two words to anybody since his wife died. But look, I thought we would have to beg for a ginger cake and he gave us a sackful."

"I am so glad he feels better, then. I meant to give him my condolences, but truly, I did not want to see the sadness in his eyes."

"I think that best. At this juncture, if he may be happy for a moment or two, 'tis a good thing for him." She glanced quickly at Mary and looked away. "I have worried that you could never find a suitor in Mowsley, and look at you! You managed to catch the eye of the most eligible man here. I think most people assumed Mr. Horton might not be looking so quickly."

Mary darted a glance at her sister, her face warm. "Whatever do you mean?"

"Do not tell me you did not notice he could not take his eyes off of you."

"Nay, sister, I did not notice. Truly."

"If that be so, 'tis only because you could not take your eyes off of his kitchen." A giggle escaped. "To be sure, he noticed you, little sister."

Mary's heart did a timid flutter. Could that be true? Would it be possible that Mr. Horton might fall in love with her? Might want her in marriage? But what if he knew she was completely inept? "I am sure you read too much into that, Lizzie."

"Nay, and something tells me you are attracted to him. Remember, Father expects you to do as he bids. Do not get any silly ideas in your head, little sister. Besides, it would not work."

"What, Lizzie? What would not work?"

"You marrying the baker." She grabbed her sister's hand. "Now, I do not mean that in an unkind way."

"I know what you mean. His wife was perfect, you told me that."

" 'Tis more than that, little sister. You heard what he said about Ann and their beliefs. He meant they are reformers. Father

51

would have a fit. Besides, you want love, do you not?"

Mary continued in silence. Better not to say anything about the tug in her heart. Was it love? Could love cast its arrow and hit your heart that quickly? It certainly felt like that was so.

She knew there were those who wanted to reform the church. They didn't really want to leave the church, just get rid of all that pomp. Still, it was a dangerous point of view, and Lizzie might be right. Papa would have a fit.

But the bigger question was, could she perfect the womanly arts? That was an obstacle not so easily overcome. But she must strive for it, for she would not marry Robert. That was all there was to it.

They walked up the path to Lizzie's door, pink cottage roses crowding about on each side, fragrant with perfume. Ruth ran to relieve her mother of the delectable sack and Rachel jumped into her auntie's arms. Mary squeezed her and covered her cheek with kisses.

As she said her goodbyes, with promises of returning on the morrow, Zeke, with Josh close behind, returned from chopping wood.

She gave her brother-in-law a quick hug and her nephew a shower of kisses. "My, you smell of moss. I can tell you have been out tramping about in the woods." She laughed as her nephew wiped the kisses away.

She bid them all goodbye and followed the lane back home toward Saddington, admiring the bold orange and gold leaves of the magnificent oaks. Lizzie kept a perfect home. And Zeke and the children surrounded her with love and adoration. That made Lizzie the perfect teacher, did it not? Lizzie's comment about Mr. Horton popped into mind. She would work very hard. If her sister and Ann could be so capable, she would apply herself until she was too.

Lizzie was generous with her time and suggested the lessons begin with stitch work. Mary moped as they laid out a length of linen and cut out the rectangles and squares that would become a smock for Rachel.

She listened as her sister instructed her to choose a fine needle and equally fine linen thread, but her mind was on Mr. Horton. She tried to keep her promise and center herself on the task. At last Lizzie suggested that in addition to sewing lessons, Mary might benefit from accompanying her to the bakeshop.

With that, Mary's enthusiasm for all

things domestic flourished. Daily the children delighted in their aunt's attention and sampled the goodies that she and their mother brought from the bakeshop, courtesy of Mr. Horton. Rachel romped about in her new smock as Mary worked on a new one for Ruth.

With each day that passed, she came to know more of Mr. Horton and his sons. Lizzie was right. He did seem to regard her in a special way. She thought of him at odd times of the day. His high forehead and prominent cheekbones, set off by a ruddy complexion, were attractive, and his beard rather dashing. She knew she had fallen in love with him, but could he feel the same? Perhaps it did not matter. He needed a mother for those boys, and she needed to escape the impending engagement Papa planned to Robert.

As they walked home one day, arms full with breads of different grains and a sack of ginger cakes, she finally admitted her passion to Lizzie. "I find myself thinking about his eyes. Have you noticed they are green, like moss? And it seems when I look into them, they are a very window to his soul. I think he is a kind, honorable man."

"Mary, listen to you. You speak like you are falling in love. Can that be so?"

She felt warm blood flood her cheeks. "I do feel enflamed with love, Lizzie, but I know he is in love with his wife. He shan't love again. He needs a mother for his children. But still, I need a family. Sometimes I find myself sitting in the garden and dreaming about Mr. Horton and what it would be like to be married to him. I think it could be very good for me."

They approached the door and it swung open. Zeke offered to take their baskets.

"I've warned you what Father will do if you persist in this, but I know you too well. You are strong-minded, just like him. My best advice is to give Mr. Horton time to heal. Mother would tell you that too. He's like dough. It looks sturdy, and yes, it can take much pummeling. But it needs time and warmth. Give him time and warmth."

"What say you? Giving our Mary love advice again?" Zeke grinned at Mary as they entered. "Do not listen to your sister. I do not know of whom she speaks, but I can tell you, when it comes to love, give no man time." He winked. "Someone else will snatch him up if you do not."

The *stop-it-right-now* look Lizzie gave Zeke was not missed as she turned on her husband. "Of course, Ezekiel is just glad anyone snatched *him* up, though the Lord knows I would do it again." There was tenderness in her sister's tone at the last part, and her smile could not be missed either.

As she turned back to Mary, Lizzie resumed her dour look. "Do not listen to him. He will get you into trouble every time. In truth, Mr. Horton might be the perfect answer to your dilemma with Father. You would not have to marry Robert and you would not have to leave Mowsley. But I thought you wanted to wait for love."

"I want a family, like you and Zeke. And I want to choose whom I marry. Is that so terribly wrong? Mr. Horton I find to be a wonderful man. He could make me happy in so many ways."

"But you are the one who said he still loves his wife. How could you be happy? And I told you he is a flirt with the ladies who come into his shop. He's been in mourning, but he won't always be. He used to love to chat with the ladies and flirt. 'Tis who he is. Ann didn't give it a care, she was secure in his love. But how will you feel? Knowing that he does not love you as he did Ann? I worry about you."

"I shan't find love with Robert, either. With Mr. Horton I shall have a family. Besides, I shan't be hurt, Lizzie. I may love Mr. Horton, but I'm also prepared to give him time to love me. The ladies all love to prattle with him, but everyone does. 'Tisn't a bad thing." She turned quickly and took her leave, before they could see the tears that threatened to fall.

4

December 1630

December's cold was matched only by the busyness of the season. With the harvest done and land readied for the next spring, the small hamlet turned their toil to preserving food for the winter and the largest celebration of the year. Sausages were stuffed, cheese molded, butter and pork salted, and fruit dried or sugared. Tallow was rendered for candles and soap, while tree boughs and holly were foraged as they readied for the merriment of the twelve days of Christmastide, beginning on December twenty-fifth.

Attitudes about the festivities were mixed in Mowsley. Many, including Barnabas, felt that the sacredness of Christ's birth was all but forgotten with the overindulgence that accompanied the celebration.

Still, he enjoyed this season of baking and creating confections to delight young and old alike. He particularly enjoyed the frequent presence of Mary and Elizabeth and had finally told the two sisters his intention of calling on Mr. Langton.

It was no surprise to the ladies, he supposed. Elizabeth gave a knowing look to Mary, whose delight lit her face. In that moment contentment gave him a peace he'd not enjoyed for some time.

Still, when the day finally came, as Barnabas rode up the long winding road to the Langton estate, sadness seeped into his soul like flour through a sieve. He patted Baldy's withers and tried to put Ann from his mind. Mud-brown oak leaves, dry and curled inward, danced in the trees, and he watched as one skittered across the hard ground like a furry brown mouse. The Langton house loomed before him, an elegant half-timbered house with split oak beams that framed the pebble and limestone walls.

He would ask to court Mary and imagined spending many more evenings here. He dismounted, handing the reins to the young boy who emerged from the stable.

Adjusting his dark gray doublet, he knocked on the door. The cook answered and ushered him to the front parlor, offering a seat near the window. He sat forward and studied the room.

"Good morrow to you, Mr. Horton." John Langton entered from the stairwell.

He stood and bowed. "Good morrow to you, Mr. Langton. A lovely home, sir."

"Thank you. Mary tells me you are here to ask permission to court her. My daughter, Elizabeth, tells me she and her sister have frequented the bakeshop of late, presumably for Mary to learn some skills. What say you?" He folded his arms across his chest.

"You get right to the point, Mr. Langton, and I appreciate that. Indeed, I have come for permission to court your daughter. I have long held your family in high regard and, I must say, was pleased to meet your youngest once again. I've been quite lost without my dear wife. I require a mother for my children. A mistress for my home. I request to spend time with your daughter, Mr. Langton, to discover if this would be a good union."

Mary's father rubbed his chin, then pushed the intractable lock of hair from his forehead. He motioned for Barnabas to sit once more and took his own seat. "Forgive me, but I well recall the sense of loss I felt when my own wife passed. I feel it to this day. It never is easier. But, though I had a daughter to raise, I would never have married again. I could not. It would feel as if I betrayed my wife. Surely, it is very soon for you to consider another marriage, is it not? You barely know my girl, and you do not profess to love her." His look was pure pain.

"I know your sorrow, sir. My loss haunts me daily. And to be sure, marriage to your daughter will be of much benefit to me. I must take care of my sons. Ann would want that. And I can provide a comfortable home for your daughter. She would have her own needs met. It is difficult in my business to have small children underfoot. My sons need a mother to watch over them." He paused, unsure of where to go from here. "Many women in the village have offered their help, but in truth, I dislike their intrusion on my grief. Mayhap that sounds ungrateful. But I don't like to intrude on their busy days, either."

"Has Mary told you that I have been in discussions with Mistress Haskins of London, regarding a possible marriage to her son, Robert?"

He took a breath. "Aye, she did. She is not in favor of that union, sir." He did not want to say too much at this juncture. Arguing would be of no use. Mayhap her father would come to understand that he truly had Mary's interests in mind.

Mr. Langton stood up and began to pace.

He rubbed the back of his neck. "And do you not feel, Mr. Horton, she might desire to marry you in order to avoid a marriage to Mr. Haskins?"

"Your daughter may have her reasons to marry me, but the kindness she bestowed on my sons tells me of the sweetness in her heart. I would be honored if she would choose me in marriage, rather than an arrangement without choice. Though we will not know her choice, sir, if you deny us a courting period."

He stopped pacing. "I will need some time to think on these things. You understand, do you not, that I failed to have her taught many of the things you would expect in a wife?"

Barnabas stood, aware the visit had ended, but a bit of tension eased from his shoulders. He spoke gently. "It surprises me that she lacks in the domestic skills with a sister such as Mistress Fanning. But there are many things I can teach a bride when it comes to preparing a meal, and her sister tells me she gives her lessons in needlework and spinning. I truly am not looking for a replacement for my dear Ann. I could never do that." The grief that lurked behind his words threatened to surface and he donned his hat to take his leave.

"Mr. Horton, may I extend an invitation to supper this Saturday? Perhaps we can further discuss the problems of such a courtship. I do have many questions about your beliefs, your family. Over supper we might have a relaxed discussion. One that Mary could be present for. In the end, I do love my girl, very much, and I do want her happiness. Most of all I want her to be safe and secure, but her happiness is of great importance to me as well."

"Very well, Mr. Langton, supper on Saturday. I do look forward to helping you understand my position. I will answer any questions you please."

Old Baldy stood waiting, the young boy by his side. Barnabas mounted, pulling his doublet closer. The clouds moved in and he could taste snow in the air. He had not expected the hesitancy Mr. Langton exhibited. No, he thought Mary's father would welcome him. Mayhap not with open arms, but certainly he must know this would be a good arrangement for his daughter. Many parents in Mowsley would be delighted to marry their daughters to the baker. He told Mr. Langton he would answer any questions he pleased to ask, but doubt began to settle into his thoughts. What if he did not have the right answers?

■ ■ ■ ■

Mary stood from her perch at the top of the stairwell.

Papa closed the door and turned to look up. "Come down, my girl. We have much to discuss." He looked weary, a bit older. The crinkles at the corners of his eyes suddenly looked more like wrinkles than laugh lines.

She obeyed her father and sat in her favorite chair, hands folded.

"So, my girl, you have made quite an impression on our Mr. Horton."

"He has made an impression on me too, Papa."

"That is not the same as love, of course." He turned his back to her and stared out the window.

"If I were to marry Robert, it would not be for love either." She felt the sting of tears as they welled.

"There are many reasons to marry Robert, and I must tell you, many reasons to not marry Mr. Horton. Without going into those, let me just say that I know I failed your mother miserably with you. What would she think? I most certainly should have sent you to live with Elizabeth. Selfishness. It was pure selfishness that I didn't.

But I can at least take care of you now, Mary. Even Elizabeth agrees, Robert is the right solution."

"Solution? Is that what he is, Papa? I do not need a solution. And Lizzie does not agree with you anymore." She rose and stood close to his side. She tried to keep the anger out of her tone, but it seethed inside like a current beneath a restless sea. She inhaled and the words came out a whisper. "You didn't fail me, Papa. But you will if you send me off to London. And you would fail Mother. She would never do this to me." She was drained, so very tired of fighting to make her own decisions. Why must it be this way?

"My dear girl, what is so terrible about Robert? Did Mother know something I do not? I don't recall he teased you growing up or pulled at your braids. As I remember, you played rather nicely and he always seemed infatuated with you. Almost speechless."

"That's it, Papa. As we grew older, he never said anything to me. Just sat there like a lump. He is a lump. No passion, no dreams. And he just stares at me. He is . . . he is disgusting."

Papa's shoulders drooped and he took her hand in his. "You heard that Mr. Horton will come for supper?"

"Yes." She could barely trust her voice.

"I shall not promise you anything. I have many questions to ask. But I shall listen to what he has to say. Are you going to Elizabeth's today?"

"Yes."

"Tell that daughter I want to see her. Why ever would she be taking you to the bakeshop in the first place? What is she filling your mind with?" He shook his head and sat down to study his ledger.

"It was me. I made her. I told her I wanted to go. 'Tis not right to blame her. But she agrees with me, Papa. She has her own concerns, but overall she thinks perhaps to marry Mr. Horton is a good choice for me." She hoped she did not embellish what Lizzie had said.

"So be it. But do not see Mr. Horton again until I can talk to him. And tell Elizabeth to bring Ezekiel and the children for supper on Saturday. She should be here. I need her presence and perhaps advice. She would know best what your mother would do."

"Papa, I think I'm in love with Mr. Horton." Her voice was but a whisper, and Papa did not respond.

Dismissed, she gave Papa a soft kiss on

his cheek. She took her hooded cape from the peg and let herself out the door. As she walked up the lane, she turned to wave to Papa, but he was not in the window. Never had she felt so distanced from him.

5

January 1, 1631

On Saturday, Cook roasted a joint of beef, and the aroma drifted through the house, a welcome to hungry guests. Mary noted that the fires in the kitchen and parlor, kept up all morning, gave the rooms a warmth and cheer they lacked on an ordinary day. It was the halfway point of the twelve days of Christmas, and each day she, Lizzie, and Papa had exchanged a tiny token of their love for each other.

Today she would see Barnabas, and her anticipation was more than she could bear. No gift required, he was indeed the present she wished for.

A rumble of wagon wheels signaled the arrival of the Fannings. Her giddiness turned from thoughts of Barnabas to thoughts of her nieces and nephew, and she ran to the door. Zeke handed Rachel down to Lizzie as Mary joined them to unload the wagon.

She opened her arms and Ruth fell into them, but squirmed to the ground. "What, are you too big to let your auntie hold you?"

"Mama says I am." She ran her hand over her aunt's skirt. "I like your dress, Aunt Mary, so soft. Mama says you have Miss Temples make them for you."

Her ruby-hued velvet was a favorite, with its lace collar and cuffs. "Yes, that I do. Sometimes. She does good work, do you agree?"

"Yes, Auntie."

The two walked into the parlor. Lizzie set Rachel down and she toddled to her grandfather. "Bumpa, Bumpa," she squealed.

He brought her up to his knee and kicked out so she could have a horsey ride. For the moment his eyes twinkled and a broad grin spread across his face as he played with his granddaughter. "She looks so much like you, Mary, when you were but a poppet. You loved to ride on my knee too."

"You were my first horse, Papa, and then the one with the rocker that you made for me. I rode it for so long, way too big for it, before you finally gave me my first pony."

"I was jealous of that," Lizzie said. "Could you tell, little sister?"

Mary shook her head.

Papa set Rachel down and stood up. "That was the fun of watching the two of you grow up. You both were so different, but always wanting what the other had. The love you had for each other never changed, though. Your mother can be thanked for that. She knew how to instill love in each of you."

Papa cleared his throat. Now the lecture would come and the rules set for Mr. Horton's visit. Mary steeled herself, but Zeke's voice announced the arrival of the baker.

Quickly her father added, "I want to remind you both that I shall be the one talking. If I want your opinion, I shall ask for it. Understood?"

"Yes, Papa. But I think Lizzie wants to tell you something."

Lizzie's exasperation showed as she looked first at her sister, then at her father. "I only want to say that Mr. Horton is a fine man. Mother thought so too. His boys are well behaved from what I can tell. Mary could do worse, Father. She could be a spinster and a burden to you someday."

He softened his tone. "Your point is well taken, Elizabeth. Now let us greet our guest."

The three moved with Rachel to the front hall and found Barnabas removing his coat and Zeke helping Ruth and Joshua remove

70

outer clothing.

"Mr. Horton, where is Joseph?" Joshua held on to his father's leg as he wiggled from his coat.

"The boys are visiting their Grandmother and Grandfather Horton."

Mary listened to Barnabas comment to Zeke about how fast boys grow. She drew back, needing to slip away for a moment, to collect herself. She entered the kitchen and moved toward the door. Cook beat at eggs with a spoon, her back to Mary, and thankfully took no notice as she hurried outside.

She closed the door quietly and shivered, more from nerves than the cold outside. The kitchen garden soothed her as she bent to run her fingers over the winter lettuce. The last of the turnips would be pulled soon and put in the cool dirt beneath the house. Winter's sting would bring an end to what was left in the ground, so there was work yet to be done. She sniffed the air, enjoying the earthy redolence. The seasons were experienced in the garden like nowhere else and there was a pleasure in digging and plucking as they readied for winter's freeze.

She worked with the gardener every year. She found it such a pleasure. But where would she be next year? She sank onto the stone bench and pulled a rose, dark and shriveled, from the thorny bush. Long devoid of leaves, the bush looked foreboding. London was that way. Pretty in the summer, but as ugly as this rosebush in winter.

Mary raised her face to pray. She probably should be kneeling, with her head bowed and hands folded, but so far that hadn't seemed to work. Perhaps if she looked up to God, He would see her desperation. *Lord, I'm going to marry Mr. Horton. I am. This is what I need to do.*

It wasn't a very good prayer, but she did hope He understood her plight.

Barnabas appreciated the warm fire and stood with his back close to it, hands clasped behind to thaw his fingers. Mary had been in the hall when he first arrived, he knew she had, but now was nowhere to be seen. Should he ask after Mary, or ignore the fact she was no longer present? He was accustomed to leading conversations, and his hesitation bothered him.

It didn't matter. Mr. Langton excused himself, and Mistress Fanning — though polite — seemed quite occupied with her children.

His gaze lingered over the green boughs that framed the hearth and the red ribbons and balls with holly that adorned them. Where was Mary? Could it be that she had made the decision not to see him? That she would marry Robert after all? He cleared his throat. "Mistress Fanning, your sister, she is well?"

Elizabeth peered toward the kitchen. "Oh yes, she looks forward to your visit. Father would rather I not discuss this with you, but Mr. Horton, I do know she is distressed by these circumstances. Father and I both worry about her, but in the end only wish for her happiness. Prithee, have patience with Father."

Before he could answer, Mr. Langton reappeared, with Mary by his side. "Cook says supper is ready to be served. Mr. Horton, follow me please."

Mary's smile assuaged his doubts as he fell in behind Mr. Langton. He turned slightly and watched as she took Ruth's and Joshua's hands and Elizabeth scooped up Rachel.

"Are you hungry, little one?" Elizabeth rubbed Rachel's tummy.

"Yes, Mama. We eat?"

"Yes, my poppet. It certainly smells good."

Ezekiel joined Barnabas. "So good to see you. I hear so much about you from Elizabeth, I feel I've been to your shop every day for the past month." He chuckled and Barnabas appreciated the bit of levity.

"Mayhap you would come with her next time. I never tire of showing my hearth to anyone who will listen." He turned to Mr. Langton. "You are welcome as well, sir. Come and visit the shop. Stay for supper."

"Yes, very well, I may do that." Mr. Langton took his seat at the middle of the long table and indicated to Barnabas to sit opposite him. Ezekiel took the seat to his left as the women settled the children.

Cook presented the beef, fat slices with the pan juices on the side, along with bowls of steaming turnips and onions. The bread on the side table had been prepared by Elizabeth and baked by Barnabas just the day before. Elizabeth cut a thick piece for each of the children, then arranged a platter with churned butter and various cheeses.

Mary and Elizabeth busied themselves with the children, chattering in between bites. Mr. Langton spoke of his sheep and horses and the price of wool.

Conversation, light and congenial, flowed, and Barnabas wondered if Mr. Langton had decided in favor of a courtship. He could not help look down the table at Mary and was pleased to see she looked back at him. He didn't fail to notice the tinge of red that

74

flamed her cheeks every time their eyes met.

Dinner ended with Cook's plum pudding, and as if on cue, Ezekiel excused himself and took the children from the table. Mr. Horton's ginger cakes awaited them in the kitchen, and afterward they would go out to the stable to brush the horses.

Mr. Langton beckoned his daughters to move up the table, closer. Once they were settled, he turned to Barnabas. "Mr. Horton, my wife held you in high regard. My daughters obviously do as well. I crave your forgiveness, but I understand your father is landed gentry, yet you are a baker. You are the eldest, are you not?"

"Aye, I am. My father disinherited me of his landholdings. Jeremy, my youngest brother, will inherit the land and mill. My brother Thomas shares my belief that the Church of England has become very pompous and its clergy relies too much on the Book of Common Prayer, not enough teaching straight from the Bible." He adjusted his collar. "Our intent has never been to leave the church but to effect change from within. Our father has long supported reform in the church, and has opened his doors to meetings, but there are many points we disagree on. Of course, Jeremy fancies himself to be a shipmaster someday and has plans to build a ship. He has no interest in the land."

"Interesting. An adventurer, is he?"

"Jeremy has sailed with our uncle since he was but a wee lad. Thomas and I did too, but Jeremy is the one who's enraptured by the sea. I suppose there is a bit of adventurer in all three of us."

"Adventurers, yes, if you think you might change the Church of England from the inside out. That is not without danger, I am sure you know. Terrible things are happening to those who will not conform. It would worry me greatly should you marry my daughter with those wild ideas."

"Sir, I do not consider my ideas to be wild. Thomas and I consider ourselves to be conforming, rather than nonconforming."

"But your relationship with your father? You have mended the rift, regardless of your differences?"

"Indeed. In the final analysis, he and my mother are very much involved with my two sons and we were able to forgive each other long ago. We now maintain a close relationship."

"I will be straightforward with you." Mr. Langton ran his fingers through his hair, a silver lock falling across his forehead. "It is a concern to me that you have so recently lost your wife. I know Elizabeth has expressed this concern as well. She is worried for her sister."

"Aye. I do understand your concerns, truly I do. I am not quite certain what to tell you. I mourn my Ann a thousand times in a day. It is truly not something I would simply do and then move on, whether it be a week or a thousand weeks. I do not even know what during a day might trigger my grief for her. And I constantly despair that I will forget her, so I try to hold her close in my thoughts. Is it not the same for your grief?"

Mary and Elizabeth looked at their father. Mary's sorrow showed as Barnabas spoke of his wife.

Mr. Langton picked at the crumbs on the table. "You ask that with much sincerity, so I will answer in truth. I do mourn Katherine every day. Aye, 'tis true the heart cannot decide when to put grief aside. But it would seem to me you marry with haste and I desire more than that for my daughter."

"Sir, with all respect, you were rather unusual when you decided not to remarry. Elizabeth was grown, but you still had a young daughter to raise and most men would have indeed sought marriage. Mary is truly a gentle spirit. Over these weeks she has told me it is her desire that I always hold Ann's memory in high esteem. She understands that the love we shared is a rare thing and does not desire to replace it. Indeed, she is simply content to bring me some happiness. Of course, I hope I shall bring her happiness too. She is a gift to me, and I treasure her for that."

Mr. Langton regarded his daughter. She avoided his eyes. "She's a nurturer, that one." He looked back at Barnabas. "She tends to commit heart and soul. Are you ready for that?"

"My sons are in need of nurturing, sir."

"She loves pretty things, and I must say I have encouraged that. What say you about that? Do you not believe that is wrong?"

"In truth, I find her a delight to the eye. I have no qualms with her clothing. I am tolerant in those regards, I believe. God reveals to each of us what we must know, in His own time. My argument would be with the priests who wear elaborate robes with much pomp, not with a lass who enjoys pretty things. Mayhap someday she will feel convicted, but I believe that is between her and God."

"Truly? Is that not unusual for someone who has the Puritan's beliefs?"

"Mr. Langton, those of us that believe in

reform of the church do not call ourselves Puritans. It is a term used by those who would like to degrade us. I like to say I am a man of God who seeks to purify the church. But even so, if I be a Puritan, I am an independent Puritan. I have firm beliefs that I willingly share with anyone who will listen. But what is between each man and God — that is exactly what I am fighting to protect. Our freedom to have a personal relationship with God. That and the right to read our Bible."

Mr. Langton smoothed the lock of hair from his forehead. "I admire your honesty. And I will say that I admire your courage to stand up for your beliefs. But I do worry about my daughter and the reality that she could be persecuted for your beliefs."

"I shall not put your daughter at risk, I give you my word." His eyes met Mr. Langton's with conviction.

Mary leaned forward. "Papa."

Mr. Langton regarded his daughter. "Mary, we shall speak, but not now." He turned back to Barnabas. "I have considered that with the dowry I have for my daughter, not to mention the business connections that I have available, she could marry very well. Maybe even up — to a title — but Mr. Haskins of London is an obvious choice, because they have known each other since childhood, and his mother and I have a close business association. I must ponder this for a time. I promise you I will take what you have told me into consideration. Pray thee know that I will do what I think best for my daughter."

"Of course." Barnabas stood up, aware he was dismissed. "Good day, Mr. Langton. I do thank you for your consideration. The meal was superb and you a most gracious host. Mistress Fanning." He bowed. "Miss Langton, good day to you." He bowed once more, his eyes never leaving her.

Mary and Lizzie watched Barnabas depart. Papa turned to his youngest daughter. She'd remained obediently quiet during the exchange. Their conversation made her uncomfortable, but she dreaded more the discussion Papa would demand now.

"Mary, you know I want only your happiness and security. But, the reasons not to marry him are numerous and I caution you against this. I would implore you not to marry that man."

He motioned for both to sit at the fire. "I know you feel you love Mr. Horton, but you will find someday, my dear, that love is not everything. I question if he can love again so soon, and I discern that he questions it as well. Someday his feelings could turn to anger rather than love, but it would be too late for you."

He paced before them. "I have qualms that he entertains such Puritan beliefs. This is not the time for such ideas. People are being whipped and put in prison. Pray tell, if I would arrange a meeting with Robert, would you humor me? His mother buys my finest wool and I am sure it would be much contentment for her to have another woman in the household. You would always be well provided for. As children you were fond of each other. Could you not be happy with him?"

Mary leapt to her feet, hands on her cheeks. "No, I could not! Fondness is not love, Papa. How many times have we discussed this very thing? I do not know what happened. We grew up, I suppose, but he disgusts me now and I cannot feign otherwise. And don't you see what a dolt he is? He lives with his mother because he cannot fend for himself."

"That's not true, my girl. She operates a substantial business and it behooves him to remain in her household and work for her. But I see the clouds form in your eyes. I must think on these things before I will give

81

my answer. You think of this as a way to avoid a marriage to Robert, but you do not see the unhappiness that awaits you. That troubles me greatly."

Lizzie went to Mary and embraced her. "Father, please remember that if she marries Mr. Horton, she will be close by. I planned to wait to tell you this, but Ezekiel and I shall have another babe. It would be comforting to me to have her close by when it is born."

"Why, Elizabeth, how grand. Another child? You please me, truly." He came to hug her and hugged both daughters.

"Lizzie — that is so wonderful. Papa, I would be so unhappy to not be here when she needs me. I know it is difficult for you to understand this, but if Mr. Horton desires to marry me, it is his sons that he is thinking of. I know that. He is desperate to have someone help him. You know that is not uncommon. 'Tis a bit amazing he has waited all these months."

He drew back and looked at her. " 'Tis no reason to marry him, my girl. Indeed, quite the contrary."

She looked up at Lizzie and shook her head, then turned to Papa. "But he takes delight in me, he appreciates that I am well-read, and he even desires to teach me cooking. He finds me a blessing with his sons." She looked at her hands, folded in her lap. "And I love him."

He studied her with a look of disbelief. "I think he might find it charming in the beginning to have a wife that he might train, but you must realize it might get tiresome for him at some point." His gaze went to the window. "I do not mean that in an unkind way. You are my baby girl and I truly want what is best for you."

Did he want to ignore what she had just told him? That she loved Barnabas? "This is best for me. This is my chance for a family. I must tell you, though I desire your approval, I shall marry Mr. Horton, even if you withhold it." She leapt to her feet and fled the room.

John listened to her retreat, her skirts swishing as she ran up the stairs. She'd never spoken to him in that manner before. It frightened him a little, but he loved her too much to withhold from her what she wanted so desperately. He knew what he must do. Give his permission as well as his blessing. Allow Mr. Horton to court his daughter. On the morrow he must send a message to Mistress Haskins. It would be a bit embarrassing, but she was a good friend. She might be disappointed — she thought of herself as a mother to Mary already — but it would not ruin their working relationship.

He would send a message as well to Mr. Horton, giving permission for the courting to begin. Elizabeth sat staring at him. "You are quiet, my dear, I forgot you were there."

"I'm not sure who I should be more worried about. You or her?"

"Well, my dear, against my better judgment, I shall allow Mr. Horton to court your sister. How I wish your mother was still alive. She would know what to do far better than I."

He ran his fingers through his hair. The burden of raising his daughter without a wife had certainly not been without its trials, but somehow he had thought it would get easier. Mary always said she would not settle for a marriage of convenience and here she was, going headstrong into one. Would she someday be filled with regret?

6

As he left the Langton estate, Barnabas decided against going directly home. He'd made his decision to take a wife, but in the wake of that, he felt no better. He nudged Baldy left when he reached the smithy and rounded the corner down Dag Lane. He passed the Horton House and mill and rode on until he found himself at the door of Thomas's house. Thomas, the brother with his feet securely on the ground. The brother who would know the right thing to say to him. Jeremy would give his life for anyone, but he was a dreamer.

He pounded on the door, until Thomas finally appeared. "Well, well. Is it old Barn? What brings you my way? Are you all right? Come in."

He stepped in the doorway. "You've known the void I have felt since Ann died. I try for the boys to stay on course, and I still open the bakeshop. But I have done something that troubles me and I need to talk to someone. Could I have your ear?"

"What say you we go down the lane to the inn? Jeremy will be there. Mayhap the three of us could talk?"

"I had thought to speak just to you, but mayhap it would be a good thing to get both views." He waited while Thomas shrugged on his coat and informed his wife and daughter of their plans. Both Thomas's wife, Mary Jane, and their little daughter, Mary Belle, came out to give Barnabas a hug. Belle clung to his legs. He bent and gently peeled her away, giving her a quick hug before handing her to her mother.

The two trudged to the inn in silence, horses left behind.

As they drew near, Thomas turned. "I know it's been hard, Barn. Do not think for a moment that Jeremy and I do not understand. We are here for you, whenever you need us."

"Thank you. I do know that."

They went inside and found Jeremy at a table.

He looked up as they approached. "Heighho, look who joins me." He stood up and clapped both brothers on the shoulder.

"In truth, I did not plan to, but when Barn showed up at the door, I thought we should." Thomas gave Jeremy a broad smile.

They pulled out chairs and settled into them. Jeremy gave a nod to the pretty maidservant, and she brought a large platter of crusty bread, with carp and hunks of cheese. She beamed at Jeremy, and Barnabas knew what Molly was thinking. The three of them had the Horton ruddy complexions and ready smiles, and their mere presence filled the room. She frequently said when the Horton men came in, business always picked up.

Molly set the fare down and nudged Jeremy. "Do you think that be enough? I wasn't planning on a third brother here." She nodded toward Barnabas with a grin.

Barnabas held up a finger. "Aye, we've plenty. I won't be eating."

Thomas looked at his brother intently. "We know you expect a joke from us, and most assuredly we do not let the opportunity slip by often, but, Barn, what's on your mind?"

"I have asked Mr. Langton's permission to court his daughter." He put it out there simply and watched their reaction.

Both brothers stared at him, mouths agape.

"I encountered her at Webb's shop and it occurred to me that she would make a wonderful mother for Joseph and Benjamin. I have been at a loss at how to manage them, and it seems everything I do is wrong. The day I met her they were misbehaving, but she helped me in such a gentle way. I know they miss their mother. I know Miss Langton cannot replace Ann. Not for me or the boys. But my children need a mother and I need a wife."

Jeremy finished chewing and swallowed hard. He leaned forward. "It's not wrong, Barn. It's life. No need to explain."

"I know, but her father has not given his consent yet. Moreover, I worry that I cannot give Miss Langton what I did Ann. She seems a very sweet girl and is certainly attractive. She would be very easy to live with and would give me many more children. But she is not Ann." He ran his finger around the edge of his glass.

Thomas looked from Barnabas to Jeremy and back. "There's nothing wrong with wanting to have a mother for your children. And you want more children, do you not? And she is another Mary. It is a beautiful name in my book." He grinned. "I think you have made a good decision. Do you not agree, Jeremy?"

"Aye, I do. Hear me, Barn — you were very lucky in your marriage to Ann. Most people never experience love like that. You were so in love, you went and apprenticed her father's trade. No, you are right, you will not find that again, but it is exceedingly more important to have a mother for those boys and you know that."

It surprised Barnabas that Jeremy, the youngest of the three, made so much sense. "What about you, Jeremy? You do not need to work. You will inherit Father's land, and yet you have plans to build a ship and sail the seas." He looked at Thomas for agreement.

"It's not a matter of needing to work for any of us." Thomas set his mug down. "Only Father's exceedingly strict work ethic that hounds us. But Barn, you and Ann were planning on sailing with Jeremy to the New World. Is this something Miss Langton would desire as well?"

"I am sure we w—"

"It's the adventure," Jeremy said. "I have always wanted to sail since I was a small lad. There will be money for certain, of course, but it's the adventure I want. I'm working on the plans now. I'm going to name her *The Swallow.*"

"Very well, but I want you to know if Mr. Langton gives us his consent, I should like a short courtship. My plan is to post the banns as soon as we can. My mind is made up, and I do believe this is what Miss Langton desires as well. I would like to bake the wedding cake, as well as prepare most of the wedding feast. It will miff their cook to be sure, but this will occupy my thoughts and time. It will be good for Joseph and Benjamin to see their father with a purpose once again." He said it with conviction.

"I wish you the best, Barn." Thomas drummed his fingers on the table, but lowered his voice. "You know, we all need to be thinking about the colonies. Jane and I have been giving it hard consideration. We're cloistered here in Mowsley, but I hear more and more of villages nearby where people are publicly whipped simply because they're meeting in their homes, discussing teachings of the church and Bible."

His eyes darted about the room as he continued. "I have been in talks with the Reverend Cotton. He feels more and more pressure from the church and he agrees with the Reverends Davenport and Youngs. They're not Separatists, like those at Plymouth. They are men who desire to take the church to a new land, to rid it of the pomp. Without all of the harassment we endure here.

"My good friend William Pynchon left a

few months back for the Massachusetts Bay Colony. He wanted me to accompany him, and I gave it much thought. I expect to hear news from him soon. Methinks it is time to seriously consider going to Massachusetts, to join in the planting of the church." He took in a deep breath after his long speech.

Barnabas nodded his head. "Aye, Thomas, I more than agree. King Charles is, at the least, a tyrant. He's been through three parliaments in a row and now rules without one. He wants absolute power. Most certainly the Queen is bringing her Catholic beliefs with her. How insulting to the people he rules that he would marry her."

He and Thomas looked at Jeremy. Jeremy was not involved with reform of the church in any way, but he did share their interest about New England, actually the New World in general.

Jeremy looked from one brother to the other. "At least the war with Spain and France seems to have ended, but now the cost of food climbs and timber is hard to find. London needs more coal. I can tell you, the New World has thick forests and game aplenty. The ship industry is flourishing and I intend to be a part of it. I may never settle there — someone must care for our parents, of course — but I will be sailing there someday. I want to take part in the trade that is already developing."

"Very well — I can see you do have an opinion." Barnabas chuckled and stood. "There is much to talk about. For now, brothers, I do thank you for your support and advice."

His brothers stood with him and the three gave each other bear hugs.

Jeremy held his shoulders. "We will be there for you, Barn. Let me know if there is anything you require of me."

"Me as well, Barn. I will talk to Father for you, if you like."

"He is watching the boys with Mother. They already know what is on my mind. Differences aside, we have the most wonderful parents. They both support me in my decision."

The brothers trudged back to the house. Barnabas regarded his younger brother with one brow raised. "Have you told Father about your intentions of going to New England?"

"Nay. He need not know yet. I will wait until I have word from William. I do not know how Father will react. He takes it somewhat in stride that you and Jeremy will someday make the journey. I don't believe he will be happy to know I intend to do the same."

"The information will not come from me, brother. You tell him when you are ready."

They pounded each other's back in farewell and Barnabas mounted his horse. At least the ride home would be short.

Entering the kitchen he shrugged out of his coat and hung it with his hat on a peg. His parents sat with the boys, telling stories at the old oak table. He tousled each boy's hair before taking a seat near Benjamin. His son's chubby finger traced the initial Joseph had scratched into the table just a year earlier.

"Your mother saved you from a whipping that day, eh, Joseph? She scratched the heart around the *J* you made and told Benjamin he could do the same when he learned to write a *B*."

Joseph's eyes grew large. "Benjamin, you always try to get me in trouble."

"Do not."

"Do too, you baby."

"Boys, enough. You are forgiven, Joseph. You know that. Your mother always knew the right thing to do, and she loved you very much. I pray thee, apologize to your grandparents. They do not enjoy listening to your quarrels."

Grandmother Horton stood up as if to gather the boys under her like a hen. "Now, boys, everything is fine. We have had such fun today. Barnabas, do you have any of the ginger cakes? I think a treat is in order."

He rose to fetch the cakes, glad to allow his mother to relieve him of his duty to discipline for the moment and noticed as she turned to Benjamin, a kind smile on her face. "Do you think you are old enough to learn a *B* for Benjamin?" she asked.

Wide-eyed, he sat up as tall as he could. "Yes, Grandmother, I want to."

Barnabas returned with the cakes and took one before passing the bowl to his mother. He attempted a stern look at her. "What are you up to?"

She carefully removed a little cake for her grandsons. "Yours look even better than mine, crisp and tender." She started with a compliment.

He cocked his head toward her. Something was coming, he knew her ways.

"I'm thinking if Benjamin may add his initial, it might bring closure to Joseph's misdeed. I would be happy to add the heart." She looked at her son imploringly.

"Aye. Let's bring closure." He nodded to his mother and turned to his father as they bent to their task. "I met with Thomas and

Jeremy after I spoke to Mr. Langton. They are much in favor of my marriage to Miss Langton, but her father has yet to give his consent to court her. I expect he will, however."

His father's brow shot up. "Why would he not? He knows your circumstance."

"You expect people to see things your way and fail to understand when they do not. But not everyone thinks as you do. He is very careful with his daughters and favors a more cautious approach with any decision that affects them. Miss Langton agrees to our marriage and will be a good mother to the boys. I expect he will come to see that." He decided not to delve into the misgivings her father had toward his religious tendencies.

Joseph jumped up, nearly knocking the ginger cakes to the floor. Miss Tilly dashed from underneath the table and disappeared. "I don't need a mother. Why didn't you ask me and Benjamin first?" His shoulders shook.

"Joseph! This is the second time today I must tell you to watch your tongue. Go to your room. I do not want you to come back out until you are asked to do so. Do you understand?"

"Yes, Father. But Miss Langton might not wa—"

"To your room and now!"

Long after Joseph went to his room, long after his parents went home, doubt assailed him. A messenger rode in with a summons to come to the Langtons' on the morrow. What if Joseph were right? The decision came quickly. Mayhap Miss Langton had changed her mind. It would not take her long to realize there were many men who could offer her far more than he. Men with social standing. He was but a disinherited baker.

7

January 2, 1631

Baldy stood hitched to the wagon. A second message, sent early that morning, requested Barnabas bring Joseph and Benjamin with him for a small repast at the Langtons' following church services. Though long ago discontent with the formalities of the Church of England, Barnabas was still present every Sunday morning. To not attend would bring suspicion with serious repercussions, so he conformed. But the secret meetings held on Wednesday nights in homes, where they worshiped and studied the Bible void of the pageantry, he considered his church.

He lifted the boys into the back of the wagon. "You will like the Langtons. You know Mistress Fanning, of course, and her son Joshua will be there today. And Mr. Langton has all manner of animals, but mostly sheep and horses."

"Do they have babies?" Benjamin bounced as his father took a heavy blanket from beneath the seat and wrapped it around both boys.

"Hold still." Barnabas chuckled. "Do you mean the sheep and horses? They do, though they are quite big now. Mayhap more babies in the spring. There now, are you warm enough?"

Joseph pulled the blanket higher. "Yes, Father. Do you think Joshua will want to play with me?"

"Oh, yes, I do. I think you will have a fine time."

"I'm sorry for what I said yesterday. But, Father, I do hope you know that I'm happy with just you and Benjamin."

He placed his large hand on the top of Joseph's head, turning it so his son looked into his eyes. "Happy? Really? You have not acted very happy, and you have very good reason to not be so happy. That is all right, truly. But I hope to make things better for you and Benjamin. Remember to watch your manners. I do not wish to discipline you again in Miss Langton's presence."

Joseph rolled his eyes and Barnabas tousled his son's thick hair.

Certainly the request to bring his family was a good sign that Mr. Langton had decided in his favor and the doubt that weighed heavy the night before lifted. He would need to make arrangements with his parents to care for the boys on the days he spent courting Mary. The good women of the town liked to talk. No, he would not be asking for their help. Mayhap his mother would come to stay with them for a time. Yet another reason for a short courtship.

After the service, he led the boys to Ann's grave, behind the church. It sat at the top of a hill, the blue slate looking cold and bare. He wished there were flowers along the path to pick, but the blooms were long spent. Even the seedpods were empty.

He held the boys close. The slate would last through the centuries, and the words he'd carved upon it he hoped would tell generations to come of the remarkable woman he loved so much.

He loosened his grip and knelt down. Touching the stone, he remembered his promise to her. He would take care of their sons. He would.

Large, lacy snowflakes began to fall from the sky, sifting down like fluffy feathers settling about their shoulders. He brushed the white fluff from his Sunday suit and pulled the black wool doublet close. He hurried to place Joseph and Benjamin back in the wagon. Pulling the blanket tight about them, he kept them warm and safe.

Mary loved her dresses, and most days she did not have a quandary over what to wear. But Mr. Horton's opinion mattered to her, so she pulled gown after gown from her wardrobe. Running her fingers across the fabric, she studied the garnishing trims and textures of her brocade and silks.

From the casement window she could see the gray clouds quickly moving in from the west. The air was cold and damp, a storm on the way, no doubt. The dark green wool, with a simple white linen collar, should be suitable. She preferred the delicate lace collars and shiny fabric of a satin, but she did not want to appear frivolous on this day.

In church the urge to look across to the men's side, where she knew Mr. Horton would be sitting with his boys, nearly overcame her. But she folded her hands and kept her eyes toward Reverend Barton, though to actually listen to his sermon was just too much.

Papa had not mentioned Mr. Horton again, beyond telling her that he and his sons would be joining them after church. Lizzie gave her the details, explaining that after she went upstairs, following Mr. Horton's visit, Papa relented and sent a message to Mr. Horton. His invitation included the baker's sons.

As they walked home after church, Mary skipped ahead with Ruth and Joshua. As huge snowflakes began to fall from the sky, she twirled about. "Ruth . . . Joshua . . . angel's tears!"

"That's what Mama calls them, Aunt Mary." Joshua looked to Ruth and she nodded in agreement.

"I know. When we were little, our mother, your grandmama, told us about the angel's tears. She said when angels are sad, they cry great torrents of tears, and we have rain. But when they are happy, so very happy, the tears come down all fluffy and white, dancing about on the wind. An angel is crying tears of joy today, I am certain."

She took their hands in hers and together they entered the house. Tantalizing smells greeted them, a promise of a delicious meal prepared by Cook. Mary waited for her sister, Zeke, and Papa to come in, and then ran up the stairs. She needed a moment to consider what she might say to Mr. Horton. *I am honored for your consideration?* Oh, no. *I am pleased we shall be courting?* How silly it all sounded. Perhaps she could not prepare and needed to take it a word at a time.

Yes. Word by word.

She held her looking glass and pressed her lips together firmly. A cherry hue sprang up. She studied her reflection. Might he kiss her? The warmth flooded her cheeks before she saw the crimson in her reflection. Oh goodness, such thoughts! Not likely, and most certainly he would have more decorum, even if he felt so inclined. Still . . .

A commotion downstairs brought her back from her reverie and she placed the mirror on the bed table. Mr. Horton had arrived, and if she could believe the chatter reverberating up the stairwell, the children were excited to see each other. Smoothing her skirt, she started down. Halfway, Lizzie met her and the two embraced.

They descended the stairs arm in arm. Mr. Horton looked up, and as Mary arrived at the landing, he offered his hand. She took it and leaned into a slight curtsey. "Mr. Horton, 'tis a pleasant surprise to see you again so soon."

"Ah, indeed, it is." He gave a gentle squeeze and slowly released her hand, turning to Mr. Langton. "Thank you, sir, for asking me to bring the children. I can see how much they enjoy each other."

" 'Tis good for your boys to be involved with — ah, but I have a small sitting room

102

off the parlor. Shall we let the ladies settle the children and we men adjourn for a chat?" He looked from Mr. Horton to Zeke, and the three retreated.

Mary looked to Lizzie. "Do you think Papa will tell Mr. Horton of his decision? Now?"

Her sister laughed. "Your eyes are as big as saucers. You are not frightened, are you? This is what you begged Father for, is it not?"

"Oh, yes. But I cannot explain what I feel inside. Hopeful and scared all at once. Do I sound silly? Is that how you felt when Zeke asked to court you?"

" 'Tis not silly and yes, dear sister, 'tis exactly how I felt. And look how beautifully everything turned out."

"You always know what to tell me, Lizzie. What would I ever do without you?" She gave her a big hug as Rachel tugged at her skirt. "Come here, little one. Let your auntie hold you."

She tried to distract herself with the children, but her thoughts were on the men in the other room. Every time she looked at Joseph, she was reminded of how much he was like his father. He was playing well with Joshua, but she noticed he preferred to ignore her.

Lizzie nodded toward him. "Joseph is old enough that he will most likely avoid you, rather than act out, I believe. His father is strict and insists on good manners, so I don't think he would openly be unpleasant to you."

"Do you think he will warm to me though, in time? Perhaps after the wedding, he will relax and know that I'm nothing to be dreaded." She wiggled her brow at her sister with a smile.

"Listen to you — you don't even know what the men are agreeing to and you are planning the wedding. Such a headstrong girl you are. 'Tis why I love you so much, I am sure."

Their laughter was interrupted by Cook, who announced dinner.

As everyone gathered again at the table, Mary knew she would be too excited — distressed? — to eat much. She could not tell from Papa's or Mr. Horton's face what the decision was, but Zeke gave it all away in his broad smile and eyes that danced. He winked at her too, when he noticed her looking at him. Why didn't they just come right out and tell her? She certainly was half of the equation, was she not?

Papa led grace, then rose and stood behind his chair. "I would like you all to know I have given Mr. Horton permission to court Mary. My daughter's happiness and her security are most important to me, and I find that Mr. Horton can assure me that he will provide for her. Mary, my girl, you give me much joy." His eyes watered, but he cleared his throat to continue. "Mr. Horton, please call me John." He extended his hand.

Her heart pounded as the two men clasped hands with a shake.

"Thank you, John. And, of course, I wish you to call me Barnabas. I am honored, sir, and look forward to getting to know you and your daughter over the next weeks." He looked at Mary, a smile creasing his face. "And so we begin."

The afternoon stretched out as the children made a trek out to the barn with Grandpapa Langton to visit the animals. Barnabas fretted over the cold air on the children, but John assured him the barn would be warm.

Lizzie and Mary sat opposite Zeke and Barnabas next to the fire, engaging in light conversation and a bit of local gossip.

Snow accumulation mounted and goodbyes could not be delayed any longer. Mary walked with the Hortons to the door, and her family trailed behind them. Joseph made plans to see Joshua again, and Ruth had to be told once again to put Benjamin down. He wasn't a baby anymore and too big to be carried. They all laughed as she rolled her eyes but eased him gently to the floor.

Mary handed Joseph his coat and bent to bundle Benjamin in his. As she wrapped a neck cloth about him, she told the boys her story of the snowflakes. "My mother loved the snow. She would run out and twirl when the flakes began to fall. She said when it rained, it was angels crying, but when it changed to snow, the angels smiled. The snowflakes are angels' happy tears and they coat the world in beauty."

Joseph raised an eyebrow. "She could have gotten sick out there in the snow."

Barnabas turned and took her hand in his. "The snow is beautiful indeed, Mary. Your father suggests I return Tuesday, after the shop closes, for an evening of checkers or mayhap chess. Is that something you would favor?"

There was safety in his question. He would not rush events if she were uncomfortable. But when he raised her hand and grazed it with his lips, she knew Tuesday would not be soon enough.

As Zeke dressed the children for the walk home, Mary and Lizzie bounded up the stairs, shoulder to shoulder, whispering and giggling all of the way. "He kissed me, Lizzie — I did not think he would kiss me."

"Oh, goodness, Mary. He barely touched your hand." She held her sides as she stifled her laugh.

"No, Lizzie, I felt it. His lips are so warm and soft. It was a kiss."

"If you must declare it a kiss, so be it. But Tuesday! 'Tis just two days away. So soon. Does it not concern you?"

"I wish it were tomorrow. I think he wants to move with haste into marriage, and Lizzie, my mind is made up, so why should we wait?"

"He has told you he loves you, has he not?"

She looked away. "It depends on what you mean by that."

"Just that, Mary. Has he told you he loves you?"

"Nay, but I wouldn't want him to say it if he does not feel it. I know 'tis important to him right now to have a mother for Joseph and Benjamin. Perhaps love will come someday. You told me in London that people often marry and that love comes later. And remember, you said to give him time."

Elizabeth's eyebrows shot upward. "My

107

goodness, Mary, I meant leave him alone for a while, not marry him."

"I need you to be happy for me. I crave your approval. You must be my advocate to Papa."

Her sister's arm encircled her. "You have my blessing, and I am forever your advocate."

"Thank you. I think I shall go to bed, so could you tell Papa good night for me? I'm so tired. Give my love to Zeke and the children too."

"Of course. Sweet dreams, little sister, if you can sleep." They hugged once more and she watched Lizzie retreat.

She eased out of her dress and pulled on a sleeping chemise. Chilled, she crawled beneath the covers and pulled them close about her chin. Tuesday. She could not wait until Tuesday.

Mary spent Tuesday evening with Barnabas. She sat contemplating her next move in their chess game, but how difficult to concentrate when he was sitting right there, opposite of her. Her hand hovered over her knight as she looked up into his moss-green eyes. His eyes held hers until she willed her concentration back to the board and quickly moved her bishop up two squares diagonally.

Her gaze returned to him. His eyes teased with delight, a grin on his lips, but he looked at the board, not at her. She looked down at the game. The proximity of her opponent obviously affected her strategy.

He deftly moved his rook to four squares in front of her king. "Check."

She could see his rook was protected and she glanced at Papa. Papa smiled. She turned to face Barnabas. "Why then, I resign."

The next Tuesday evening they read Shakespeare's *The Comedy of Errors*. When Barnabas departed that night, she stretched to her tiptoes and hoped for what Lizzie considered a real kiss, but she contented herself as his warm breath skimmed her cheek.

The following Tuesday evening they finished the play. "It was not his best, do you agree?" He cocked his head back and the firelight played across his features.

He looked so handsome. Could she be this lucky? She picked a chestnut from the pan, popped and roasted, and she peeled it back. "Yes, Papa says it was one of his earlier works and it shows." She looked from him to Papa. Her father gave her a smile and a nod.

But that night, after their farewells were done, Mary overheard Barnabas and Papa speaking in the hall. As she pulled her chemise over her head, she put her ear to the door. Their words were loud but garbled as they drifted up the stairwell. She lay awake, afraid of what the morrow would bring.

Early the next morning she dressed in a simple yellow gown, covering it with her cape and hood. She left a message for Papa with Cook, took a bite of biscuit, and slipped out the door. Lizzie expected her for a morning of sewing — a bit of feather stitching and point lace — but she needed to talk to her first.

Standing at Lizzie's door, she caught her breath and waited for her sister to answer her knock.

"You are early. Come in, come in. 'Tis so cold out there." Lizzie helped her with her cape, hung it on the peg by the door, and led her to the fire.

Mary lifted her hands to the warm flames. "Prithee, may I go to the bakeshop alone?" She hadn't quite meant to say it that way.

Lizzie raised her eyebrows. "Nay, that would not be good. You know how Papa feels about you being alone with Mr. Horton. Why would you suggest that?"

"We'd had a perfectly lovely evening last night, but when Mr. Horton left, he and Papa exchanged loud words. I was in my room and I don't know what they said. It did not sound good."

"Mary, calm down. Shall we sew a bit and then perhaps I will need to stop at the cobbler's on the way to the bakeshop. He's working on some boots for Ezekiel. I should check on his progress." She winked at Mary and the two embraced.

Mary entered the bakeshop. Her cheeks burned and her heart fluttered, but here she was. She clutched a basket filled with her needlework, an alphabet sampler on top — her gift for Joseph and Benjamin.

"Heigh-ho, there. And wherefore is your dear sister, Mistress Fanning?"

"She shall be here soon. I — I — heard you and Papa last night."

He stepped close and cupped her chin in his hand, drawing it up. "Then you know, do you not? You look worried. Mayhap you have second thoughts?"

Tears pooled and wet her lashes. "Second thoughts? About you? Nay, I thought Papa told you our courting was over. Is that true?"

"If you will have me, Miss Langton, your father gives his consent. Is this too soon for you? For me, I wish not to tarry. It is a difficult thing, children without a mother. Will you have us? Will you marry me?"

His fingers, shaking slightly, caressed her chin. Her tears let loose and he dabbed her cheeks with his fingertips, then took the basket and set it on the table. "I do not mean to cause you sadness."

"Kiss me, Mr. Horton. Please kiss me."

He drew her close once again and she breathed in his scent of toast and spice. His lips hovered over hers as he looked into her eyes. "I think I'm learning what your sister has always known. I can see your thoughts in the color of your eyes."

His lips fell gently on hers and the warmth of his kiss spilled over her like sunshine on a chilly morn. She'd thought she had known love before, but Nathan did not come close.

8

February 14, 1631

A wind swept through the bare limbs of the oaks and the smell of rain hung in the air. Even so, the snowdrops were in bloom, poking up here and there, papery white petals adding light to the dreary landscape.

Barnabas strode up the lane with his sons at his side, Baldy and the wagon secured at the livery. Jeremy emerged from nowhere to walk with him. They joined the small group huddled together at the church. Elizabeth and Ezekiel stood by Joshua, Rachel, and Ruth. Barnabas's parents, Joseph and Mary Horton, arrived, along with Thomas and his wife and daughter.

The group turned as John Langton walked around the bend with Mary tucked beside him. A long white brocade cape, trimmed in matching fur around the hood and along the open front, lifted in the breeze, giving a glimpse of her pale yellow gown with a high neckline trimmed with point lace.

The wedding party stepped inside the church and John helped her remove the cape, revealing billowy sleeves with small slashes, tied above the elbows with blue ribbons. Her high-waist bodice, laced with more blue ribbon, narrowed into the full brocade skirt. The open front, scalloped with lace, revealed layers of silk petticoats, the top one as creamy as her glowing complexion. She was beautiful.

Barnabas's throat grew tight. Why did it feel like a door was closing, when indeed a new one stood open before him? He was leaving Ann behind. He'd anticipated this day with a measure of joy, so the sadness surprised him. He must hold onto Ann, keep her by his side. Never forget her. She wished him love, that he knew. She always would.

The rain pattered, lending a cadence to the vow "With this ring I thee wed." The two became one in the sight of God. Barnabas held back tears that were of what might have been, but he ardently prayed Mary's were tears of joy.

The sun broke through the clouds and the wedding party made their way to the Langtons' home with much dancing and singing. As the merrymakers entered the house, the servants — Cook's family — laid out platters. Barnabas would have been more comfortable with a civil ceremony, and far less gaiety, but to see Mary smile and laugh was a good thing.

Succulent beef, seasoned with herbs from France, wrapped in a flaky, buttery pastry, was accompanied by roasted carrots, parsnips, and leeks swimming in butter. A joint of pork encrusted with blackened spices, a roast duck surrounded by six doves all nestled in a currant-cherry sauce, and several savory pies filled with pigeon, mutton, or beef filled the table.

Salads with borage and violets dressed in oil, lemon juice, and salt were served, as well as breads, puddings, and mincemeats of every kind. Cherries, apricots, pomegranates, and figs and pippins complemented an array of cheese.

Sugared plums, oranges, and lemons as well as fruit tarts and sugared violet candies loaded the long oak side table.

Barnabas arranged to have a tray piled high with small, crisp ginger cakes sprinkled with sugar for the children and the wedding cake kept out of sight.

The guests took seats at the long table, with Mary and Barnabas in the middle, Joseph and Benjamin on each side. Hands were joined and heads bowed in the Langton tradition for grace.

He squeezed his bride's hand as her father led the prayer. How wonderful to have found a woman who came from a righteous home. She would understand in time his desire to worship God, free from the pressure of government.

Benjamin wriggled and squirmed during the prayer and Barnabas snuck a glance to see his new bride lean down to plant a kiss on his young son's forehead. He smiled at them. At least one of the little Hortons was glad that she was joining the family.

John raised his glass and announced, "Hear, hear. To my lovely daughter, who on this day has married a man of fortitude, honor, and devotion to God. And to Barnabas, who is a lucky man, indeed. To their good health and cheer."

"Cheers," came the echo.

Barnabas finally stood and raised his glass. "I am indeed a very lucky man this day. To that I give tribute to Mr. Langton, who has raised her to be such a fine and lovely woman, and to her mother, God bless her. And lastly, to Mary, my sweet. God blessed me far above rubies when I found you. I am, indeed, a rich and lucky man."

A smile wreathed her face and a deep, red

blush crept across her cheeks. Her eyes were as bright as emeralds. "Thank you, my husband, I so want to please you."

"Aye, Mary, and that you will do when you accompany him and the boys to Massachusetts." All chatter ceased as Jeremy clapped Thomas on the back. "Eh, Thomas?"

John's face turned to stone as his eyes slowly riveted between Jeremy, Barnabas, and Mary. Barnabas shot a warning look first at Jeremy, then at Thomas.

Mary's eyes widened, the smokiness in them unmistakable to Barnabas, but he looked steadily at Jeremy.

Benjamin jumped up and down in his chair. "Where are we going, Papa? Where? Where?"

Joseph's long face shifted to a scowl.

He did not want to lie to Mary, but this was clearly not the moment to approach her about sailing to the colonies. He swallowed hard as he searched for something to subdue her. "Mary, forgive my brother. He always is one for fun, but he has misjudged his humor this time. Jeremy, please apologize, for you have misspoken." He glared once again at his brother.

Thomas remained quiet during the exchange.

Jeremy stood up. "Pray pardon, my dear sister-in-law and Mr. Langton, do forgive my jest." He returned to his seat and looked expectantly at his brothers, as if relying on them to take over the conversation.

John leaned toward Mary just as she turned to Barnabas. Her father had more to say about Jeremy's comment, he could see that, but he hoped it could wait until the morrow. Or longer. He needed to talk with Mary, he prayed she would understand.

The meal progressed with much gusto, culminating in the presentation of the much-awaited wedding cake. "For you, my sweet."

The traditional wheat cake towered, covered in an almond paste and shimmering in sugar. Delicate sugar roses, created with rose water, sugar, and pomegranate juice to match Mary's ruby lips, crowned the cake and cascaded down the side. To those he'd added a sprinkling of candied violets.

"But, Barney, 'tis the most beautiful cake I have ever seen. I want to keep it forever — we cannot eat this."

He chuckled, grateful that his bride could make him smile. He leaned over the cake and tenderly lifted her chin until her dewy eyes met his. He swept a wisp of hair from her cheek as his lips brushed hers, tentatively at first, then passionately as he claimed them for his own.

A twitter of laughter pulled them out of the moment, and together she curtseyed as he bowed. He took her elbow as she again sat, and he dried the tear caught in the corner of her eye with the tip of his finger. "Nay, my sweet, do not weep over our cake. For you, I will bake one every year. You will have wedding cakes forever." A deep pang cut through his chest. He would do anything to see her smile, but truly there was no such thing as forever.

After the meal, Joseph and Benjamin went home with Aunt Lizzie and her family. Mary told them they were cousins now, to Joshua, Rachel, and Ruth. Joseph almost grinned at that.

Thomas and Jeremy were not so easily persuaded to leave the party.

Barnabas's earlier displeasure forgotten, Jeremy was up to his usual pranks. "Heigh-ho, brother, can we not follow you home to toss the stockings?"

Mary turned to Barnabas. "Toss stockings?"

"Aye, to see who shall marry next. Jeremy, you and Thomas go home. Thomas has a wife and I would pity the woman who marries you." Great guffaws erupted and Barnabas pounded his brothers' backs.

Mary and Elizabeth exchanged a look, and it occurred to Barnabas they were not used to the playful banter brothers could engage in. "Mistress Fanning, I believe we are now in the same family. It would be a privilege if I may call you by your given name."

"Indeed, call me Elizabeth, and may I call you Barnabas?"

"I would be honored." He bowed as an elegant carriage, provided by his parents, came into view. He turned to Mary. "Are you ready to go to your new home, my sweet?"

She cast a shy look — or was it trepidation? He would have been surprised if she was not a little anxious. But she managed a brave front and accepted the hand he stretched out to her. "Yes, I'm ready to go with you."

Mr. Langton shook Barnabas's hand. "You take care of her for me."

"I will do that. Our door is always open to you, John. Please, visit soon."

"That I will do." He gave Mary a firm hug and cleared his throat. "You come see me."

"I will, Papa. Often."

In the carriage, Barnabas offered Mary his shoulder, where she rested until arriving home. He jumped down and swept her into his arms. She hugged his neck as he carried her through the house toward the bed they would share. Her dainty feet peeked out amongst the petticoats, and he was pleased to see that the sugar roses matched not only her red lips but a petticoat as well.

9

August 1632

Mary longed for Barney's love and a babe but took much comfort in the sweet love Ben bestowed on her. Almost five, he still snuggled with her whenever he could, never letting her far from his sight. Joseph remained sullen. Why did it need to be so difficult? Had not they at times touched with their hearts?

She hauled the bucket of freshly drawn water up from the stream. Sweat trickled down the side of her face as she lowered it to the ground. She dipped her hand into the cool water and splashed her face. Joseph watched her — she could feel his eyes upon her. He would think she was intruding, but she needed the chance to talk with him.

"Why, Joseph, you surprised me. Those are pretty flowers. Shall we find a vase? You may use some of this water."

He fingered the yellow coreopsis and blue

bellflowers he'd picked in the meadow and the petals wilted at his touch. "They are not for you."

"I did not think so. I do love them, even though they are not for me."

"No, my mother loved them. She always loved all kinds of flowers. Why do you always think you can just take over and be my mother?"

"Oh, Joseph." Pain jabbed at her heart. "Please do not think I want to take over for your mother. I can't do that and I know that. She was a fine person, your mother, and I know that you miss her. It wouldn't be right if you did not miss her. She loved you so and she deserves that."

"You didn't know her, so don't tell me what you think about her."

She stiffened. She must say this right. "Yes. I did not really know her. I hear all of the lovely things people have to say about her, and I wish that I had the chance. But you know something, Joseph? I know how much your father loves her and that tells me she was quite wonderful, indeed. I know her through your father's eyes and heart and that tells me everything I need to know. Promise me that you will think of her every day. Share with me all of the wonderful things about her that you know, so we can both feel close to her."

Joseph's eyes misted and he blinked. He would think tears were babyish. His sullen face was an attempt to hold those feelings in. But she could see he was losing that battle. A tear wound its way down his cheek.

"Let me hold you, Jay, let me bear some of your pain, please."

His eyes jerked toward her. "How did you know?"

"How did I know what?"

"Jay. My mother called me Jay after I scratched the *J* in the table. No one else has ever called me that. Not even Father."

" 'Tis my way to shorten names. Have you noticed I call your father Barney and Benjamin Ben? I like that. May I call you Jay?"

"I think so. But I still do not want to call you Mother. You're not my mother."

"Of course. For your father's sake and mine, just be respectful. 'Tis all that I ask. Thank you for allowing me to call you Jay. Now, I shall fetch something to put the flowers in, but I think perhaps you should take them to your mother's grave. 'Tis a bit of a walk up that hill — I shall go with you. She will love them, and it shall give you a moment to think about her and remember her love for you. I'll be right back, wait here by the bucket."

She started up the path to the house, but glanced back. He squatted next to the bucket, his back to her. His soft words, meant for his mother, drifted to her on a gentle breeze. "I wonder if it would be all right to like her. Only like her, that would be all. Mother, I could never love her like I love you. But mayhap it would be all right to like her."

She brought back a red slipware jug, and he rose to meet her. He handed her the flowers and lifted the bucket to pour water for the thirsty nosegay. Mary lifted her apron and wiped a dusty tear from his cheek as the two set off to the cemetery.

Grass grew in tufts around the blue slate headstone, but it was recently trimmed and she knew Barney had been out to tidy up around the grave as he often did. She was sure, too, he'd stayed awhile, perhaps sitting on the sod and soaking up some sun. He felt close to Ann at those times and she was glad he could have the moments to himself.

She picked out the dried lilies from the clay pot next to Ann's grave, tucking the fresh coreopsis and bellflowers in their place. Jay quietly poured the water from the jug, and she stepped back to give him his own precious time.

They started down the hill and she smiled

as Jay ran ahead. He finally slowed and turned back to her, offering his hand, the red jug swinging in the other. A sigh that could shake the heavens escaped her as she clutched his hand, and she looked up, wondering if the angels indeed were taking note.

Barnabas swept crumbs into the fireplace. The last of his customers had left over an hour ago and he was able to close a bit early. Miss Tilly rubbed her side against his leg and he bent to give her ear a scratch. He untied his apron, wiped his hands, and dabbed at his damp forehead before he hung it on the peg. On a warm summer day like today, the heat of the oven drove him to the open door often. A breeze stirred as he watched Mary and Joseph step into the house. Her hand was tucked in his and it gave Barnabas cause to smile.

The past year had been difficult at times between his son and Mary. He'd made the decision early on to give her time to spend with the boys, and of course for visits and sewing sessions with Elizabeth. He'd kept control of the kitchen tongs and the duties that went with them. Every time he thought about passing the tongs to Mary, he remembered Ann and the day she received them.

But mayhap it was time. He could at least begin teaching her a thing or two about baking. The oven was still hot and a good fire ought not be wasted. Besides, the sun would set and the England mist would settle in to chill the air.

Yes, now would be an excellent time, but he had to give her due. She'd made a bit of progress already. When they first married, she did not know the difference between a simmer and a boil.

He entered the parlor and found her settling in to mend a stack of breeches. She looked up and smiled.

"I am thinking mayhap we should go to the bakeshop. I know it is hot, but 'twill cool off soon and it's a good time for a lesson."

"Do you not know I married you for your culinary skills and that two cooks can spoil the pot? I know when I am better off." Green twinkled in her hazel eyes. She looked happy.

"You will not get your way that easily. Come now, wife, I will show you what I know, but do not expect to master all of my skills. I know how to keep the mystery alive in a marriage," he teased.

They entered the bakeshop and he helped her with a fresh apron. As he tied it around her waist, she reached up to catch wispy tendrils escaping her comb. He marveled at her slim figure and, forgetting momentarily why they were there, put his arms around her in a tight embrace and kissed the nape of her neck.

"You are, Barney, so, so . . . shameless. Was this a trick to get me alone? You know the minute we think we are alone, both boys shall suddenly appear."

"Pray pardon, but you do inspire such things in me. Ah, now, what were we doing? Cooking — ah yes, cooking."

"Ah, yes. Cooking." With a grin she dipped her fingers in the powdery white flour and flung sprinkles across Barnabas's nose.

"Oh, ho! Two can play at this." He scooped up a handful.

Mary scampered around the table, her green eyes sparkling like emeralds. She darted back and forth giggling, teasing Barnabas. Finally she gave herself up to him, as if ready to accept her fate. A shower of flour landed full in her face, coating her eyelashes like new-fallen snow.

"Ah, my sweet, I am so sorry. Let me wipe that." He removed his handkerchief from his pocket and with great tenderness dusted her eyelids.

She leaned back in his arms, and as he

moved to her nose, her eyes opened and met his. "Barney, if ever I wonder why I married you, it would be this. You are the sweetest, most gentle man I have ever known."

"I am fun too, am I not?" His grin was mischievous.

"Yes, fun and smart and the best baker I know. Now let us get to the matter at hand and you show me all that you know. About cooking."

Turning toward the massive fireplace, he picked up the bellows and handed it to her.

Mary took aim at him, but he was quicker than she this time.

He redirected it to the fire. "No, my sweet, practice has begun." He stacked some logs over the coals. "Now then, give it some air with the bellows. Do you remember what I told you about stacking it so the fire gets air? The logs form a tent. If you stack it tight, one on top of the other, the fire will smother. You will know your fire is not going anywhere if you do not see smoke or flames lapping about your wood." He watched as the flames began to lick about the logs. "Aye, that's good, Mary. You have a fire."

While they listened to the music of the fire snapping and crackling behind the closed oven door, Barnabas explained his inventory of implements and supplies in his bakeshop. Oh, he'd done that many a time for Mary, but he never tired of the tools of his trade.

"This copper cauldron I've had for as long as I've had my shop and is the largest. Here on the table are my other kettles and pipkins." He waved at various iron and earthen pots that sat stacked next to his collection of sieves and skimmers, colanders and chopping blocks.

He pointed to the salt box that sat in a cove next to the chimney.

" 'Tis to keep it dry, is it not?"

"Yes, my salt comes from Southwold and is costly. 'Twould not do to have it ruined." He picked up a whisk of bundled birch twigs and swept some ash back into the hearth. "You remember well. And the more you practice working with the dough, the sooner it will be second nature to you."

"Lizzie told me 'tis important to use all of the senses in cooking."

"She is correct — the art of baking bread or preparing a proper dish is to remember to use your senses. You must feel the texture to know the consistency and taste it to know if you have the right amount. The aroma will tell you when it is done. Experience will teach you."

He turned to the oven and opened the door. Mary drew back from the heat, but he nudged her to look inside. The soot had turned to a white-hot ash on the walls of the oven and he nodded toward the slice. She fetched the long hoe-like tool and scraped the embers to the pail below. He handed her several wet rags, and she brushed as much of the ash as she could from the floor of the oven, making it ready for the loaves of dough. She raised her brows and winked at her husband. "I feel like a scullery maid."

Barnabas chuckled. "Yes, yes. Well done." He took the slice from her and handed her the long wooden paddle. "This is the peel — just put your loaves right here, one at a time, and then place it on the oven floor."

Mary removed a loaf from the long, wooden molding board and placed it on the peel.

"Now, make your cuts across the top and put it in. Close the door quickly because you want your oven very hot. Once we can smell the bread baking, you will want to check it often." He watched her expertly position four loaves in the oven and close the door.

She looked about the kitchen. "So what is next? Cakes?"

"Nay, we shall put a joint of beef on the spit to roast." He pointed to the jack positioned at the top of the hearth, with the long chains connected to a wheel.

"Papa was amazed you have this contraption. Cook was too. Her son always turns the roast."

"It is an amazing invention, to be sure. The smoke vane keeps it turning. Preparing the beef for the spit is the most work required."

"Roast of beef is my favorite meal. 'Tis Joseph's and Ben's too."

He liked it when she mentioned the boys. They were always close to her thoughts, he knew. "That it is. Methinks they are adjusting to our new life. I knew Benjamin would, but Joseph surprises me. I saw the two of you today, holding hands."

"He and I had a chance to talk today. He told me I may call him Jay."

A pain jabbed across his chest and the familiar sorrow he felt with thoughts of Ann settled over him. "Indeed?"

Mary moved close to her husband. "Yes, is that all right? 'Tis but a nickname I picked for him, but he told me Ann would call him that too. I did not know."

He settled his cheek atop her head. The scent of jasmine teased his nostrils and he remembered the day long ago when he first took her into his arms in his bakeshop. "That she did. And he is all right with this?"

"Yes. We had a conversation about remembering his mother and I told him I would be pleased to go with him to the cemetery, whenever he should like to think about her. I think it helped him, Barney, and I know it helped me."

"Very well, then. He misses his mother, to be sure."

"He is very much like his father."

"Shall we make a pastry for our roast beef?" He didn't wait for her answer but pulled out a crock of flour. "Could you fetch me a pot of butter?" Trouble creased his brow as he waited for her. "Aye, Joseph is much like me. At times I wish he were not, for I can be very stubborn. This reminds me of something, Mary. I have something exciting to tell you. I have been talking to Jeremy and he tells me he's begun work on his ship."

"He is such the adventurer. I did not realize he was that serious, though."

"He is in talks with the Petts and plans to be shipmaster of his own ship."

"Truly? How extraordinary."

"He is, he is. He tells me it will be a few years, but he says he will sail for the Massachusetts Bay Colony and he's brought me word about the Reverend John Youngs."

"Oh?"

"Yes. Do you recall me telling you about him? He is curate in Reydon, near Southwold. He plans on leaving from Yarmouth for Boston sometime in the future. Thomas and Jane speak of that too. Jeremy thinks his ship could be ready by then. We could be on the same ship."

"By your leave, I pray thee, explain what you mean. You are speaking of sailing to New England? Is it true, Barnabas, what Jeremy said at our wedding?"

Her eyes were the flinty gray he had come to know as trouble. It had been over a year since their wedding and Barnabas had not brought up a desire to go to New England again. Apparently, she had never forgotten Jeremy's indiscretion.

"Mary, you know it is hard times these days. Do you recall my good friend Peter Hobart? He plans to sail to New England as well. The persecution from Parliament is intolerable for him. You are well aware that last year I myself had to petition the courts on behalf of our good friends the Tuttles. Simon was reported to Parliament for nonconformity. Can you imagine? They are inventing things to go after the people they want and I do not believe it will improve. To a degree, when that happens to our friends, it happens to us.

"Word is John Cotton is nowhere to be found. Mayhap he has already sailed for New England. I feel I can do great things in Massachusetts. Churches are being established, townships founded. I desire to be a part of that. I have been much interested in what Reverend Youngs has to say. He supports Reverend Davenport in his decision to go to the New World."

"Why have you not been speaking to me of such? Why am I just finding this out now? Why did all of your family seem to know this of you before our wedding, yet you did not share any of it with me, Barnabas? Did you not deem it important? You, who feel so strongly about your faith, do you not feel you were lying to me? Do you not feel you have betrayed me?" She threw her hands up in disgust.

He squared his shoulders. Her outburst was uncalled for. "Jeremy was out of place when he spoke. There is danger in too much talk." He folded his arms. "Besides, it is not my duty to tell my wife everything I might be pondering!"

"Oh, 'tis not, Barnabas? 'Tis done, then." With that she picked up the crock of flour, ceremoniously dumped it over his head, and stormed from the kitchen.

10

The memory of her wedding drifted like a rose petal in a bubbling brook, overtaken much of the time by day-to-day chores, but surfacing from time to time — mostly when Lizzie came to visit with her children in tow.

Each year on February 14, Barney presented Mary with a wedding cake as beautiful as the one he'd made for her the day they were married.

Each year Mary's longing for his babe in her arms deepened, though she became more practiced in hiding her disappointment. Most of the time.

Lizzie's fourth baby was another little girl, named Hannah after Zeke's mother.

Three years of lessons in spinning and sewing, and embroidery still challenged Mary. Such a lesson was the backdrop for their chatter on this cold winter day. The children played all around them, with little

Hannah determined to keep up.

Mary stuck the needle through her cloth. " 'Tis so good to hear Joseph playing with Joshua and the girls. It seems to be the only time he is able to relax and enjoy being a child." She looked up from her needlework to smile at her sister.

"He is a good boy." Lizzie lowered her voice. "But much troubled, I think."

Mary watched as the girls chased the boys out of the parlor. "That he is. He misses Ann. He will not call me Mother, although he is polite about that most of the time. I have grown to love him as my own, though, and I grieve for him."

"Just be patient with him and pray for him. 'Tis all you can do." Lizzie looked over at her sister's work. "Your stitches are looking very even, but shall we turn it over and review the underside? What is underneath is very important as well."

Mary peeked underneath. "Nay, do not look. I can do better." She picked up a new cloth and began again.

Lizzie's laugh tinkled like raindrops on crystal. She stood and stretched. "You've mastered stitching a straight seam on garments, indeed they are almost invisible. But without some pretty embroidered flowers or birds, they shall be plain indeed. Let me show you how to hold your fabric." She bent over Mary's work.

"Ben misses his mother too, but he does seem to be doing very well. I think he would like to have a little brother or sister." Mary paused as Hannah took a tumble and picked herself up again without a whimper.

Lizzie looked up and caught her tender look. "I know we have spoken of this before, but when do you think that might happen?"

"I think about it all of the time. I don't know. Barney says in God's time. He is right, of course, but I do find myself impatient. I know he wants another child, and I feel sometimes I let him down."

"Do you take the honey mixture?"

"Yes, I have. Occasionally."

"Do not fret too much over how Barnabas feels about it. Sometimes when a woman relaxes and lets nature have its way, things happen." She nodded at Mary.

"I try not to fret about it, but I fear Barney does." She sighed and pushed away a fallen tendril from her face. "Not to change the subject, but have I ever told you Barney still holds to some of the old ideas of bloodletting and such. A bit antiquated, do you not think?"

"Barnabas is not likely to change. But you are his wife now and should be taking charge of all his care and the children's." She looked directly at Mary to make her point.

"I know that, Lizzie, and I take all of your instruction to heart. But Barney has not even given me the tongs yet. I feel like he runs the house and almost prefers it that way. I try and try, but look at me. No babe, no kitchen tongs. But someday, Lizzie — I just need to keep working at it." She said the words with conviction, but could she really try harder?

The door swung open and both Mary and Lizzie lowered their needlework to their laps. The children gathered quietly as Barney came through. "We've a message from Jeremy. He tells me Reverend Youngs would like us to stay with him in Southwold on holiday."

Lizzie's eyes lit up. "Mary, a holiday at the beach?"

"That shall be lovely, Barney. When would we be going?"

"Not for a fortnight. I will need to arrange to leave the bakeshop for a few days."

Lizzie rose and motioned her children to say their goodbyes. She leaned close to Mary's ear. "You take the honey mixture with you, Mary. 'Tis an elixir." She winked as she pulled away.

Barney harped constantly. Not Lizzie too. Mary's cheeks tingled with the blush she knew all could see.

Lizzie hugged her tight. "Forgive me," she whispered. "See you soon."

Mary watched the little family hurry down the lane and sighed. She was giving it her all. What more could she do?

Mary spread her gowns on the bed. The dinner invitation had come by messenger the week before, and every day since she'd taken her frocks from the wardrobe, fretting over what to wear. They had been to visit Papa, of course, but this was special, this was his birthday.

"You spend too much time on your apparel, my sweet." Barney stood at the door. "You will look pretty in whichever you choose. Mayhap the gray?"

"The gray? Yes, I like it very much. I shall have to decide."

"Very well. It will be good to see Ezekiel once again," he said as he walked to the parlor.

She picked up the gray and held it to her. She twirled a bit, then set it down and put on the green silk.

Picking up a comb, she padded out to the parlor. " 'Tis been a long time since we were all together at Papa's." She sat and combed each boy's hair and scrubbed Ben's chubby face, wiping it with her apron. He squirmed, but grinned through it all. She handed the rag to Joseph and he quickly ran it over his cheeks and chin.

She heard Baldy out front and pulled on her silk slippers. She pulled on her cape and tucked her hair beneath the hood.

She held out coats for the boys. "Come, boys, your father is ready."

He helped Mary up first, eyeing her gown as he handed her a sack of ginger cakes. "You wore that dress the day you came to the bakeshop with Elizabeth."

"Yes, I did. This is my favorite dress, can you tell?"

"Aye. I like the color. It is very becoming on you. But do you not feel the lace calls attention too much? And the shine of the fabric? Might it be above our standing? We've been over this before and you know how I feel. Why do you persist?"

His words bit at her like Baldy's horseflies. "I like to look pretty for you. You never forbade this dress. Do you not enjoy seeing me in it? Besides, Papa likes it. Please, Barney, I'm looking so forward to our visit. Can we be happy?"

He handed Ben up and turned to find Joseph eager to climb up front. "May I handle the reins, Father?"

"Aye, Joseph, good idea. Be sure to let him know who is in control. Baldy is a wise one."

"I know how. I watch you."

Barney climbed up with a smile and looked back at his wife. "I will have to remember that. You are right, my sweet. I do like the dress on you."

As they pulled up in front of the Langton house, Joshua and Ruth ran out to greet Jay. Lizzie followed with Hannah on her hip, as Rachel ran to keep up. "The children could not wait until you were here."

"Lizzie, 'tis so good to see you. Where is Papa?"

"He's out at the barn with Ezekiel. He has something to show you. Barnabas, good morrow to you. You shall want to see this as well."

"Good morrow to you, Elizabeth. Benjamin was just talking about the lambs."

"Oh, he does have lambs out there, to be sure." She winked at Ben and received a big smile from him in return.

Lizzie put Hannah down and they all followed Barney along the path behind the house.

The ash and birch trees lent shade to the walk, and the scent of roses and lavender drifted from the garden beyond. As they entered the barn, Mary breathed in the aroma of sweet hay mingling with the pungent odor of dung, a familiar scent that she loved. She walked past the row of stalls, Barney, her sister, and the children behind her; Northstar, a yearling, put his head over a stall door to greet her.

"There, baby, you are a good boy." She patted the bold star on his forehead.

They continued down the corridor and she could hear Papa and Zeke speaking in quiet tones. Both men turned to them and stood as they approached. Mary was the first to reach the stall and peered in. "Oh, Papa. Look, Ben and Rach. See how small he is?"

"It is a filly. A little girl," Papa said.

"What shall you name her?"

"I believe Starlight. Do you see that faint little star on her forehead? Yes, I like Starlight."

"Oh, I do too." Mary bent to trace her finger around the star. The filly raised her delicate nose to nuzzle her fingers. "Why, hello there, little Starlight. You are a beauty."

"Good you like the name, my girl, because she will be yours someday." Papa looked pleased with himself.

"Thank you. So much." She hugged Papa

and turned to Barney with a grin. "I shan't have to ride Baldy anymore."

"Heigh-ho, and Baldy thought you loved him."

The clan celebrated their patriarch's birthday with a fine dinner, and after much fawning over little Hannah — and the new filly — Papa turned to Mary. "So, my dear. What about you?"

"What about me?" Her smile was expectant.

"A babe. When shall you give me another grandchild?"

Her face burned and she looked away. She could not think of a proper reply, and Barnabas just stared at her.

Lizzie stood up. "Father, for shame. 'Tis not right to make poor Mary speak of such things here at the table with children present. She shall decide when the time is correct for such matters."

Mary pushed back from the table. "No, Lizzie, I am fine." She knew her eyes would betray her and she kept them lowered as she turned to her father. "I do pray for that, Papa. I think about it all of the time, it seems. Barney does too. Perhaps it is not in God's plan for us to have one of our own."

Barney stood and came to her side. "Nay, my sweet, do not think that. He will bless us in His time."

"I think that is true." Papa stood. "Children, you are excused. You may play outside, but until I join you, please stay out of the barn. We need to make certain little Starlight has her time to rest." He turned back to Mary. "You have always been so very good at nurturing. I have always loved that in you. To be sure, you will be a good mother. You are now, my dear. If God does not bless you with a child of your own, He will bless you in many other ways. Of that I am certain."

On the ride back home Mary was quiet, lost in her thoughts. Jay and Ben bantered back and forth over who might ride Starlight first. As they approached their home, Barnabas drew back on the reins. "Enough, boys. Starlight has plenty of growing before she is big enough for you to ride, and by then I daresay neither of you will care who is first."

He helped Mary from the wagon and sent the boys to put Baldy in the barn. "I was surprised your father told you God might bless you in other ways."

" 'Tis true, do you not think?"

"We desire a child so much, Mary, I do pray that He will give us one. I am patient. I know it will be in His own time."

"You do not sound patient to me, Barney. It seems you are always talking about it.

Asking me, just like Papa did. Lizzie knows how much that hurts me."

"I do not know why the question should hurt. It is an honest question."

"It makes me aware how much time has passed and still no babe. There is only so much time and then . . ."

"Then what?"

"Why, then a woman no longer can. She is old."

Barnabas finally chuckled. "You have a long way to go until you are old. If that is your worry, please stop it."

" 'Tis not funny and do not tell me to stop it. Or perhaps you should like to sleep with Baldy tonight!" She flounced to the door.

"Gracious, woman, and how would that solve anything?" He charged for the barn, in a fume.

"There is nothing I shall want solved tonight," she called, but hoped he did not hear.

11

October 1636

Wind swept through the wheat with a gentle rustle as Mary looked out across the field. Thomas and Jane had been in New England for three years now. Barney talked daily of his plans for their migration to the New World, but it was all so much to take in. Somewhere to the west would be the ocean they must cross to their new home. She shuddered. A new home, if they survived. It was a long way across that ocean. Barney told her she must trust in the Lord and He would provide. But so far her world kept shaking.

A twinkling star appeared, followed by another. Would the stars follow them to the colonies? She hoped God would. She closed her eyes in prayer as the wind stung a tear trickling down her cheek. She wanted God to listen, but at times He seemed so far away. Like the stars. Like her mother.

Barney slid his arms around her waist. She caught her breath as he pulled her close. "I didn't hear you come up. Do you think my mother and Ann look down from heaven, from the stars?"

He scanned the sky. "God gave us stars for navigation, to find our way in the dark."

"Mother said they are like little windows to heaven."

"Aye, I like that. She had many stories, did she not? Mayhap that's heaven's light shining down."

"I shall miss my family so much, Barney. Papa, my sister, Zeke, and the babies — they are all I have had for so long."

She waited for his reply while he rubbed her arms, bringing warmth to the cool fall evening. After a moment she added, "I'm tired of planning and quite ready to go, and it's helped me so much talking things over with Lizzie. What shall I do without her?"

"You will have me, Mary. I know this is a hard thing for you to do, to follow me. As long as there is the very breath in me, I will take care of you."

A cool, wet wind whipped her skirts about. She shivered and once again imagined crossing the ocean to a place she could not fathom. Jeremy had made the voyage twice and even his stories left her wondering.

Barnabas hovered over her and rested his chin in her hair. "You remember meeting Reverend Youngs when we went on holiday to Southwold? How he requested passage on *The Mary Ann* out of Yarmouth and was denied? His plan is now to depart from Hingham over in Norfolk. Of course his wife and six children will accompany him. Several members of his vicarage plan to go with him, as well. They are bound for Boston, but likely it will be next year before they sail. It must be kept silent, of course, not even your father should be told."

"He tells no one of our plans. He would do nothing to endanger us or any of the reformers, Barney."

"Of course, but the fewer who know about Reverend Youngs, the safer it is for his family. Your father has been very tolerant of the meetings we have, but mostly to protect you."

"He's not happy with our plans. He would have us stay if he thought it safe, but the dangers across the ocean are just as frightening to him. Lizzie tells him of the stories she hears about how wondrous the New World is and tells him I must support you."

"The stories are true, Mary."

150

"Do you believe that?"

He chortled. "Jeremy might embellish, but Thomas tells us straight. Yes, indeed his letter states it is true what they say. I promise you. It is truly God's paradise."

"Are you not happy here?"

"It is not about being happy here. I believe God's hand is in this. We see the dangers here compounded every day. I worry much more about persecutions from the church and government than Indians and wild animals in the New World."

Mary drew back. "We hear so many stories about whippings and jail, yet I feel so isolated here."

"That's the danger, Mary. We can become complacent. I promised Ann. I promised her I would take care of the boys. Prithee, it is what I must do. There are many things in this life I do not understand, that I do not know. One thing I have learned. Sometimes we must step out in faith. Is it not what we did when we pledged our lives to each other?"

She rested her head against his shoulder, his breath warm on her hair. "I want to be strong for you and have your faith. But we are not without problems, and they will follow us. We have yet to find a way to ease Jay's pain. He misses his mother and it hurts him. He is like you. You both hold your pain inside until it rises up to overwhelm us. I try so hard to understand, and to anticipate, but sometimes I feel lost and helpless. Those things will not change by running away. And far across that ocean we shall have no one to turn to."

His arms tightened around her. He was silent and she wondered what was on his heart.

"We shall have God. God is who we must turn to." He hugged her tight.

"Then I shall go with you and always work beside you." She turned to look into his dark green eyes. "Barney, I don't know why, but you carry much guilt over Ann's death. You know much more than me about spiritual matters, but pray thee, you need to forgive yourself. You need to do that before we leave."

"Ann and I had a beautiful life together. We were much more fortunate than most of our friends. We found love. A true love we delighted in and thanked the Lord daily for." He paused. "Can you not understand why I would want to leave this place? There are so many memories that it holds. It haunts me."

"The memories you must keep, not run from. You shall find a time when they make you smile. You shall remember the good times, the happy times. But it does not mean you cannot create new memories."

"It is more than that. At times I watch you as you clean and rearrange things to your liking. You are but building a nest, and I understand that — yet I want to correct you. To tell you, nay, that's not how Ann did it . . . that's not where Ann kept it. I hold my tongue and hate myself for those thoughts, but they are there."

Pain pricked her heart like a thorn. "I — I know that. I can tell what you are thinking. But 'tis all right. I don't wish to change things for you. Only —"

"I see that. I do. We both can start anew in Massachusetts. But more than that, God has laid the church on my heart. My father and I will never agree. He gave me his Bible years ago, yet our thoughts on the church are at odds. If I cannot convince my father, I cannot convince the Church of England. Unless by going to New England we might establish the church there and show the king what God intended."

"But you have reconciled with your father."

"Certainly. But to the point, it is time for me to seek my own way. To not just say the words, but to act on my beliefs."

"You are an honorable man. 'Tis one of the reasons I adore you, Barney."

"Pray thee, if we go to the New World we have the chance to build the church as God would have us to do. A chance to build our own home. Without the memories. We will do as you say, make new memories. Give me your agreement. Give me your support. That is the balm I need."

She leaned on her husband as they gazed out to the west. If this is what he needed, she would indeed be his balm. And perhaps God would grant him a second love of a lifetime. "You are the kindest, sweetest man I have ever known and I am so blessed to have you. It makes me feel guilty when I think about you losing the love of your life and I have just found mine. I long for you to love me like you loved her. I pray thee that you understand."

He looked down at her. "But why does that matter? I try to understand. We never seem to get past the wondering and the guilt, though. It perplexes me to think you cannot understand how I care. Do I not show you daily? What else can I say? I fear you do not believe in yourself. Do you not understand how much you give me? For that I am truly indebted."

"That means much to me, but I'm still

struggling to find my place with you. I think I understand how you care for me, and then I find pieces of your soul that I know nothing about, and that scares me."

He pulled her closer. She turned in his embrace and met his kiss. "You have been strong for years for your father. And now you have stood by me and pulled me from my grief. You are a strong one, to be sure, but mayhap it is time for me to be strong enough for both of us."

They stood together and watched as myriad stars popped from the darkening sky. A savory aroma wafted down from the house and Barney inhaled deeply. "Gracious, it is getting dark."

"Are you hungry?" She reluctantly broke away. "Supper shall not be long. I put the meat from dinner in a pottage and left it simmering on the fire. Gather up the boys for a washing while I put it on the table."

"The smell makes me hungry."

She hugged herself and grinned. Was he saying he liked her cooking? Perhaps he would pass the tongs. Perhaps he would love her.

The Horton clan gathered at their well-worn oak table. Mary put the pottage, brimming with thick pieces of mutton, onions, turnips, and parsnips, at the center of the table. She set the crusty bread, hot and fragrant, next to the freshly churned butter. As she sat next to her husband, they joined hands and lowered their heads.

Barney led the prayer. "Lord, I pray that You will guide us in our preparations for the trip to the colonies. It will be long and arduous. We will be risking much. We pray that You will be with us each step of the way and that we may not waver from Your plan for us. We ask Your blessings in all things. Amen."

Jay and Ben eagerly mopped the gravy with their bread. It pleased her to see them eat with gusto. Barney would disapprove of their manners, but it was good to see Jay enjoy her meal. Usually he feigned a stomachache when she cooked.

"Joseph, Benjamin. When I grew up, we ate with our hands, but now that is what we have spoons for." Barnabas took a heaping spoonful of stew and savored it. Carefully, he put down the spoon and scratched at his beard, winking at the boys before turning back to her. "Aye, I see. We shall all want to soak our bread in the sauce to get every bit. Gracious, I shall lose my place as cook and baker in this family if I am not careful."

She basked in the compliment. In the

New World he would need to devote his attentions to building a house and a church. She would become mistress of the hearth and home.

Supper finished, they settled near the fire. Barney picked up the Bible and leafed through the pages. He looked dismayed. Or was that indignation?

"The ribbon. Ann's blue hair ribbon. Where is it?" His voice was sharp, so far different than just a few moments ago at dinner. His look was leveled directly at her.

"I — I don't know. I didn't take it out of the Bible. I did read from it this morning, but I am sure I did not remove the ribbon." She looked frantically about, spotting the frayed ribbon resting at the leg of the oak table. "There it is. Perhaps it fell as you opened the pages."

He sighed and looked a bit sheepish. She picked it up and he accepted it without comment.

She listened as he read a passage, but his angry words echoed in her head.

12

March 1, 1637

A frantic flurry ensued with the necessary planning and preparation for such a long voyage. Mary bent over the list at the oak table, twirling a ringlet of hair around her finger as she studied the account intently. Dried beef, salt pork, beans, wheat, oats, peas, oil, vinegar, and butter. Sugar and spices. Ginger, pepper, cloves, mace, nutmeg, and cinnamon were on his list, but she knew she would need far more spices than that. And herbs. Sweet oranges and lemons were recommended for their fragrance and health. Implements included an iron pot, kettle, a frying pan, gridiron, another skillet, a spit, wooden platters, trenches, and spoons.

"This is a good start. But in truth, I worry more about sleeping down below with all of those people. People that cannot bathe and are sick. I've heard the terrible stories,

Jeremy. I shudder to think of the conditions."

"Aye, life on the 'tween deck is dangerous. The seas will be rough and the voyage long and people do get very sick. It's not easy, but you are strong and healthy, as the boys are. I promise you I intend to make it as easy upon you as I can. I would like to offer you the master cabin. It's not large, with only one bed, but it would offer you privacy, as well as safety."

"Oh, no, you cannot do that. That wouldn't be right. Where would you sleep? What if you became ill?" Mary looked to Barney for agreement.

Jeremy was quick to answer. "Do not worry for me. I'll sleep in the scuttle hatch with my two ship's officers. As long as I'm not sleeping on the beakhead, I shall be fine."

Jay looked up, showing interest in the conversation for the first time. "What's that, Uncle Jeremy?"

"That is where the sailors work the foresails. And they use it as their chamber pot." He laughed at Jay's obvious disgust. "The scuttle hatch is forward of the foremast."

"What's the foremast?"

"It holds up the sail. Barn, your son will be a sailor for sure. I'll teach you all about sailing on the voyage, Joseph. You can learn to use the cross-staff and learn all about the stars." He turned to Mary, obviously satisfied that all would be well with this journey.

His sincerity softened Mary's heart. No matter how hard the next months would be, she knew Jeremy would do everything he could to make it bearable for her. He was so much like Barney.

"What of our furniture, Jeremy?" She eyed the old oak table.

"Nay, the furniture stays. It is too heavy and bulky. There are plenty of trees of all kinds in Massachusetts. The forests are endless. No one even knows how vast they are. Barnabas can build all of the furniture you could ever want for." He turned to his brother. "Do you have a cask? It would be best to pack your necessities in one, but with a wife and two children I could allow you two. Cargo room is limited, and we will have livestock on board, so I want you to be careful in what you plan to bring. I will have final approval, so it shall be best for you to tell me early on."

"Aye, brother. I know the cooper. He will build what we need. We will look at your list and make revisions. I shall let you know next week what we require."

■ ■ ■ ■

To her surprise, she enjoyed working on the list. To Jeremy's basics, she added biscuits and cheese. How had he not mentioned them? Although she loved her dresses and hats, the kitchen cloths and other various linens were far more important for their home. She would try to fit in as many folds of fabric from the mercer as she could, perhaps worsted and linen. In gray and black? Yes, if she were to start over, she would dress for Barney. Dress in the conservative style he preferred her to wear. But her favorite green gown would not be left behind, and the silver looking glass, a must. And seeds. She must ask Lizzie to help her gather seeds. Perhaps they could do some cuttings. How to transport, though. Hmm . . . she must ask Jeremy. She would miss her English garden.

Barney looked over her shoulder. "Do not forget we will only have two casks."

"I know, Barney. I do wish we could bring the table, though." She lovingly traced her finger around the hearts that contained the *J* and *B*.

"You heard Jeremy. That is not possible. Too heavy, too big. I will make you a fine table when we get there."

"But you are missing the significance of this one. Someday you shall realize it, but it will be too late. Jay and Ben both know the importance. It is a very real expression of their mother's love. Beyond their memories and their quilts, they do not have much to cling to as they travel so far away."

"I am touched that you care, I am. You remind me of why I need a mother for my children. But we simply will not have the allowance for the table. You must abide by that." He kissed the top of her head and listened to her sigh. "Truly, I do understand it. Now cheer up, my sweet. On the morrow we leave for London with Elizabeth and Ezekiel. It will be a holiday for you ladies. Jeremy plans to meet with me and Ezekiel. There is much to discuss."

"And the children?"

"Joseph and Benjamin will stay with Grandmother Horton, and Elizabeth's children will stay with their grandpapa."

While Barney, Jeremy, and Zeke met for a game of bowl, Mary and Lizzie took to the shops. After their supper, the five walked the path next to the Thames and leaned on the same stone wall where she and Lizzie had stood over six years ago. Mary searched the docks for *The Swallow.* Lizzie quietly put her arm around her sister.

Jeremy stepped close. "You cannot see her from here, Mary. On the morrow I will take you to her before we set out for Mowsley. She is bigger and grander than any of these. That one across the way is *The Hector.* Reverend Davenport will be on that ship and *The Hector* will sail with us, as our sister ship."

Barney came to Mary's side. "Reverend Davenport is the minister I told you about who knows Reverend Youngs. They will work together in Massachusetts."

" 'Tis comforting to know there will be another ship close by."

"Aye. It is always planned that way, for safety."

"I have been thinking, Jeremy, of the people who will live down below, on the 'tween deck."

"Oh?"

"I should like to be of help to them in some way. It shan't be much, but I was thinking I should like to bring a few barrels of lemons, if I may, and share them daily with the passengers down below. It might ease their condition somewhat perhaps. For their breath and to help fragrance the living area. There is not much I can do, but with your permission, I would like to make that my mission."

"That would be most kind of you, but of course, you do not mean to go down there yourself, do you?"

"Oh, yes, I do. I would not feel I was being of help to stay on the main deck."

Barney touched her hand. "Jeremy will take you down when we board. If you can see firsthand the conditions, I believe you will know it best to not go down with any regularity."

"Aye, Mary, I am trying to spare you that. It's kind of you to offer barrels of lemons, but limit it to one and we'll add it to the larder. Or if you would slice the peels and dry them, we can bring more."

On the night of their return, over a supper of cold meats and carrots, Barney discussed the trip with Mary. The boys listened eagerly, asking about the bowling and ships. Jay and Ben took turns telling of adventures they had with Grandmother and Grandfather Horton.

Supper finished and Scriptures read, Barney closed the Bible. "Boys, it has been an exhausting day. Time for you to change into your nightshirts."

Jay gave his usual look of disdain but did as he was told. Ben looked at Mary and she nodded toward the bedroom with a smile. He followed closely behind his brother.

"Jeremy and I stopped at the cemetery and I knelt beside Ann's grave."

Mary looked up. "When was that?"

"Coming home, when you were in the carriage with Ezekiel and Elizabeth. We got so far in front of you that we found we had some extra time. Did you not notice we disappeared for a time?"

"No, I suppose Lizzie and I were talking too much. It was difficult in the city, knowing this would be the last time we were there together. We had so much to say to each other on the way back. 'Tis good you stopped."

"I was looking at the blue slate I put over her grave. I told Jeremy it would mean much to me if I could bring a similar piece with me for my own tomb." He studied his cup as he fingered it.

"Is there something about your health you have not shared with me?" She hoped the sarcasm she heard in her voice did not sound so sharp to him. "You know it hurts me when you do not share important matters with me." She reached out to touch his hand.

He pulled back. "If you please, there is nothing wrong with my health. My good doctor tells me I am hale and actually very sound. Nay, this is about wanting the blue slate in New England. I know what I want engraved on the stone and I must make haste to have this done before we take our leave. Jeremy is in agreement."

She wanted to be kind, but she felt herself slipping. "Barnabas. Is there no end? Jeremy tells me that I cannot bring the oak table. A table that means so much to your sons and should to you too. And you agreed with that. Now you tell me that you want to bring a slab of blue slate — the weight we cannot even guess — and — Jeremy tells you that he approves?"

"It is his ship, Mary."

"I do not understand. 'Tis quite beyond me. If thou thinks I will follow thee to the end of the earth, methinks you should think again! I love you, but if you do not value my judgment, then by your leave, plan on what you will take, but do not plan on taking me!"

Barney jumped to his feet and raked his hand through his hair, then scratched at his beard. "Pray thee, where does this come from? This anger that boils up?"

"Why would it not anger me? It seems you and Jeremy have both gone behind my back and planned this. 'Tis not a matter of thinking I cared not. You knew I cared. Did not that matter to you?"

He began to pace and it reminded her of Papa.

"I do care, you know I do. Have I not stood by and let you make that confounded list? I have remained silent while you make your lists and purchases. And did not Jeremy give his permission for you to bring an extra barrel of lemons?"

"They are not for me. They are for those poor people in the holds of the ship."

"Very well, but even so, I have been patient with what you intend to bring. You know I have."

"Perhaps you don't understand how important the table is."

"Please know I would not sail without you. Let me go to Jeremy on the morrow and ask if we might bring both. The blue slate is important to me. I cannot say wherefore, just that it is. But I would not choose the slate over you. Never, Mary."

"I thank you for that." She managed a weak smile. "Yes, please, I want you to ask this of Jeremy. Truly, I want to bring the table. Tell him he has upset me greatly."

"I will do that. I will beg of him to reconsider the table, on the morrow. Mary, when the weather improves, will you come to the cemetery with me?"

"Of course I shall. And bring the boys?"

"We will, but I would like to make a trip there with just the two of us first." He stood and picked up the candle. "May we get some sleep?"

"I'm so tired from the trip, sleep shall be good."

As she walked toward their bedroom, she heard him pause. He said good night to Ann, as he always did.

Spring arrived, wet though it was, and while the morning was still fresh, Mary set out to pick flowers. She and Barney would go to the cemetery today, and she wanted a bouquet to place on Ann's grave.

Jay and Ben climbed in the cart as Barney whistled to Baldy, and they started down the lane. "You know, boys, Miss Tilly will not be able to make the voyage with us." He glanced at the boys.

"What? Why can't she come with us?" Their plea was almost in unison.

Mary pulled Ben close and leaned toward Jay. "Miss Tilly is old. It would not be nice to her to bring her on the ship. She will be much happier with Aunt Lizzie and your cousins."

Barney nodded. "Mayhap Joshua will take

her under his care. What do you think, Joseph?"

"Yes, Father. Joshua would be good to her. Those girls are too jumpy and noisy. Miss Tilly needs someone who will hold her and not squeeze her."

Lizzie came out when they arrived. She laughed as the boys scrambled off the wagon and chattered to their cousins about Miss Tilly. Lizzie would never complain about one more to take care of.

"Don't worry about the boys, Mary. Joshua has been looking forward to playing with them all morning."

"We shan't be long. Barney wanted a bit of time at the cemetery and then we shall be right back." As they pulled away Mary waved, but only Lizzie returned it — the children too busy to notice.

As they entered the cemetery, they stopped for a moment. The grass, green and tall from the rains, swayed with the breeze. Ann's grave was up the hill and Barney urged Baldy forward.

He helped Mary down and she gently put the nosegay across the blue slate. They stood in prayerful silence, his Bible tucked under his arm.

He cleared his throat. "Mayhap this is not the time to ask this of you, but I do not know what would be a good time. May I share with you the words I wrote for my slate?"

He knew the words he wanted on the slate? He had never answered her question about his health. In fact she had asked it in jest. But perhaps she should ask again. "Barney, are you ill? Why do you plan your epitaph?"

"Nay, it's not that. Certes, I would tell you if I were ill. Gracious, it is not about that at all."

"Then I should like to hear it." She chose her words carefully. She still smarted from the words they had exchanged weeks ago. " 'Tis important to me that you are at peace when we leave Mowsley. I know no matter how hard you try to believe to the contrary, it will be hard for you to leave. Tell me now, what you intend for your tomb."

"I want my name, place of birth, and the date of my birth and death to frame the face of it. Of course, the date of death would be added after I'm gone."

She raised her brow. "You have this well planned, Barney."

"Aye. I am thinking in the center I would like to say that it is with God that I now abide, and that our children should trust and obey our Lord so that they may come to rest in God's holy place with me."

"My, but that is a lot to say and methinks you have put much thought into this."

"I have, my sweet. In truth, I have penned it. Here, read it and tell me your thoughts." He opened his Bible and carefully removed a folded parchment and handed it to her.

He looked flustered as she took the paper. It seemed important to him. She lowered herself to the damp ground and unfolded it. The paper fluttered in the wind, and her eyes, reflecting the blue sky, began to mist.

Here lies my body tombed in dust
till Christ shall come to raise it with the just;
my soul ascended to the throne of God
where with sweet Jesus now I make abode;
Then hasten after me, my dearest wife,
to be a partaker of this blessed life;
And you, dear children all, follow the Lord,
hear and obey His public sacred word;
and in your houses call upon His name,
for oft have I advised you to the same:
then God will bless you with your children
    all,
and to this blessed place He will you call.

She hugged the paper to her chest as tears trickled down her cheeks. "Barney, I do not know what to say. This is beautiful. I love that it is a message for all of your children and their children to come. Generations of Hortons. Why did you not tell me of this?"

"It means much to me and I was not sure you would understand. I want to bring the blue slate. I do want you to have the table, though, and I have petitioned Jeremy to bring it."

She grabbed his hand and squeezed it. "I see two messages here. Am I correct?"

His smile was broad and genuine. "Aye, you see that? I pray for you to follow me to this new land, our new abode, where our children can grow up hearing God's sacred Word and be able to worship Him in our home, free of persecution. If we do this, I truly believe that God will bless us with many children."

"I like that." She smoothed the paper and studied the words once more.

"And then when He calls me to my final abode, I pray you hasten to join me in heaven, and that all of our children, and their children, under our covenant with God, will join us too. I feel we are beginning a most significant journey going to the New World. I know it is hard to leave behind our family and possessions, but the Church of England believes it can control the minds of men, and it cannot. We are ordained by

God to have a free will. Aye, it is time for us to leave. The blue slate will endure forever. I want all of my children for the generations to come to know of me and why I came to the New World."

"I love you, Barney. What you have written here is testament to your faith in God." She searched his eyes to see his soul. "I am troubled though, with one thing."

"What is that, my sweet?"

"Ann has gone before you to heaven. She is waiting there for you. When you join her, what becomes of me?"

"I would never forget you. That is why I wrote that for the blue slate. Aye, I will be happy to be joined with Ann once more and I do celebrate that thought. But I will not forget you. I believe God brought us together for a purpose. I will be waiting for you."

"But who would be married to you? Ann?"

He looked at the blue slate covering his Ann's grave. "On this earth I am married to you. In the Bible, I believe God teaches there is no marriage in heaven. I will wait for you and rejoice with all of the angels when you are at heaven's door."

She took his hand. "I need you, Barney. I have you now and for that I am thankful. I pray we have many, many children, and that from our seed there will be generations to come that will gaze upon your blue slate and know you were a man of God, obedient to His ways and one who truly loved his children. But I hope 'tis a long time from now."

He swept her into his arms and kissed her nose, then her waiting lips. "You understand me so well. Thank you for that. I have not had a reply from Jeremy, but surely he will grant us our requests. There must be some merit to being the shipmaster's brother."

Mary squeezed his hand. Ann had been blessed. She had a husband who was honorable and loved her very much. Would Barnabas ever love her the same way?

13

May 5, 1637
London, England

Standing on the pier, Mary could taste the salt on the dank air. The wooden ships bobbed like apples in a water bucket. *The Swallow*'s sails flapped in the wind.

She held on tightly to Jay's and Ben's hands as the crew heaved cargo up to the deck. Crates of oranges, turnips, and winter lettuce were hauled on board. Heavy barrels of salted meat were rolled up the plank, and bags of beans, too many to count, were tossed from one sailor to another.

"Mama, look." Ben's voice rang with excitement. "Look, our table!"

She attempted a smile as the table was hoisted to the deck, followed by two weighty oak casks. Everything they would have in the New World was in those casks. The family joked they were filled with gold, they were so heavy. "Yes, Ben, the table goes with us."

Jeremy had responded that the blue slate should stay and granted Mary's request to bring the oak table, provided the legs be removed. He commiserated with his brother, but promised he would do much importing in the future and would make delivery of the blue slate a priority.

Jay's hand wriggled to escape her grasp and she clung tighter. He disliked holding hands, but today he needed her. Ben's love came so easily. Would Jay ever return her love?

She looked up and down amongst the crowd for Papa, Lizzie, Zeke, and the children. Everything she'd done this past year prepared her for their journey and she'd visited her family as often as the days would allow, but nothing could have prepared her for the ill she felt in her stomach this day. She spotted Josh first, running ahead of his sisters and Lizzie. Zeke brought up the rear with Papa.

Allowing Jay to run up ahead to greet his cousins, she wrapped her arms around Ben and kissed his blond curls. "It shall be hard saying goodbye to everyone. Help me through this, Ben."

"Why don't they come with us, Mama? Why must we leave them here? Father says it's not safe. Why would they stay?"

"I wish they could come. Perhaps they shall miss us too much and decide to follow us." She squeezed him harder.

Lizzie pushed through the crowd, her crystal blue eyes dry, but her cheeks red and tearstained. Just like Lizzie to hide her pain. Rachel and Ruth pulled at Ben until he was obliged to join them in a game of tag.

Tears collected in Mary's eyes as Lizzie and Hannah joined her. " 'Tis good for him to run off some energy. It shall be a long journey without much chance of such play."

"That is true. I cannot imagine life on a ship. 'Tis like a prison, is it not?" Lizzie smiled with a tease in her eyes.

Mary giggled despite herself. "I could not know yet, but thank you for the thought. You've an odd way of alleviating tension, my dear sister."

The wind whipped the sails around the tall masts as if impatient, and Mary looked up at the ship that would carry her small family away to the New World. How many ships had she watched labor out of this very harbor? To think she would now be the one waving from the deck. Would it be a prison? No matter, as long as they lived to tell about it.

Lizzie followed her gaze. "You always said you loved the ships."

She forced her attention back to the pier, searching for Papa. "What was I thinking? I must be a romantic at heart."

Lizzie stepped close. "Mary, you do not have to do this. You still have time to say you must stay."

She looked at her sister, so beautiful in her sapphire blue dress, her black ringlets pulled high under her wide-brimmed bonnet. How she would miss her!

Mary caught sight of Papa. He was holding on to Zeke's arm, his silver head lowered. "He looks so old, like he has aged ten years overnight. Family would always win over ships, Lizzie. No, 'tis Barney I love and he feels a calling to go to the New World. I must go. He is my family now, and his boys my sons."

Reaching out to take Papa's hand, she whispered in his ear, "This shall not be the last time we are together. Jeremy says that I can come back to visit — he shall be back and forth so often." If only it were that easy.

She straightened. "I know I have said this a thousand times in the year past, but I want all of you to consider joining us when you can. I want you to see the New World's beauty and abundance for yourself. More than that, I cannot bear to be apart from you."

"I'm afraid I am too old for such a journey and I could never leave your mother. Who would bring her flowers? Nay, this is my place. This is where I will stay." Papa looked back, away from the pier, to the gentle, heather-covered slopes, toward home.

Tears fell as she threw herself into his arms. "I shall miss you."

"Aye, daughter, there now. Look what I have brought for you. The dolly that Mother made for you. She always made you happy and brought you comfort. Your place is with your husband now, but I wanted you to have something of your childhood. Where is he, by the by?"

Mary took the cloth dolly she had treasured as a little girl and held it close. Its curly yarn hair meant to match her own and the legless body covered with blue cloth and a red heart she had treasured since she was no bigger than Rachel. "He is on the ship. He wanted to see how they stored the casks. We shall have very little in the cabin itself, most of what we bring will be down on the 'tween deck. We shall keep the Bible his father gave him in the cabin, of course, and Jeremy says Barney should keep his old musket there." She turned toward the ship.

Lilting laughter erupted from a small group of ladies as Barney strode up to them.

"What — ? Mary, I thought you said he was on board." Papa frowned.

"Tsk, I told you, little sister, to take things slowly. You never listen to me. Now he is dragging you across the ocean, away from your family, and look, he's surrounded by fawning females. He needed time before settling down with one woman again. Men always wonder —" Lizzie stopped herself. "Prithee, forgive me. I should not put such notions in your head."

Mary hugged the doll tighter. "Nay, he's done on board. Most certainly those ladies are imposing on him. That always happens at the bakeshop. Remember how he loves to chat with the ladies? Nothing has changed. He still enjoys that. 'Tis nothing."

Zeke moved closer to Mary. "No harm in old Barn saying goodbye to the ladies. He has been their baker for years."

"How do you know they are not traveling as well?" Her sister's frown matched Papa's.

Barney turned, his eyes meeting Mary's, then darting back to his audience. He made a slight bow of his head to Miss Patience Terry, and turned to join his wife and her family.

Extending his hand first to John, then to

Zeke, he thanked them for coming to say goodbye. "This means so much to Mary and to me as well." He wrapped his arm about her shoulders.

She leaned into him. He was by her side and that was what mattered. Everything would be all right. Would it not?

"Mary, I almost forgot," Lizzie said. "The girls have something for you. Something we spent the last several months working on. Rachel, Ruth! Come at once." Her thin voice floated over the din.

The girls gave up their chase of Ben and rushed to their mother's side. Lizzie handed Mary a large basket. Inside she found a stack of carefully hemmed handkerchiefs. Delicate, embroidered red and purple roses decorated each. Layered between the hand-kerchiefs were sprigs of lavender. Mary held the scented cloth to her nose.

"We know it will be trying on the long voyage. I hope this will ease the stench you no doubt shall endure."

"Oh, Rach, Ruthie . . . Lizzie. Thank you so very much. I am beyond words. What a thoughtful gift. I will think of you every time I use these. The embroidery is exquisite. They are beautiful." She looked to Barney and he nodded his approval.

Ben peered into the basket. "Mama, look

underneath. Oranges."

"Yes, there are a few oranges in the bottom and I made some sugared ginger. Perhaps it will help with the seasickness they say is such a problem."

"How very generous of you and your family. Thank you again." Barney gave Lizzie a hug.

"I pray thee to take good care of our Mary, Barnabas. I shall not be there to catch her, as I always have been."

"Aye."

John looked him straight in the eye. "I told you she is very strong, but she has a sweet and gentle heart as well. It makes her vulnerable." His voice caught. "She will always desire to believe the best in you."

"To be sure, Mary helps me to be a better man. I know that. You have my promise, John. I will take care of your daughter. And Elizabeth, it is now my turn to protect her and that I will do, with God's help. Now stay a moment, my sweet, and let me go ahead to see to our cabin. Jeremy awaits me." He kissed her forehead.

She watched as he trudged up the plank. He looked eager to begin their journey.

Her gaze followed Barney until he disappeared. "He is a good man and he needs me." She gently put her doll in the basket with the handkerchiefs and oranges. "I shall send letters with Jeremy and tell you all about the colonies. And, I hope to soon have another grandchild for you, Papa."

"I await that news eagerly, my girl. I shall miss you greatly, you know that, eh?" He pulled her to him.

"Papa, oh please do not cry. I do know that, and I shall miss you terribly." She put her arms around him as his trembling arms wrapped about her shoulders.

Lizzie moved toward them, loud, anguished sobs escaping, and they brought her into the embrace. "I wish you could stay."

Barney's voice resonated above the milling crowd, calling the children to gather. Mary dabbed her eyes with the handkerchief as she broke away from Lizzie's embrace and gathered her nieces and nephew to her.

A familiar elderly couple made their way toward them. Grandfather and Grandmother Horton pushed through the crowd. How sad they looked. How hard it must be to lose yet another son to that vast unknown. She joined her husband as he greeted them.

"Father, Mother — I worried you might not make it here before we embarked." He gave the Horton bear hug to both parents at once, kissing his mother on both cheeks.

He pulled back and shook his father's hand.

Grandfather Horton held tight. He lifted his walking stick and pressed it into his hand. "This is for you, son. I have used it a good many years and it has helped me walk tall and straight. It's yours now, to take to that New World."

Barney turned the stick over in his hand, running his fingers over the ivory head. He traced his father's initials, *J.H.,* and looked from his father to his mother.

"Your mother gave it to me as a gift, one that I have treasured. She wants you to have it now, son. We both want you to have it."

"Father, I shall always strive to live up to your example. Thank you, Mother. I know this is difficult, but you both have always shown me support, even when you disagreed."

Grandmother Horton's eyes were wet as she turned to Mary. "Jeremy will keep us in touch. Prithee, write to us often. You are a good wife to our son. You are always in our prayers." Her words sounded broken, a reflection of her heart.

The grandparents bent to say farewell to Jay and Ben, a moment so tender and heart wrenching, Mary wondered if Barney could watch. He could not.

Grandfather Horton tucked a small,

carved horse in each of the boys' pockets and turned to embrace Mary. "You will take good care of them, I know."

"This is difficult, but it is time to board. This does not have to be a final farewell. Lord be willing, we will all be together again. Come, Joseph, Benjamin, say your goodbyes and then we must take our leave." Barnabas clapped his father on the back and gave his mother one last kiss.

The boys, with tearstained faces, hugged their step-cousins and kissed Aunt Lizzie goodbye. They grabbed Mary's hands once more and turned toward the ship that would take them far, far away.

Mary's heart ached and she felt she had no breath as they walked up to the ship. Walk. Just put one foot in front of the other. One step at a time. You can do this. The Lord would help her do this. She squeezed Jay's and Ben's hands until they both looked up at her. She hoped her nod was reassuring.

Elizabeth stood with their father and watched her sister ascend the plank. She dabbed at her eyes with a handkerchief that matched the gift to her sister. As she leaned into Ezekiel, she caught notice of a young woman trailing behind an older couple as they were boarding the ship, reluctant to leave her girlfriends behind on the dock.

"Ezekiel. Isn't that Miss Terry?"

14

The Swallow

Captain Jeremy Horton escorted Mary, Barney, and the boys to the roundhouse on the upper deck. He made the necessary introductions to First Officer Bennett and his wife, Mistress Bennett. "Barn, mayhap Joseph and Benjamin would enjoy inspecting the masts and sails, whilst I give the ladies a tour of the ship." He turned to Mary. "Mistress Bennett will be disembarking before we set sail."

Mary leaned toward the older woman. "Oh, truly? I was thinking how painful goodbyes are with my family, but to think you must say farewell to your husband." A farewell was just that, to be sure — you prayed the other would fare well until you met once again. One did not know if that would be on earth or in heaven.

Her brother-in-law took his duties as shipmaster seriously, and she tried exceedingly hard to pay attention as he spoke of the fine merits of his ship. He took great measure to ensure the safety of his crew and passengers. If they arrived safely in the New World, and it was as wonderful as the adventurers claimed, perhaps someday he would bring her family across to join them. That would be her daily petition in prayer, but she would also work very hard to that end.

They arrived at the shipmaster's cabin and Jeremy explained that it would be the Horton family's quarters. Both ladies viewed the small, curtained berth. It would be bed for her, Barney, and both boys for the duration. Pity dripped from Mistress Bennett's face.

Mary turned again to her brother-in-law. "I am sorry you shall not be able to use your cabin."

"Nay, I will be fine. Someday I hope to have a wife myself, and then I won't be eager to be so generous. But it's only a small sacrifice to sleep on the officer's deck for this voyage if it gives some comfort to you and my nephews. Come, I will show you the rest of the living quarters. It will give you some perspective when you think about comfort." He gave a meaningful look to Mistress Bennett.

Descending to the 'tween deck, Mary's

breath caught. "People will actually live down here? For almost three months? How many are on board?"

Already masses of people filled the small, close space. A handful claimed the few bunks lining the edge of the deck. Most piled their bedding on the wooden floor. The air seemed warm and clammy from the sea of humanity, and the plank had not even been drawn.

She eyed the pails. Were they to be chamber pots for all of these people? Quickly she gave thanks for her cabin with its porcelain chamber pot, tucked inconspicuously into a corner.

"There are ten and hundred souls on board, counting crew. Some have paid good passage." Jeremy took her arm and directed her up the steps behind Mistress Bennett. "A few will work off the cost of the voyage in the colonies. They are indentured to the Massachusetts Bay Company and have signed a contract. After five or so years of working for the company, the contract is returned, and the land they have built on is theirs. Conditions have been so poor here in England, they are willing to gamble on going to Massachusetts. But many seek to do God's will as you and Barn do."

As they climbed to the top deck, she

scanned the people still crowding the dock. "Is New England really better? It sounds like a magical place someone has dreamt up."

"Aye, it is. But ye know God is the Creator. He dreamt it up. Beautiful — I have seen it with my own eyes. Barnabas believes he and John Youngs's followers will be caretakers of God's gift. But ye know that."

"I do, as Barney pointed it out to convince me. But only if we survive the journey. I've heard the stories of other ships and the families who have perished. If someone has boarded with the pox or measles, we could all die. If a storm comes up, the ship could sink. I like adventure, but this is not something I would choose for myself." She grinned at her brother-in-law. "Do you think 'tis for love?"

"Certes." He lowered his voice to a mutter. "Barn is a blockhead to not see it." He picked up his pace to the main deck. "We are at God's mercy, true. But my ship is sound." He knocked on the rail. "I take immense care in maintaining it. You won't have the comfort of home, but it will be bearable and safe, on my oath. I will be here for anything you will need. I wouldn't take the risk with you and my nephews if I did not believe in the safety of my ship."

Barney, with sons in hand, emerged from the crowd.

"Ah, and here he is. We will lift anchor soon, so I must make haste and go to the stern. Reverend Thomas Reeve will be delivering a sermon and then I will give the command to set sail."

"Mama, the sails are so big." Ben ran up to her. "We climbed the ropes. The topmen let us."

She looked at Jeremy, then at her husband. "They climbed the ropes?"

"Not even half a rod, to be sure." Barney grinned at his brother. "But at sea it will be forbidden."

"Thank goodness." She hugged Ben. "Oh, what fun. 'Tis exciting, is it not, to be on a big ship?"

Ben beamed, but Jay turned and leaned on the rail, his face sullen.

The times Mary had been on the other side of the rail, down on the dock, watching the ships depart, seemed ages ago. She joined him now to look down at the crowd.

Her cape fluttered in the salty breeze and she pulled it tighter around her shoulders. She inhaled deeply to fill her lungs with the fresh air. She searched the crowd on the dock for her family. Spotting them, she jumped up and down, both arms waving frantically over her head. "Papa, Lizzie — I'm here. Look this way! Oh Jay, there they are."

It was Lizzie who caught sight of her first. Mary could almost hear, but had to concentrate on her lips, to make out the words. "Mary. Father, there's Mary! We love you. We shall miss you. Barnabas! Take good care of her and the boys. Mary, write to us." She hugged Hannah to her as the last words faded on her lips.

Papa stood silently waving, his eyes red and dry like they no longer had tears to spill.

Mary watched as Rachel spotted Jay and waved at him and was quickly joined by Ruth and Joshua.

Barney and Ben joined them in waving their goodbyes and then turned to bow their heads as the prayer service and sermon began.

Mary reached to pull Jay to her, but he wrenched out of her grasp. She winced but bowed her head. She touched her forehead, heart, and then her left shoulder followed by her right, in a sign of the cross as she slightly genuflected. A tradition of her Anglican upbringing, it seemed irreverent to begin worship without the ritual.

She allowed herself a small sideways glance at Barney. She could conform while attending Church of England services and Barney showed leniency when they attended the services held in secret midweek. But now they were on their way to a New World. In the end she had left her pretty green gown behind. Would he expect her to leave her heritage behind too?

After what seemed an interminably long time, she peeked over the rail once more and mouthed, "Goodbye, my family. I love you too." A strong breeze swept across the deck and Mary quickly grasped her hood and clamped it to her head.

"Amen" resounded and the order rang out for the first mate to raise all sails. The canvas flapped as the deck groaned. The small ship slipped from the dock and departed for open seas. God must be with them. The wind and tide certainly were.

Mary's family gradually melded into the shoreline. She waved from the deck until her arms ached. The clouds darkened as they huddled together. Bewilderment crumpled Jay's and Ben's expressions. Surprisingly, she saw it in Barney as well, and she knew they all felt the same chill she did. The journey had begun. Now what?

The dusky sky turned to ink and Barnabas stared at the masses of stars that blinked as a canopy above. Mary said the stars were God's windows to heaven, where loved ones shone down to let them know they were happy. He knew it helped her feel closer to her mother. He wished it were true and the brightest one was Ann's. It truly was a miracle how the same stars they gazed at in Mowsley followed them across this vast sea.

But Ann should have made this voyage with him. Their sons needed her. Benjamin was young and clung to Mary, but Joseph — he missed his mother so. Barnabas had promised he would always protect them. Why did it feel as though he'd failed?

Ten days at sea and each night had been beautiful. A large white moon rose and sent a shimmer of light across the dark, rough sea. Barnabas clenched his hands and leaned further into the ship's rail. He shivered as he tried not to think of Ann.

He should go see if Mary was back from the 'tween deck. She insisted on spending time down in that dank hole. She worried about the people who shared the cramped quarters and brought them lemons from the larder. Elizabeth had told her the juice could save them from scurvy and the fragrance would clear the air. He just asked that she not spend too much time below and she keep a handkerchief over her nose.

His sons needed a mother and she was all they had.

Long, scorching days stretched into torrid, interminable weeks. Sunburn gave way to a leathery tan only to burn again. The smell of rotting food competed with the stench from the buckets of human waste from the 'tween deck.

Mary's attempts to thwart the ravages of the relentless sun seemed woefully inadequate, but the peril from the storms when the rain came was worse. One crew hand was washed overboard in a great wave, and a search was not possible without risking more lives. Illness struck almost every family below, and half the crew.

Two young sisters, Alice and Catherine, became delirious, and their hands and feet had to be fettered to their pallet with strips of petticoat. Sadly, they died and their bodies were buried at sea.

Spoilt fruit and bags of soggy, festering rye were tossed overboard and the ship's larder became alarmingly scant.

Mary brought out the few remaining biscuits from their personal larder and picked at them. "They are quite hard, but I do not see any maggots."

Barney laid out fresh cod caught by the

men that day on a particularly calm sea. "Mayhap maggots do not like their biscuit so hard." He chortled at his joke. "You've tended our supplies well. We still have a goodly amount of dried meat."

She eyed the fish. They looked beautiful as their bodies writhed and scales glinted in the sunshine. Her stomach used to turn when she and Papa would fish from Mowsley Brook, but at this moment nothing looked more appetizing. "I prefer the fish to the dried meat, to be sure." She did miss the oranges though. The memory of biting into a luscious wedge and the squirt of its tang made her lick her dry, rough lips.

Her stomach grew queasy and she looked away from the barrel. "Last night was terrible, Barney. My stomach was so sick. I would have gone out to the deck, but I remembered Jeremy warned us against the rheumy air. He thinks the weather is beginning to change. 'Tis so terrible about those two young girls. I wish I could go down and comfort their mother."

He sliced the stomachs of the fish and scooped out the guts, tossing them into a pail. "Aye. But you must not go to them. We don't know why they got sick. The girls were behaving very peculiarly before they died. They were hallucinating and could have hurt someone. We shan't risk it. Jeremy asked if you were feeling better today. He has more dried ginger. After we have our meal, you should make some ginger tea. Mayhap 'twill ease your stomach."

"I shall do that."

"I know you tell me you are not, but I do think it highly possible you are with child, my sweet. You are much sicker than any of the rest of us, and nothing seems to help. What think you?"

Mary peered down the deck. "Where are the boys?"

"Are you avoiding my question? The boys have gone with Jeremy to the stern. 'Tis helpful their uncle has taken them under his wing, is it not? Now, to the point, are you with child?" His look held a tenderness she rarely saw.

"I pray I am. I want to make you happy, Barney. I hope I'm wrong, but I do not think I carry a babe. 'Tis been six years now and sometimes I think I shall never have one."

"That can't be. Of course, we shall have children. In the colonies it will be important to have many, many children."

She sighed at his words. She knew how much this meant to him. "I know you say that. And I pray daily we shall have a babe.

Perhaps 'tis why I am so sick."

He handed the gutted fish to her. Her small metal box with a sand pit inside worked well to cook the fish and boil beans, as long as the weather stayed calm. Though she could improvise a tent should it rain, Jeremy would not permit a fire in a storm with wind.

"The embers are low — what say I take a bucket down to the fo'c'sle and fetch some? The boys should be back soon."

"Thank you, Barney." She watched him cross the deck and disappear down the step.

Barnabas scooped the glowing coals into his bucket and climbed the stairs. He wove back and forth as the ship pitched about and, as he emerged, ran straight into Miss Terry. "My apologies, Miss Terry. I pray I did not burn you with my pail."

"Oh, no, Mr. Horton." A tinkle of laughter followed.

As he stepped aside for her to pass, Jeremy approached with Joseph and Benjamin.

"Heigh-ho, brother." Jeremy's voice boomed over the waves. "Miss Terry." He bowed to the young lady.

Joseph looked at his father, then at Miss Terry.

"Son, you remember Miss Terry? She has

been to the bakeshop often with her mother."

"Yes, Father."

"Then say hello to her properly."

Joseph mimicked his uncle with a bow, but his brow furrowed and a scowl threatened. "Good morrow, Miss Terry."

Jeremy nodded to the pail of embers. "Be careful with the fire tonight, Barn. We don't have wind, but the seas are high. Cook your fish and put it out."

"Most certainly. Mary is looking forward to the fresh catch. We won't dally with it." There was so little she looked forward to eating, and he worried for the babe.

The ship pitched and rolled through the night. Mary lay rigid and listened to Barnabas's rhythmic breathing as she prayed for daylight. At long last, she swung her feet over the bed, glancing at Jay and Ben, stretched across the end. She knew Jay had tossed about for a while, but now he slept soundly.

The wooden floor was cool on her bare feet as she padded to the table. The family Bible lay there, and she traced over the worn binding with her stiff fingers. She picked up the book, but set it back and reached for her dolly propped against the wall. Hugging it, a tear crept down her cheek. How long had she prayed for a babe? She looked toward Barney.

He did not stir.

A wave of nausea made its way up her throat. Still grasping her doll with one hand, she covered her mouth with the other and crept out of the cabin to the rail. She bent over and heaved as the side of the ship came up, rolling on a wave.

Trembling, she leaned further over the rail, still cradling the doll. Tears flowed while she waited for the next wave of nausea to pass.

"Mary, you should tell me when you are this sick."

She jumped. "Oh, Barney."

He pressed a handkerchief from Lizzie into her hand and slid his arms around her, as much to keep her from going over the side as to comfort her.

"You — you frightened me. I am not sure how much more of this sickness I can stand."

"I know the waves are high and many people are sick from it, but you have not been well since we started out. You are with child, I am certain. Let me help you back inside before we are both swept overboard. You are drenched and the wet night air is certainly not good for you."

She allowed him to lead her back to the cabin. "It hurts me more than I can say that we don't have a child." Why was she saying this? Did it not make things worse?

"We will. And we will build a house big enough to hold a dozen more children once we are in Massachusetts. Now, pray thee, put down that doll and come to bed." He wrapped her in her cape.

She placed the doll next to the Bible and crawled in beside him. She snuggled close.

Barney stretched out, eyes wide open.

Was he thinking of Ann? Or could he be thinking of Miss Terry? She looked so pretty on the dock the day they departed. Mary had seen her once or twice since, but they never really spoke. Miss Terry always seemed to remember something she needed below deck when a chance meeting did occur. Why was her mind leading her to all of these terrible thoughts? She prayed she was with child. She prayed Barney would love her.

The night calmed and the rhythmic rolling finally lulled Mary to a fitful sleep. Dawn arrived like a blessing and she got up to get the day underway. Barney had been up and gone from the cabin before the sun rose.

Ben squirmed and curled into the spot she'd vacated. She smiled and pulled the well-worn quilt over him. Jay appeared asleep as well, and she tucked the quilt about his shoulders. He stirred and looked up.

She smiled and pushed a lock of hair back from his forehead. "Sorry, I did not mean to wake you."

"You didn't wake me. I've been awake for a long time, since Father got up."

"Oh, I did not realize. You seemed to be enjoying your slumber."

He sat up. "Nay, I was wondering where Father would be off to so early."

"He feels a responsibility being the ship-master's brother. We are more fortunate than the others on the ship, you know — we have this cabin. He wants to be of help to anyone who is in need."

"Oh."

" 'Tis something on your mind?"

"Nothing I could talk to you about — I miss Mother. She always would listen to me."

She took a step nearer. "Jay, I'm listening. You can tell me anything."

"I saw Father with Miss Terry. I know that must trouble you."

"It troubles me more that you think you

must inform me. Your father is a good man and he loves you and Ben. I know you miss your mother, but it hasn't been easy on your father either. He misses her very much. 'Tis quite possible Miss Terry reminds him of your mother, when she was younger."

With that, she made her way out of the cabin. Why was she so good at making excuses for everyone but herself?

She made her way to their larder and pried the lid off. Ugh. Dried, tough beef and beans with worms. She was so tired of picking out the worms.

"You did well planning your provisions, little one. You'll do well in the New World." Jeremy bowed.

"Oh, you startled me, but thank you, Jeremy. Speaking of the New World, I've had something on my mind about Massachusetts. I should like to establish a place where women could come and discuss the problems they encounter when we get there. I brought lemons down to the 'tween deck and 'twas a nice idea, but truly only a gesture. I should like to do something more meaningful in Massachusetts."

"Aye."

"I miss Lizzie greatly. She's always been a support to me and I hope to be a support to others. I should like to offer a place where we could share our concerns and help each other. I've heard the story of Dorothy May and her unfortunate drowning. I've heard she jumped. There are other women like her that need help. We need a way to reach out to each other."

"That is indeed a singular ambition. I can certainly make it known to all of the ladies for you."

"Thank you. Perhaps one of the meeting-houses in Boston would allow a group of women to meet from time to time."

"I will see what can be arranged. Now, I should go check the charts and see just how close we are. I expect to see land in a day or two." He turned to leave, but faced her once again. "Barn did tell you we lost sight of *The Hector* after the storm?"

"Yes, yes he did. He told me this should not be a problem for us, only that we do not know if *The Hector* or the people on board are all right." She glanced about as the ship dipped to the side.

"Aye. I'm sure Barn told you we spent days circling, hoping to find them, or at least the debris. But it would have been dangerous to continue the search. We are now overdue and we are most certainly off course at this point. Depending on the shoreline itself, we may or may not go ashore when we have it in sight."

"I understand. I know you will make the best decision for us all. To walk on land again seems only like a dream."

He nodded and trudged up the stairs.

She watched him disappear to the upper deck. Finally, satisfied they would have sufficient food for the remainder of the voyage, she picked at the beans. With a grimace, she plucked out the worms. There was a time in her life she would have completely recoiled. It seemed so very long ago.

She paused from her task. Why didn't she ask Jeremy what he thought of Miss Terry? Had he noticed her spending too much time with Barney? She climbed the stairs back to the upper deck and looked skyward. No, time to forget about such things. Too many other worries.

Two days later, as the sun hovered on the western horizon, "Land ho!" broke the silence.

Barney instructed Mary to bring Jay and Ben to the main deck.

Reverend Reeves led the crowd in prayer and thanksgiving. Jeremy instructed the men to settle their children and womenfolk and report to the quarterdeck for a meeting.

Mary remained riveted at the rail. She strained to see into the distance what must be the shoreline of New England, the New World. She turned to Ben and Jay. "This is to be our new home, our new life. Are you not excited?" Most likely she sounded stronger than she felt. Did she possess what would be required to settle in this new land? She certainly would find out. Lizzie thought she was strong. She prayed she was.

Barney gathered her and his sons and led them to their cabin.

"Shall we be able to go ashore tonight, Barney?"

"Nay, my sweet. I am sure Jeremy will want women and children to stay aboard, whilst the men — or at least some of us — go ahead in the shallop and determine if this be a safe harbor. I venture he will not want us to go until the morn, and certainly we have to put the shallop together and it will require some time. I think 'twill most likely be suppertime tomorrow before everyone is brought ashore."

"We should have a big feast. A celebration, do you not think so?"

"To be sure. This is the land of plenty. We will be feasting tomorrow night. Now, boys, be good for Mother, and I will be back shortly with news."

Jay watched his father as he disappeared through the door, then turned to Mary. "I hope he won't be long. It would be too bad if he were to worry you again."

She rolled her eyes. "Please behave. I shall worry, indeed, but not as you intend. Pray, let's sit and talk about all of the things we look forward to when we are in Massachusetts, shall we?"

Ben snuggled next to her. "I want to run. And climb a tree."

Mary grinned and hugged him close. "Yes. Me too. And you, Jay, what will be the very first thing you want to do?"

"Not climb a tree. The ropes on this ship are more fun than an old tree."

"That could be true. So, what is it you would long to do? Pray tell, anything at all."

"Why, I would go home to Mother if I could. Yes, that would be the thing."

Ben looked with sad eyes at the woman who was a mother to him. "You mean what do we want to do in Massachusetts, right? Joseph, won't you be glad to get off this ship? Why are you always so mean?"

"He is not mean, Ben. He is unhappy, and sometimes, when people are not happy, 'tis hard to be nice to people. And sometimes harder the closer the person is to your heart. Jay, I think you are frightened by what you do not know, and 'tis natural to want to cling to that which you do. I'm a little frightened myself. I miss my family. But we have your father, and we have our belief that God shall take care of us. We shall be fine."

"What I want most, right now, is to be left alone."

"And that we can do." Mary motioned for Ben to scoot over, leaving Jay some room on the bed, should he choose to sit down. She listened to Ben as he said his prayers, and soon, with the gentle sway of the ship, he fell into peaceful slumber. Closing her eyes, she tried to sleep too, hoping Barney would come back soon to wake her and share the details of the meeting with her and Jay. It wasn't likely they would sleep anytime soon.

Time seemed to crawl and she knew Jay wearied. Slowly she became aware he slept soundly on the floor, propped against the wall. She turned her head toward Ben's cherubic face, drool trickling down his cheek. Taking a corner of the soft quilt, she gently mopped his face.

With care, she swung herself off the bed. Her back toward the wall, she slid down until she sat next to Jay. Trying not to wake him, she shifted him toward her and cradled his head in her lap.

Anticipating the journey's end, she drifted toward sleep, hoping the morrow would bring the joy of release. Not just from the voyage, but their journey to be a family. She would work very hard in this new land. And perhaps, as Barney liked to say, the Lord would bless her good works with a babe. Perhaps Barney would present her with the tongs. Perhaps he would fall in love with her.

15

July 16, 1637

Mary opened her eyes. Her back ached and she tried not to disturb the still sleeping boy in her lap as she stretched. Barney and Ben slept side by side. When had Barney come back to their cabin? She tried to hold still, but her arms cramped from holding Jay. She tried to gently shift his head.

He woke and sat forward quickly. "Why are we on the floor?"

She touched her fingers to her mouth. "Hush, your father is sleeping." She pulled a blanket up over his shoulders. " 'Tis all right. You fell asleep on the floor, and you are too heavy for me to lift. So I slept with you here. 'Twill be a busy day, I am sure."

The ship swayed and the gentle sound of the water lapping against old wood soothed them. The bay was calm, a most welcome respite from the volatile ocean.

"Are we going ashore today?" He kept his

voice low.

"I don't know. Your father will, I believe. He and Uncle Jeremy shall take a look with some of the other men. Perhaps gather some food, do some hunting. Our larder is low. Fresh food will be such a blessing. Hopefully, we shall cook a feast on the shore tonight."

"It makes my stomach hurt to think of eating beans for breakfast again."

"That I shall agree with. Before we left England, I heard such stories about the corn and strawberries here. 'Tis what I desire first when we walk on land."

"And a juicy piece of roasted beef." Jay looked up at Mary. "They do have cows, do they not?"

She buried her mouth in his thick, dark hair, suppressing a giggle. "Shhh, do not make me wake everybody up. I think we shall have a cow or two someday. But I think we shall rely on the deer and elk for our meat until Uncle Jeremy sees fit to bring us cows."

Barney opened an eye and peered at the two, a grin spreading across his face. "Are you two talking about food?"

"Father, we are starved. May we go with you today?" Jay stood up, stretching.

Mary held onto the table as she raised

herself up, her legs stiff. Every muscle ached.

Barney rolled off the bed. He stretched forward and rubbed her shoulders. "I wish I could take you with me, but your uncle has been firm in his instructions. Women and children will stay on the ship, and a party of no more than twenty-five men will go ashore to scout the area. This is not, of course, Boston Harbor. We need to hunt, but we need to ascertain how safe we will be here. If all goes well, we will bring you ashore tonight for a large feast. We hope to build fires and roast whatever we bring in from the hunt."

He pulled Mary around to face him. "I will see what vegetables and fruit I can find. We have heard all of the stories, but we don't really know what is out there until we look. A squirrel or rabbit would be as welcome as anything, to be sure."

She nodded in agreement. " 'Twill be a blessing to taste real meat again, but I cannot wait until I touch the ground. You shall hurry back to fetch us?"

"It depends on what we find. Whilst I should like to assure you we will feast tonight, either on shore or aboard the ship, 'twould be prudent to cook a pot of beans. Of course, we sleep on the ship tonight."

She looked at the small bed. "When do we go to Boston?"

"Much depends on how far off course we are. It will take some time to decide where to build tents or if we can go straightaway to Boston."

Jay stood up and turned to Mary. "I'll go with you to sort the beans and put them on to cook."

Warmth spread over her like she had not known before. It seemed her prayers were being answered. She wanted to throw her arms around him, like she had held him last night, but he would object, to be sure. She resisted the urge. "Yes, Jay, I should like that. One more pot of beans, and then I promise you we shan't have beans for a long while."

Barney moved toward them and opened the old Bible. He searched the Scriptures until he found the verse he needed. "Mary, Joseph, listen. Psalm eighteen, verse thirty through thirty-three, 'The way of God is uncorrupt: the word of the Lord is tried in the fire: he is a shield to all that trust in him. For who is God besides the Lord? and who is mighty save our God? God girdeth me with strength, and maketh my way upright. He maketh my feet like hind's feet, and setteth me upon mine high places.' "

"Barney, you should share that with Jeremy and the other men. 'Tis like God speaking directly to you."

"He is. That He is. Now, before we take our leave, let us pray." They bowed their heads. "Lord, be with our family today and be our strength. I pray for safety, for our food, and for Your guidance in all that we do. And Lord, we pray that our angels who watch over us today will always be with us. Amen." He looked at Mary and they exchanged a knowing smile.

He picked up his battered musket and drew Mary to him once more, kissing her soundly. "My sweet, I will be gone before your breakfast is ready. Jeremy already waits on the quarterdeck. We will have our prayers and then depart. He is anxious for an early start, as I am. How long we shall be gone, I don't know, but we do need to be back before dark. And I promise you, we shall be laden with food."

Jay stood, straightening his shoulders to stand tall. "I will take care of her today, Father."

Barney tousled his son's dark hair. "You are growing up. It gives me much relief to know you will watch over her and your brother too."

All three turned to Ben, barely visible

214

under the quilt.

"He sleeps so soundly, I wish I could do the same," Mary said. She bent toward Jay. "Shall we go so we can be back before he wakes?"

With one more kiss, Barney headed for the quarterdeck, while Mary and Jay turned toward the main deck and larder. They walked without speaking. Such a change in his attitude. Perhaps the end of the journey gave him much relief, but it did not matter what prompted it. She was thankful.

They paused at the ship's rail and tried to make out what the lay of the land was. A gray shroud hung close to the water, eerie to the view. The men would be going ashore in a shallop, a much smaller boat, while the women and children waited on the ship. She prayed Barney would be safe.

A sob escaped from Jay.

"Pray thee, 'tis all right. This is a happy day for us. We were just talking about all of the good food we will be filling our bellies with and how wonderful it will be to put our feet on the dirt of the earth. Are you afraid?" She touched his chin with her hand, raising it to look in his mossy green eyes. "Your father shall be safe. God is watching over all of us. Or 'tis something else troubling you?"

"I'm not afraid." He pulled away. "I dreamt about Mother last night. She was holding me again. When I woke up, it was you. I miss her so, but she would not have liked that I was mean to you and Benjamin last night."

"It is good to try to do the right thing, always, for God and for your mother. He watches over us, Joseph. And your mother would be proud of you."

A gentle rain fell and Mary smiled as she looked toward heaven. She glanced at Joseph's sad face. She slid an arm around him and they watched as the drops fell. "Your mother wanted the best for you and I know it would have made her glad that you are choosing it for yourself too. Now, let us fetch the beans and thank the Lord for them."

"Thank the Lord for them? I thought we are sick of them."

"Oh, yes, we are, Jay, but we can be thankful we have them or we would not have survived."

They slowly made their way to the larder and stared at the beans. Bugs and worms slithered freely about.

"We do thank Thee, Lord, for our sustenance. Amen." Her stomach revolted and she could pray no more. It comforted her to know God heard her prayers anyway, spoken or not.

Jay picked through the beans, and Mary offered up one more silent prayer.

Barnabas quickly stepped up to the quarterdeck. Everyone stood in prayer with heads bowed. Jeremy acknowledged him with a nod of his head as he joined the men. With a hearty "Amen," the group divided the provisions for the day.

"Take some of this dried beef, Barn. We will all need our strength today. You look terrible."

"Aye, I am sure of that. Not much sleep, I fear."

"How is Mary? Is she feeling better? The bay is much calmer than the ocean."

"She doesn't complain like a lot of women do. That is both good and bad. I never really know what goes on in her head."

"Mayhap you should just listen to her once in a while, Barn. She loves you very much. I thought with all her sickness she might be with child, but I suppose not, eh? Surely after more than two months of heaving up everything, she would know if she was with child? But I don't know about these matters. What say you?"

"I think she waits to be certain she keeps

it. I do not believe she has felt the quickening. There have been many times she thought she be with child, but was not. Very distressing for her."

"No reason to speak of it until she feels ready. But enough of this. If we are to conquer a new land, we must take the first step, eh?"

Barnabas thumped Jeremy on the back as they turned back to the men. "To the wilds we go."

Eager laughter broke as each picked up his musket. A bag filled with provisions slung over their shoulders, the assembly made their way as one to the shallop. Working together, they lowered it to the water and proceeded to climb one at a time over the side of the ship.

Twenty-five men set out to explore their new world. As they rowed toward the shoreline, Barnabas pondered the dangers they might encounter, but his excitement was palpable with each stroke. Before wading the last few feet to the shore, he pulled his Bible from his sack and shared Scripture with them. Their heads bowed in humble prayer and then over the side they slipped, sloshing toward the shore.

Ben woke when Mary and Jay returned to

their cabin. Under the quilt, his big blue eyes were the only thing visible. "I thought you left me."

"Aye, we thought we would, but we needed some provisions." Jay chuckled. He sounded more like his father each day.

"Jay, don't tease your brother. Ben, get up and let us get you washed and dressed. Your father is already ashore."

Ben's eyes grew wider. "Without us?"

She poured a bit of water from the red earthenware pitcher into the bowl. "Yes, just some of the men went. 'Tis raining, but there is no wind, so I must try to keep our fire lit for a pot of beans. Pray that our supper shall be a feast from the shore." She helped Ben with his clothes and they returned to the deck.

A bucket of embers from the galley supplied the flame for her pot of beans. As she stirred them up, Miss Terry made her way across the deck.

Jay looked at her with a steely glare.

"Jay, Ben. Bid Miss Terry good morrow, please."

Ben bowed with his pleasantries, but Jay barely muttered before he turned back to Mary. "May Benjamin and I go and climb the ropes? We could see the shore better."

"Nay, you know you are not allowed. But

you may find the ship's mate and ask him if you might go to the top deck to look. I don't think you shall see much with the rain. I must stay with the fire. Be careful now."

"Yay, let's go, Joseph." Ben took off at a run.

"It was my idea, Benjamin, wait." Jay took off as well.

"I'm sorry for their manners, Miss Terry. We do work on that, but 'tis best, it seems, for Barney to correct them."

"Yes, he tells me it has been difficult since their mother died."

Mary shifted. "You have spoken of such things with him?"

"Oh, only a bit, to be sure. He's a wonderful man, is he not?" Her smile evoked a dreaminess that riled Mary.

"Of course I find him to be wonderful. He is my husband. 'Tis something you should remember, perhaps."

Miss Terry tossed her head. Without a reply, she flounced away.

Rain pattered and wind gusted along the deck. Mary readjusted the makeshift tent that protected the fire. She should put out the fire, but perhaps 'twas just a gust and not a storm.

16

Before the sun set, the scouting party came into view. Most of the passengers crowded the deck to watch with anticipation. Those who were too ill remained below.

Mary scanned the small group, looking for Barney. Several men carried butchered deer on poles, which they eased to the ground. Others carried armloads of dry wood — a difficult find even in the endless forest, considering the rain that had fallen earlier in the day.

She turned her attention to the men approaching in the shallop. There he was. Even from the distance she could see he sat with reed baskets brimming with the biggest red strawberries she had ever seen and fat corn still in the husks. Her stomach clenched at the sight of food and reminded her how long it had been since they had partaken of fresh food.

Barney gave her a big wave when their

eyes met.

She waved back. "Jay, Ben, wave to your father."

Ben cupped his hands around his mouth. "May we come down, Father?" He looked as if he might jump over the rail any moment. His shout was carried away by the wind, lost on the vastness of the ocean and forest, which came together as one on the rugged coast.

She put a hand on his shoulder. "Nay, Ben. He cannot hear you. We must wait."

The three met the scouting party as they came up over the side of the ship. Barney looked so happy, so exhausted. He cradled a berry-laden basket roughly woven of reeds. "Come, let us go to the cabin. I will tell you all about the day. The stories we have heard are indeed true." His breathing was hard. "We had to take great care to mark the trails we chose. There are many. Some would be deer trails but others surely are made by man. They must belong to Indians living nearby. We did not see any, but they most likely saw us. We have gifts to give them when we do make an encounter."

"Do you think they are friendly, Father?" Ben's face looked more excited than afraid.

"Mostly, but we have to be careful. We do not need to look for trouble. Some accounts of the Indians to the south have been unfavorable, but for the most part 'tis an internal war between tribes. Nothing for us to fear, I do not think. And like I said, they are to the south."

They entered the cabin and he brought his family to kneel with him as he offered a blessing to the Lord.

He passed the strawberries to Mary. She held the basket out to Jay and Ben and allowed them to pick several berries first. She then selected a large, bright red berry for herself. She bit into the soft flesh and let the juice dribble on her chin in sheer delight as she closed her eyes. "I have never tasted anything so perfectly wondrous. So sweet, 'tis almost like licking a loaf of sugar. I could eat these every day for the rest of my life."

Jay nudged her arm and pressed a rag into her hand.

"Nay, Jay. I shall forget my manners for a time." She proceeded to wipe her chin with her fingers and relished licking the last few sweet droplets.

Barney passed the basket around again. "We found fields of corn, cultivated by Indians, we think, but yet abandoned."

She set the basket on the table. "How do you know they were abandoned?"

"Most of it was going to waste. Corn rotting on the stalk, plants trampled by what must be elk or deer. We found no evidence of humans nearby. Does not mean they are not out there. Now come, we must put on boots and bring blankets as well. Jeremy told me we are to be on the first shallop to go ashore. Mary, fill your apron with whatever from our stores you might need for our feast. More corn and venison await us on the beach. We will eat well tonight."

She watched anxiously as Jay and Ben climbed over the side of the ship into the waiting arms of crew aboard the shallop. This was far different from when they boarded *The Swallow* at the port in London. But the promise of solid ground gave Mary the courage to follow them over the side and into the little boat that awaited her. Barney was right behind her.

The shallop made three trips from ship to shore to bring everyone who was able. Weapons and provisions accompanied each run and additional trips brought the remainder of their supplies.

A roaring fire beckoned from the shore, and Mary laughed like a child as she lifted her skirt and splashed the last few feet to the small beach. She dropped to her hands and knees, scooped the sandy soil and held it to her face, breathing in the moist earthiness. They had made it. They were here. Praise be to God. Barney picked her up and swung her about.

Jay and Ben attempted to run up and down the shore, only to discover their sea legs would not permit it. They expected the ground to sway like the decks of the ship.

"Boys, come here. Your father wants to say a prayer with us."

Joined in a circle, heads bowed, Barnabas gave thanks for a safe journey, for their health and the abundant food on the shores of this new land. As the waves gently washed the beach with a rhythmic slap, Barney's deep baritone rose above with a hymn.

Mary listened in awe as, one by one, all who were on shore joined in and the strains flowed through the men rowing back to the ship until the music reached those still on board *The Swallow*. As the chain of voices linked, the notes blended in unison, a choir before the Lord.

Men and women worked side by side to feed the fires and prepare the meat. Supper would be a banquet of fire-roasted venison, pheasant, and rabbit. Corn nestled whole in the coals and fresh berries bulged from their baskets. Everyone gathered; only the sickest

225

did not come ashore.

"Mary, I will bring back some of the food to the ship. Some on board will not be able to eat much, they are too ill. But we can make a broth from the meat and bones. Would you gather a meal together before we sup? I'll ready the boat."

"Barney, may I go with you? I should like to help where I can. And it would be good to see Goodwife Jennings again and her babe."

"Nay, not in your condition. You need to gather your strength. I understand you want to be of service, but you must take care of yourself first. Wrap up the provisions, and I shall take them."

She set to work and sent Jay and Ben to deliver the baskets to their father.

She lowered herself to the ground near the fire and clasped her arms around her knees. The voyage had been rife with starvation, illness, and death, and with the storm much longer than planned. But those who survived were safe for now, and while they landed far north of Boston, Jeremy thought they were very close to the port settlement of Winnacunnet. Hopefully, that was a good thing. She peered into the dark forest that edged the beach. Her shoulders shuddered and she looked quickly out to the shallop.

Barney promised he would not tarry. She watched the men who stood guard with their muskets. How could she feel so alone with so many around her? God was with her too. She would never be alone.

Women huddled around the fires scattered across the beach, many with young children or babes in their arms. They nodded their recognition to Mary, but their pain and exhaustion were evident. There would be much to do as they settled in to their camp, but she would not forget her pledge to Jeremy to create a place where women felt they could gather and unleash their emotions. They all shared one thing in common: they'd survived crossing the ocean. They could not give up hope now.

She gazed at the flames dancing through the logs. Papa and Lizzie, what would they be doing right now? Would her sister be mixing her dough, the children tucked warm in their beds? Zeke reading from the Bible? Would Papa be sitting next to his fire, his belly already full, and Cook bidding him goodbye for the night? How she missed them and longed for a home where she could be safe and warm. And loved.

Barnabas gave a full report as to how those on board fared and their appreciation for the feast he brought to them. He didn't want to share with Mary that Goodwife Jennings's babe had died. She'd been present for the baby's birth and she would want to leave the fire and go back to the ship. Mary looked fragile and she needed this time near the fire with some good food.

He watched his wife help the boys fill their bowls. She was a good mother to his children. She had learned much over the years. Pride in her accomplishments filled him. God had been good.

An old familiar ache settled over him. Leaving England should have lessened the pain. But Ann was the one who shared his dream of coming to the New World. How he loved her, and nothing, not even an ocean, would change that.

"Barney?" Mary laid her hand on his arm, but he sat still with no response.

He watched Joseph and Benjamin as they ate. Joseph was in a rare mood, with contentment on his face. Benjamin chattered to no one in particular. He was thankful the boys were so healthy after such a long trip.

He studied Mary and rubbed her dry, weathered hand. She looked too thin. It would not be good for the babe. He rose to cut off another slab of meat and picked up a juicy ear of corn, roasted golden. He sat down next to her and offered the food. "Here, my sweet. Eat some more. Eat well now, we do not know what tomorrow will bring. Not a good thing for you in your condition."

"Barney, I am about to burst. I cannot eat another bite."

She was embarrassed, he could tell, but he plunged on. "You're not just eating for yourself now. You must think of the little one."

"Little one?" Joseph looked from his father to Mary.

Mary's cheeks flushed. "You must not speak like that in front of the children. May we discuss this later?"

"Only if you will eat." He thrust the plate to her. He looked to his sons. "Your mother is not ready to share this with you. We will give her the time she needs."

Benjamin looked at his stepmother, wonder in his eyes. "Are you going to have a baby?"

"Barney." She put her hand on his arm, this time with gentle pressure. "There might not be anything to share. 'Tis not right to bring up such a thing in front of them."

Barnabas looked into the glow of the fire as he warmed his hands. "You are with child, are you not?"

229

"I only had the seasickness most everyone had. There is no babe." She looked from Barnabas to Joseph and Benjamin, her eyes the same soft gray as her simple gown. "I'm sorry, Barney, I know this is not what you want to hear."

His eyes scanned her belly. "You seemed much sicker than anyone else. I thought you were with child." He rubbed his forehead with stiff fingers, then gently took her hands. "My apologies. God will give us a child. I cannot imagine not having a houseful someday." He rubbed her hands, smiled his encouragement. "We are serving God. He will bless us."

She returned his smile with strength in her eyes. "I pray 'tis true. I pray He blesses us in that way. Whilst I wait for the blessing, I intend to work beside you."

Later, Jeremy insisted they remain in the cabin that night. He intended to sleep under the stars — close to the fires, musket beside him. Mary and the boys, exhausted from the excitement of the day, settled into their small bed and soon slumbered. Barnabas could not. He sat for long hours on the edge, head buried in his hands as he prayed. His back ached.

He pinched the corners of his eyes to stifle the moisture that collected. He needed to get out of the cabin. He was finally here. The New World he and Ann talked about. Here without her. He looked down at Mary and pulled the quilt gently about her shoulders and eased out of the cabin.

He made his way to the starboard side and grasped the rail. Staring down at the fires burning low across the beach, the day he met Mary rushed back to him. A day so filled with emotion.

The ship gently swayed and he looked at the water below, then up to the stars that blazed. The early days after Ann died were excruciating. He could not fathom how he'd go on. By the grace of God he'd done it. But it did not feel any easier on this night. No, she should have been here with him.

17

Late Summer 1637

The first weeks were about survival. Too many were sick from the long voyage and in need of shelter and good food. Tents were built of sailcloth, food scavenged from sea, land, and air. Mary appreciated the fresh venison and duck, but the oysters, shrimp, and lobster — bottom fish of the ocean — rather repulsed her. Fires were tended with a passion.

Soon after that first night, Barnabas and Jeremy encountered a small band of Indians. Though not particularly amiable, the natives did not threaten them. The rugged cove *The Swallow* anchored in was discovered to be close to the tiny English settlement of Winnacunnet, far north of Boston. Because it was built on a protective bay, ships frequently stopped with provisions.

The few hardy residents offered their homes where they had room, and their labor to those they could not accommodate. Together the families harvested corn and prepared beds for the flax that would be planted in early spring.

Barney desired to remain there, waiting for word of Reverend Davenport and Reverend John Youngs. Some of the families, bound by their indenture to the Massachusetts Bay Company, continued south to Boston. The Terrys, though not indentured, decided to travel to Boston as well. It was embarrassing how much relief it gave Mary that Miss Terry would not be around.

Everyone worked from dawn's first light until the fire was banked late in the evening. But when word came *The Hector* had arrived safely in Boston Harbor — days before *The Swallow* anchored — work ceased and a feast was prepared in celebration. Contentment beat in Mary's heart as she watched Barney preside over the festivities. There were times she longed to take over the kitchen tongs, but today she was happy to watch him in command.

Each afternoon as they prepared food, Mary encouraged the women to talk about what they personally thought to be the most difficult part of living in the New World. Nay, 'twas more about surviving than living. She asked them to express their emotions and fears, and their dreams as well. What he dreamt of most was more sleep.

Barney set about clearing land with his sons by his side. The small community came together for a log-rolling and then a stone-piling. Soon he began building their cottage. Each night in their tent of sod and sailcloth, he would fall onto the pallet of hickory branches covered in pelts. "A hard day's work makes for a good night's sleep," he said many a night.

The stormy season would come soon enough and he told Mary he was determined to have his family safely within the walls of their cottage before the first freeze.

"Remember, this will not be the house I've promised you. 'Twill be rough logs quickly put together, and it will be but a tiny cottage. We shall not be here long."

She snuggled close to hear him as he whispered. The boys slept on their pallets nearby.

"Reverend Davenport sends word he is not finding Boston to his liking, though they have made a great effort to keep him there. He has already sent scouts south to look at another harbor to plant a church and build a township. He has word back the Indians are cordial and amenable to trade. I don't know for certain, but mayhap I will want to go there. Already I worry there are too many people here for my liking, and that all they think about is how to become rich."

She propped up on her elbow to look into his face.

He continued. "We've come here for a new start, but surely we were richer in England. My focus is the church. It might be we can better serve God if we follow Reverend Davenport. I hear Reverend John Youngs is now in Salem and plans to unite with him. Much is happening."

"But what about the people here in Winnacunnet? Do they not need a minister of the Word? Why would Reverend Youngs not come to plant his church here?"

"He never intended to plant a church this far north. He will be down in the area of Quinnipiac. Reverend Bachiler, of Old Hampton, will be coming here. As early as next year, I am told."

A pain built in her chest, an ache for a home, wherever it would be. She wanted to be established, to begin to put down their roots. Perhaps Lizzie and Papa, upon hearing from her the wonders of this new land, would decide to make the voyage and join them. But first they needed a home to bring them to.

She rubbed his shoulder as her mind

drifted back to a day when he tried to share with her how Ann felt about coming to the colonies. She would have loved the adventure, the chance to be on the verge of something you could not quite imagine, yet surely was something grand. Mary wanted to share that with Barney too, but when would they know they were there? How long would this go on?

She buried her face in his shoulder. "I will follow you wherever you go. I do not want to fail you."

"You have not failed me. If the reverend's scouts find a suitable location, we shall go soon. Do not be troubled." He reached for her.

Mary scooted close. "I dream of a home, but I want more than anything for you to build your church."

"John Davenport has many ideas for the church, and I very much want to meet with him when he is ready to establish it. There shall be a legacy for our children and our children's children. All will be well. Take care of yourself and we will have the babe we so desire."

"I pray for that, Barney. I just pray it shall not take too long."

Mary lay quietly beneath her husband's

strong arm until she heard his heavy, rhythmic breathing. She lifted his arm and crawled from the bed. Heart aching, she needed to walk. She wrapped her cloak about her and picked up her doll. Walking a short distance from the tent, she came into view of their little cottage, almost complete. She sank to the earthen floor of the front hall and drew her knees up to her chin. Leaning back against the wall, she clutched the doll until tears fell in more torrents than the summer squall that had ripped through the night before.

Every time he brought up children, specifically their children, her heart cracked a bit. What would happen if she never bore him a babe? Her forehead dropped to her knees and she brought her arms over her head. In time he would resent her, just like Papa said he would. Barney expected her to carry his babe and he was patient now because he had much work to do. And Ann. He never stopped thinking of her. She prayed for forgiveness from her selfishness, but truly, she wanted her husband to think of her for once.

Barnabas rolled over and looked about. No Mary. He checked the boys and left the tent. He walked briskly through the dank night air and found himself in their new cottage, somehow knowing he would find her there. There she lay, curled in her cloak. Even her sleep did not prevent the dry sobs heaving from her chest. She held the doll in her arms.

He pulled it up by an arm and let it drop to the floor. Gently, he scooped her up and followed the path back to their tent. Thick clouds parted for a moment and a thin slice of moonlight fell on Mary's face. She looked so fragile, so vulnerable. He remembered his promise to John, to keep her safe. How could he do that when he could not even fathom what troubled her the most? Her hood blew back in the breeze and he pulled it about, tucking it beneath her chin. Keeping the cloak wrapped around her, he set her down on the pallet and lowered himself beside her.

Sleep would not come for him. What was he doing wrong? Why did nothing seem right? But more importantly, what could he do to change it? His prayers were not for himself. Ann still surrounded him, but he prayed he could be the husband Mary wanted. What on earth, dear Lord, did she want?

She woke the next morning to bright sunshine. The storm had moved on. Barney and the boys were gone. Stiff and spent, she recalled the night before. How had she gotten back into bed? Her cheeks burned with embarrassment. He must have found her in their cottage.

Her mother's silver looking glass lay on the small table and she peered at her reflection. Her eyes were a watery blue. She gave her papery cheeks a little pinch and gently bit her lips to bring color back to them. Donning a pale yellow garden chemise, she brushed out her tumbled mass of hair and secured it into a knot. She looked outside for signs of Barney.

He was up on the frame of the roof, stacking the rocks that would be their chimney. It would be a small cottage, but he wanted a real hearth. "Good morning, my sweet. You have slept in quite late, but I do believe you needed to." His voice was strained.

"Yes, Barney, I am sorry. You must have put me back in bed?" Squinting upward into the blinding sun, she shielded her eyes with her hand.

"That I did. You worried me."

"Did you find my poppet?"

"Yes, the doll. You had the doll. That worries me as well, Mary. It seems to me you

spend too much time coddling that poppet."

"Yes, but where is it?"

He looked off to the distance.

"Barney, where did you put it?"

He looked back down at her and she could
sense his regret.

Agitation crept slowly into her voice. "I
said, where is it?"

"I threw it away. 'Tis gone."

"What? No! Where? Where did you throw
it? I shall retrieve it."

"You cannot. It's gone for good. Prithee,
forget about it."

Her chest heaved, breath squeezed from
her lungs. Tears burned her eyes but would
not flow. She had never been this angry in
her life. "By your leave, I shall not forget
about it. She was mine. My mother made
her for me. How could you? How could
you!"

Barnabas almost fell from the roof as he
tried to scramble down. But he was too late.
She had already run from him.

He pried the lid from the oak cask and
gently removed the doll. He would never
have thrown her doll away. It meant too
much to her. He only wanted to make a
point. What was he thinking?

The paths made by the Indians were numerous, some quite invisible unless one already knew they existed, but he knew her favorite. It wound through berry bushes and past a grove of oak to a gentle stream. No doubt she chose it and he would find her there, in a heap. Remorse at his own harsh words drove him down the path, praying as he went that she would forgive him.

The reeds danced in the breeze as he scanned the opening. Nestled in their midst, he found her curled up, lying very still. He'd almost tripped over her. Her face was buried in her arms; her hair entwined with the damp grass. He scooped her into his arms. She turned toward him, eyes wild and wet.

Her arms flailed against his chest. "Put me down. I do not want to look at you. I do not know why I ever came here with you anyway. You have lied to me from the start. You never explained your intentions coming to this awful place and you made decisions that should be mine to make. You threw away my doll! You are vile! I want to go home. I pray thee, let me go home."

"Forgive me. It was not right of me, not right at all. I don't know what possessed me to speak to you in that way. Here is your poppet." He held the doll up. "I would never destroy it. I know how much you treasure it. It was unconscionable of me to say the things I did. Do you forgive me?"

She grabbed the doll and hugged it to her chest. "Did it even cross your mind that my mother made the doll for me? That the memories and keepsakes I treasure of my mother are just as important to me as the keepsakes you have of Ann? Of all people, I would think you could understand family and the things that keep us tied to them."

She looked wide-eyed from his face to her doll and pressed it to her cheek. Her body wilted against him as if the last ounce of her strength left her.

He ran his fingers down her temple. "There now, let me take care of you, Mary. I have not done well. I can, by God's grace, do better. Come let me take you to the tent where you can rest."

Her voice sounded dry and rough. "I miss my family so very much. Papa and Lizzie I can hope to see someday. Mother will not come back to me, though. I have so few pieces of her — I cannot bear to lose what I do have."

Barnabas bent to gently kiss her forehead. "Aye, I understand, I do. I will not do this to you again, you have my promise. You do know, my sweet, you will see your mother in heaven again someday, do you not?" He started up the path, toward their home.

Mary hugged Barnabas's neck and nodded. "You can put me down now, really you can. I shall be all right." He set her down and held her hand as they continued up the trail.

She hiccupped as she tried to speak. "Barney, you will see Ann in heaven too."

"True and that gives me comfort. And I will be waiting there for you too."

A shy smile crossed her face. "You told me that once before. How does that work?"

"I do not know. 'Tis one of God's mysteries. I do not believe there will be any grieving up in heaven, so I know I will be waiting there for you with a kiss."

He looked down at her as they approached the clearing to their home site. "I know I am not the husband you hoped for, but I do care about you. Please believe that. I may not always act like it, but I do. I despise myself when you are unhappy. I truly want to see you smile."

18

Fall 1637

Fall gave scant relief from the humid heat and summer thunderstorms, but no one complained. The reality of spending over two months on a ship, crossing the Atlantic through high seas and storms, spoilt food, and rampant illness gave the Hortons and their neighbors an appreciation of how horrendous living conditions could be.

And there was much to do to ready for the winter and not much time to ponder it. They worked hard during the fall months to prepare their shelter and their food stores and to ready the ground for the spring planting.

The stories about abundant forests and wildlife were true, and there were expanses of salt marsh, too, covered in cordgrass that offered protection for mussels and birds. Mary pulled the grass to make mats and busied herself gathering eggs and mussels for their meals. She delighted in her discovery of purslane growing amongst the grass. She'd missed the salads they enjoyed in England, and this wild, leafy green made a tasty substitution.

Late in October, when the chill of the night took a decided turn from just crisp to bone-chilling, Barney swept Mary off her feet and carried her into their cottage, the boys close behind them, wide grins on their faces. It was small, but Barney had built a loft for the boys. The hall contained a hearth, large for the size of the room. The clapboard siding — hewn from the logs with the help of the townspeople — was topped with a thatched roof, but the chimney and hearth were of stone.

When Barney and the boys carried the old oak table in, a hush fell over the household. Barney set it across two fat logs, and Mary wiped off the dirt and grime with a kitchen rag. Jay and Ben stepped closer to study the *J* scratched in one corner and the *B* on the opposite side, both encircled with a heart.

Tears gathered in the corner of Mary's eyes and she swallowed hard before she turned once again to tend the fire. She threw another log on and kicked it into place with her booted foot. Picking up the fire iron, she rearranged the logs to allow more air and studied the orange flames as they licked upward.

Barney joined her and slipped his arms around her waist. They both stared at the fire, its warm and sumptuous glow fragrant from the fruitwood.

He bent toward her. "Thank you. You were right. The table is important. I was being selfish. Are you all right?" He kissed her behind her ear.

"Yes, Barney. Just a bit overcome. We are all here safely and we are in our home. How I prayed for that."

"Aye, God has been good to us."

"It would be all right with me if this is where we stayed."

"Aye, I know you long to know you are home. This will be home for a time."

"I'm glad we have the table." She turned into his embrace. "Barney, we need to speak to Jeremy about bringing the blue slate. I know how much it means to you to have a gravestone that matches Ann's. We should tell him to bring it at his next sailing."

"I can wait for the slate, my sweet, until we establish ourselves. There is much going on. Reverend Youngs is in Salem with talk of relocating with Reverend Davenport in Quinnipiac. I'll be traveling there off and on whilst plans are put into place. There is still so much to be decided. I wish I could tell you where we shall be in a few years, nay, even in a few months, but that is for God to show me. Can you be content to know this is home, if only for a little while?"

"There is no choice then. But I have a garden to tend and I told Mistress Browne I would help her plan a wedding for young Emma. I shan't have much time to be discontent, Barney. But I pray we are here through harvest and the wedding."

She regarded Jay and Ben as they sat at the table and played with their carved horses. "The boys are of an age they can help me when they are not working with you."

"Aye, they can do that. Now what say I help you with dinner? There is still a thing or two I can teach you about cooking, though I dare say you are most capable." He picked up a small pot, attached it to the trammel, and swung the lug pole to the back of the hearth. With the tongs he rearranged the logs beneath for added heat. "Joseph and I will go down to the stream and bring back some buckets of water."

She offered him a kiss and turned to Ben. "Help me grind the corn and be thankful 'tis not beans."

Later that night, after they had supped on

a pottage made up of bits of turkey, corn, and turnips left over from dinner, she sat at the oak table and penned letters. The first one was to Papa, then one to Lizzie. She did her best to sound happy, and in many ways it was true.

She wrote to Lizzie that Patience Terry, although a nuisance on the voyage, had not settled in their small hamlet but in Boston with her parents. She asked her to be sure to tell Ruth and Rachel that the handkerchiefs proved invaluable on the ship, and the seeds her sister had so lovingly prepared for her would be planted in the spring. Jeremy would bring her more, and did Lizzie think the plants from the English gardens would grow in New England as well? She hoped so; they were planning a wedding in the fall for one of the young women who came over on the ship with them.

She went on at length about the abundance of the land, telling them that everything Jeremy had told them she found to be true, but left out description of all of the work and toil it took from sunup to sundown just to survive. She thanked her father again for giving her the dolly, but left out the argument she and Barney had regarding it.

Dwelling on the good helped to lighten her burden, but more than that, she hoped someday her family might come to New England. She hoped by the time they arrived, she and Barney would be settled and able to offer them a more comfortable existence than what they had experienced when they arrived.

She had no idea when these letters might be delivered. Jeremy hoped to be back in the spring. She planned to write from time to time, and when he returned, she would send all of the letters with him. When she mentioned this to Barney, he laughed and reminded her there were other ships that came in occasionally and he would be happy to take the letters for her whenever he was traveling to Boston. She declined. To put them in Jeremy's care and know he would hand deliver them was important to her. After all, letters often did not make it to their destination. She would wait for her brother-in-law.

Jay and Ben were excited to climb the ladder up to their room. It was just large enough for two small pallets, but they said the fact they had their own room — and moreover, they did not share a pallet — was much like living in the turret of a castle.

Mary and Barney slept close that night on

their pallet at the back of the hall, thankful to be snug in their new cottage. It was difficult for her to sleep, though, as she thought of her letters to Lizzie and Papa. Sometime during the night she heard the wind whip through the birch and she got up to peek out the window.

There were no stars, but as she stared at the sky the first few snowflakes of the winter flitted to and fro as they fell through the night. She thought of her mother and angels, smiling and laughing until they cried as the lacy flakes danced. Her mother had always loved the snow, and she had too.

But this first winter — in this wild, wild land — she feared the coming cold and all of the snow it would bring. In this season of her life, the joys she remembered from her childhood, her mother, and her family seemed so far, far away. God did too, even though Barney was certain He held them in the hollow of His hand. She hoped so. On the morrow, she would work harder in hopes of making it so.

Despite her fears for the winter, May of 1638 arrived warm and pleasant, and with diligence Mary attacked the weeds threatening her sprouts. She'd hoped Jeremy would be here with the much-needed plants for her garden. To occupy her, Barney brought her some fledgling carrots and leeks for starters in her garden when he returned from Boston. He fashioned a hoe for her but stifled his chuckles at her attempts to use it.

"What now, have you never used a hoe before, my sweet?"

"I loved to work in Papa's kitchen garden, you know that. But there were not so many weeds. I fear I am overwhelmed. I cannot keep up."

His suppressed chuckle exploded into an outright guffaw. "Mary, you had a gardener. Whatever weeds you found to pull were an oversight of his." His look was one of pure delight.

Her face warmed with indignation and she tossed the hoe down. "Why, Barnabas Horton! Do not laugh at me. I know that. I just did not know how fast they could grow. I just cleared this when you were off to Boston."

He pulled himself together and bowed. "I do apologize — I didn't mean to tease you so. You have worked hard by yourself and accomplished much — I'm amazed by you, truly. I do hope the hoe makes it easier for you and less strain on your back. Let me show you how to use it." He picked up the hoe and placed it in her hands. Wrapping his arms about her, he guided her movements, working the stubborn rock-strewn ground with ease.

"I like this, Barney."

"Mmm. I do too."

"I mean, having you close. 'Tis been awhile. You are gone so much, you know."

"Mmm. 'Tis what I mean too." He closed his eyes and nuzzled her hair. "I smell lavender."

"I made a lavender water to rinse my hair with. Barney, when you decide where we shall live, do you think you will travel less? I have been praying hard for the babe we both want."

"I pray for that as well. The settlement I told you about to our south, the one that has a port. The Indians who occupy the area have been attacked and harassed by their neighbors and have agreed to sell their land in return for protection. I hope to purchase property so we can make plans for our house, a timber-framed one. It will take some time, so you and the boys will stay here. I hope to have it done by winter next year. So much depends on Reverend Youngs though, so I but dream at this point."

"If God blesses us soon with a child, winter would be perfect for our new house.

But why must everything depend on Reverend Youngs? Is he not removing to Quinnipiac with Reverend Davenport?"

"He's in Salem for now, but that is the plan. Reverend Davenport does not have a Charter from England for the settlement, but there is fear the Dutch in New Amsterdam will settle it if he does not. So it's with much haste he travels there. The land has inlets that could be quite valuable as ports and it is important we claim them for the Crown."

"It seems so complicated."

"But once we are in Quinnipiac, I see little need to travel. An occasional trip to visit Thomas, but we would make the journey together with the children."

"Oh, Barney, that would be wonderful. I would love to see Jane and Belle again."

He pulled her closer. "It will be good to travel less, my sweet. I do believe once we are settled and you feel you are truly making a home for us, the Lord will bless us with a child."

Mary's spine stiffened, her eyes stung with tears she willed not to appear. "I — I pray for that, Barney. I pray 'tis soon. There are times I think if Papa and Lizzie came over, I could accept that God does not give us a child. But I fear they will never come, and I do know how much you desire a child. Do you think He punishes me because I want the wrong things?"

"Nay. The longing in your heart is for family. God would want that for you too. And He may give us the desires of our heart, but in His own time. We must be diligent and do His work. To be sure, we are in God's will here in Massachusetts, but I know there is so much more to be done. I did not mean to make you unhappy, I only wanted you to know I understand how difficult it is here for you."

She leaned into him, bringing the hoe to her chest.

He kissed the top of her head, smoothing a strand of her hair caught by the breeze. "Speaking of Thomas, Reverend Youngs tells me he plans to travel to Agawam later next month. He invited me to come. Would you like to come with Joseph and Benjamin to visit Thomas and Jane?"

"I should like to see them. How long a journey is that?"

"Two days, mayhap three, if we borrowed an ox to pull the cart. The Henrys would let us use theirs, I believe. I have helped Miles enough with his fence. Or mayhap 'tis time to buy a good horse of our own. It seems I borrow a different nag for every journey."

She turned in his arms, and he smiled as he looked down at her.

She reached a hand to his brow and smoothed it. "I know it would be a long journey, but I would not mind."

"Very well, then. The plan is to meet with Reverend Youngs in a fortnight. Let me see what can be arranged. I will need to get a letter off to Thomas. He built their house to be temporary, so it is small and would not accommodate company. But there must be someone who could accommodate us."

Mary anticipated the trip with pleasure. She would bake some bread and persuade Barney to bake his ginger cakes. Perhaps she would sew a poppet for Belle. The excitement she felt for the journey reminded her of the anticipation she felt before the trips to London with Papa and Lizzie, though Agawam was not London, she was certain.

19

Late May 1638

A fortnight later, the Hortons were on their way to Agawam. A large wagon pulled by two oxen — Mr. Henry insisted they take both of his — served as their bed the first two nights.

Finally they pulled in front of the widow Moore's boarding establishment. A hot meal and a comfortable bed, how good that would be. Not quite The Swan, but at least she would not be doing the cooking and cleaning.

Finishing Mistress Moore's breakfast of cheese, butter, and fresh-baked bread, Mary looked up to see Thomas, his wife, and their daughter walking through the door. Her joy at seeing family, the first familiar faces in this wild land, made her breath catch and she clutched her hands over her heart.

Barney jumped to her side and helped her to stand.

She rushed to the arms of her sister-in-law, Belle caught between their skirts. "Oh, my, Jane! 'Tis so good to see you. I have bread to give you. I baked it myself. Do not let me forget to give it to you."

"Mary, let me see you!" Jane held Mary at arm's length and gave her an approving nod. "You look well. Barnabas has been taking good care of you."

Belle grinned at her aunt but hid from her cousins.

Mary bent to her niece. "My, I wanted to pick you up and hold you, but look how big you are. But indeed, not too big for a kiss from your auntie." She gave the little girl kisses on both cheeks. "I have a treat for you. Uncle Barney baked the ginger cakes himself."

She handed the bag to Belle and turned to the boys. "Jay, Ben, say hello to your cousin."

With a nod from their father, they both stepped forward and offered a timid good morrow.

Mary exchanged a hug with Thomas as Barney greeted his sister-in-law.

The rest of the morning Barney spent in meetings with Reverend Youngs until he could join Thomas and the ladies at the riverbank. The children chased each other until exhaustion, then made little boats from leaves and floated them at river's edge.

Thomas turned to Barney. "It was exceedingly difficult to live in Boston. His Majesty kept imposing tax after tax. First it was a tax on anything we traded with the Indians. Now a ship's tax. Can you imagine? We decided to follow William Pynchon up the Connecticut River. The natives gave us land on the east side of the river and a plot to grow crops on the west side. In return, we gave them eighteen fathoms of wampum, along with eighteen hatchets, eighteen knives, and eighteen coats."

"How much land to build on?"

"Ten acres each."

"Amazing. Eighteen, eh? What is the significance of that, pray tell?"

"It was a small tribe, eighteen families in all."

"Aye, I see."

"You should come here, Barn. Agawam is a beautiful place. Come live with us." He looked at his sister-in-law as he spoke.

Mary gazed at the water, a breeze caressing her face. She did not care what Barney might decide. Just that he decide where home was to be.

"Nay, brother. I have plans to go to Quinnipiac. And gracious, I have not seen anything here in New England that has not been beautiful. I want to be near a port, and of course Jeremy will be making frequent trips."

"True. What do you hear from him?"

"We expected him sometime this spring, truth be told. Now that I have the house built, I am anxious to begin receiving supplies from home."

"Pynchon is the man for supplies. He has just about anything you can have a need for. I shall have him load you up, if there be room in the wagon, of course."

Mary's attention turned to the business at hand. "Does he have thread? And scissors?"

Thomas chortled.

"Is that yea or nay?" She grinned back at her brother-in-law. It still amazed her how much alike the three brothers' laughs were.

"Aye, I am certain he would be able to get you thread and scissors."

"My sweet, I will need to meet with the reverend once more. It would be the opportune time for you to seek out this Mr. Pynchon and make your purchases."

"Oh, yes. Shall you be able to take me to see him, Tommy?"

"It is my Jane's favorite pastime, is that not so, lovey?"

His wife grinned sweetly. " 'Tis true, we

must go see him."

The end of the day found them together again, in Thomas and Jane's tiny home, their stomachs full with good food, and contented to be with family.

Mary sat at the table and smiled when Jay and Ben joined the men in a discussion about life in the wilds. She enjoyed looking with Jane and Belle over the trinkets and necessities she purchased from Mr. Pynchon earlier.

"Mama says Uncle Barney filled his casks with gold." Belle's impish smile lit her face. "Did he, Aunt Mary?"

"Belle! You should not repeat such things!" Jane's cheeks reddened and she shifted on the bench.

Mary laughed. "She says that because we all said that of your papa. The Horton brothers would not leave England unprepared. Your grandparents would not allow it."

The ladies fell silent and the conversation from the men drew their attention.

"I hear the plague is raging in London once more." Thomas poked at the fire with a log, then plunked it on top of the flames.

"Aye, I know. 'Tis what I heard from Reverend Youngs. People are leaving the city in droves to escape, he says." He glanced at

Mary with a knowing look. "I dispatched a letter home, inquiring about Mother and Father's health. One to John and Elizabeth, as well. Jeremy will bring news, I'm certain, but he's overdue."

Mary fidgeted with the sewing scissors in her hands. " 'Tis been a long time since we have heard from Jeremy. News comes so slowly. I do hope everyone is all right."

"I wish we had letters — we can but pray for his safe arrival. The plague has ravaged London before and the people of Mowsley have never had to fear. They are far north, and your father stays home if there be trouble in the city."

She looked up. "Yes. He knows to take care of himself."

With much regret they bid their farewells and returned to one more night at the widow Moore's.

The following morning, Mary sang a soft tune as the oxen pulled them along. It was a jig Lizzie liked to sing to her, and although she normally would not risk singing in front of anyone, today she felt carefree.

Barney leaned in close to listen. "What is that tune, my sweet?"

"A silly old song that Lizzie learned from Mother. Something about little lambs eating ivy."

"Oh, I thought I did not recognize it." His chortle mingled with her giggle. "By the by, I have not told you about my meeting with Reverend Youngs."

Now she straightened, ready to listen.

"He says there is much indecision at the moment regarding the timing of going to Quinnipiac. I was to travel there soon, but he requests I not make the trip until further notice."

"Oh, Barney, that is so disappointing. How long does he think it might be?"

"He doesn't know for certain, but the possibility of several months to a year is not out of the question."

She regarded his profile, as he avoided looking at her. He knew she was upset, of course. She wanted to be kind. 'Twas not his fault. "Barney, do you not think we should go to Agawam, then? We know we shall not stay in Winnacunnet. May we not just settle someplace? With Tommy and Jane? We would be with family."

"Nay, my sweet. That has never been my intention. God has a plan for us. We must stay close to His plan."

She waited for him to add "in His own time." Thankfully, he did not. She settled back against the board and closed her eyes. With the boys occupied in the back of the wagon, she could at least fume in silence. Would God forgive her grumbling? She could not face another year of indecision.

20

July 1638

Mary stayed busy from dawn to dusk with cooking, gardening, and maintaining her household, any of which could be a full-time occupation. The moments of leisure she allowed herself in Mowsley were but a dream. Promising herself time for indulgence, she woke well before the boys. But once up and the fire stirred, it seemed like the day was underway and endless chores demanded her time.

Barney finally traveled to Quinnipiac. He had meetings to attend with both Reverend Davenport, in Quinnipiac since last April, and Reverend Youngs of Salem. He should be on his way home, and hopefully would bring good news that Reverend Youngs was now ready to remove to Quinnipiac. Barney had promised to arrange a land purchase if that be the case.

She rose early that morning to write letters. There was much to do in the fields, but perhaps she would have a few quiet moments to write a short missive to her family.

Dearest Papa,

It is with great love that I write you this day and pray it finds you well and in good cheer. I do miss you, my father, but have found life in New England so occupying that I do not fill my days with sadness, but rather fill them with the work the Lord intended us for.

The apples here, Papa, are the strangest thing. They are so tiny and do not seem much worth the trouble of eating. I am having dreams of the large, luscious apples from our orchard at home and wonder if you could not send seeds, or perhaps small seedlings, with Jeremy?

We will move to Quinnipiac soon and it is my desire that we will finally be at our place of abode, the place we shall call home. Once there I shall plant an apple tree for you.

Your obedient and loving daughter,
Mary

She had put on a brave front for Papa, but for her sister the façade began to crumble.

Dear Lizzie,

I am weary and missing Barney but wanted to write a short note to you. It seems work is never done. Not a complaint, mind you. If I had more time on my hands I would miss you and Papa terribly. I do, actually, but have no time to give it clear thought. Now that I am reflecting on it, I realize that not only do I not have time, I have no friends either. I miss your friendship. There is a small group of ladies that I have gathered together with the intent of giving support to each other, much like you have always given me. I hope to do good work with this, but sometimes it feels as if the ladies care more about gossip than surviving this wilderness.

Jay and Ben are schooled by a fine old gentleman, Mr. Baxter. He is well learned, like Barney, and has been marvelous for the boys. Ben continues to be the lovey, but Jay and I still have our moments. Nothing has changed there too much. Some days I think we shall be friends, but the very next day proves otherwise.

I promised Papa another grandchild, but after all of these years I start to doubt if that will happen. I used to cry and such about it, but don't have the luxury anymore. Too much to do.

Barney is a good husband to me, and works very hard, but at times I know he is thinking only of Ann. That is all right, of course, as I have always told him I would never want him to forget her. And that is still true. But there are times when his look is so very far away. I feel an ocean between us and he might as well be as far from me as you and Papa.

I'm sorry, Lizzie, I do not mean to make you sad. I have written you many letters and their tone was certainly more cheery than this. Perhaps I shall not send it. Jeremy was supposed to return last spring, but so far no word. He promised to take my letters back to you and Papa. I hope Papa is well. I have written to him as well, though it is brief, as it pains me to tell him all I have shared with you.

We will be moving soon to Quinnipiac. Barney is there now, purchasing a lot. Please keep us in your prayers as I do you. I pray daily that you, Zeke, Josh, Ruthie, Rach, Hannah, and Papa will come to join us. I have painted a dreary picture, I'm afraid, but truly all is wonderful and I just miss you more than words do justice.

> Your loving and devoted sister,
> Mary

She folded the letters carefully and placed them at the bottom of her stack. She wasn't sure if she would send Lizzie's with Jeremy or not. She truly wanted her sister and Papa to come and live in New England.

Where was Jeremy? Had he not told them he would return within the year? It was worrisome, but she also knew he would not put his crew or passengers in danger if it be in his power. She imagined him skirting a storm and waiting it out in the Canaries. She smiled at the thought as she tied a pretty ruby-hued satin ribbon around the letters and tucked them into the sturdy trunk Barney had made for her.

She stirred her fire and set her flat iron pan in amongst the hot coals. She took a slab of salted pork and cut thin strips to fry over the coals. When they were crisp, she placed them on a platter and poured a thin batter of ground corn and water into the grease of the pan. The little cakes were simple, but tasty.

"Mama, you woke me up with the smell. I'm hungry." A sleepy-eyed Ben peered down from the loft.

Jay pushed past him to scamper down the ladder. "Me too. It smells good."

"I'm glad you're hungry. We need to eat and then go out to work the garden. Your father should be home today, and I would like to please him with what we've accomplished."

Mary's hoe hit the hard ground with a thwack as the sun warmed her back. Sweat trickled from her forehead as she raised a sleeved arm to mop it. They had finished weeding the garden, but she wanted to clear a little more space for a few more rows of carrots and turnips. They should start well, even in hot July.

Jay followed behind Mary and raked at the broken ground.

She thwacked once more and felt the reverberations from the wooden handle. Her arms ached. "It shall be good to have more vegetables if we must stay here."

Jay looked up and rested on the rake. He squinted at her. "Do you think we will?"

"I hope your father has good news about the plans for Quinnipiac, but it seems our plans always get deferred."

"Mama! Joseph!"

Mary and Jay looked across the field.

Ben charged across with Jeremy in tow.

"Look, Uncle Jeremy!"

Dropping their hoes, they ran, stumbling over dirt clods along the way, to greet him.

"Heigh-ho, be careful. Where's Barn?"

Mary tried to catch her breath. "He has not returned yet from Quinnipiac. I expect him any moment. Jeremy, what is wrong? You look poorly."

He pressed his hands to his eyes. "I am well. It has been a difficult journey."

"Yes, to be sure. Let's go in and you can sit. Are you hungry?"

"No, Mary, I'm not hungry, but I would like to rest. Joseph, Benjamin, can you be good lads and go fetch my trunk? You'll need to take the wheelbarrow."

"Yes, Uncle Jeremy. We'll be right back." Jay glanced at his brother, challenged him with a look, and darted off toward the barrow.

"Wait, Joseph! Not fair — wait for me!" Ben raced after him, closing the distance quickly.

Jeremy eyed the boys with a sadness Mary could not mistake. "Come, Jeremy, we shall sit a spell. The day is too hot and I am ready for refreshment."

He followed her in and sat at the old oak table. She set two cups and a plate of ginger cakes before him. "Barney baked these."

A glint of a smile passed his lips, replaced by a frown.

He was surely tired and hungry. She could tend to that. "You cannot come to a baker's house and not expect to be offered a biscuit or cake, now can you?"

"Ah, true, thankfully, true. Mother always baked the best until Barn took over." He took a bite of the small, crisp cake and stared at the table. "Mary, I have some news from home, but methinks it best to wait for Barnabas."

She held her breath as she sat down. Grasping the edge of the table, she thought to ask about his news, but decided against it. "I don't know when Barney shall be here. He said he might make it by yesterday or perhaps this afternoon. 'Tis a long ride from Quinnipiac and the horses he borrows are poor excuses."

"Aye."

"Jeremy, there is something I have meant to ask you, and I don't want Barney to know."

His eyebrows shot up. "Oh, what is that?"

"I wanted to ask you whilst I have the chance. Do you remember he wanted to bring a slab of blue slate with him for his gravestone? I'm wondering if you could bring it. I'm hoping we shall leave for Quinnipiac and build our house."

"Do you think he still wants it?"

"Oh, yes. He wrote his own epitaph years ago. 'Tis beautiful and I wish to have it engraved on the blue slate, like he did for Ann. I want to surprise him. I know where he keeps the paper — in his Bible. Would you be able to do that for me, Jeremy? Buy the slate and have it engraved?"

"I don't see why I couldn't. Of course, it will take almost a year to bring it back. May I read this epitaph?"

Mary left his side and picked up the old Horton Bible. She opened it with care and turned to the last page. There was the worn and creased parchment. She unfolded the page and held it out to Jeremy. "Barney wrote that."

She watched him read. "I think he thought it would be a bridge to both the past and future. A link to the slate left behind and a call to the generations to come. Do you not think so, Jeremy?" She looked up at him and met his eyes. Tears. She had not seen tears, nay, even a dampness in his eyes before.

"I will take this with me and bring you back the blue slate."

"We must not take it from his Bible. I shall copy it for you."

She pulled out some parchment, a quill, and ink, and sat at the table to write.

Jeremy sat across from her, dark circles beneath his eyes, and a sadness about his mouth. "Mary, I must tell you. Barn might not be the husband you yearn for, but he cares deeply about you. He is a bumbling fool not to show you, but I know he does."

"He told me that once and I try to believe him, but just as often I feel so far from his heart. But I try not to think of myself. I have much to do for Barney and the boys. Church and the ladies keep me busy. If Papa and Lizzie would come here to live, my life would be very full indeed." She folded the paper and handed it to her brother-in-law.

"I know." He looked miserable. "Mary." His voice was gentle. "I have much to tell you, but I am weary. Prithee, may we talk in the morning? Mayhap Barn will be back."

Lord, I don't want to hear what he has to say. I don't want to hear this. 'Tis not good, that I know. Please send Barney home.

"Of course." She got up and turned to look out the window. The sun's slant sent shadows across the field. The boys needed to be back before dark with the trunk. Would Barney make it home before the sun sank?

" 'Tis just a pottage for supper tonight,

but there is much of it. And plenty of bread too. I hope that shall be enough?"

"Aye, it sounds very good to this hungry man. I don't want to be a burden."

She steadied herself on the back of her chair. "You are never a burden. I fear I am tired too. I worked with Jay all day in the fields. I'm sure I was in the sun too much."

"Mayhap I should go and see if the boys need help." He stood up and slipped the paper into his pocket.

She let him go, wanting to ask him if there were a letter from Papa or Lizzie, but afraid to ask the question.

He disappeared into the shadows that grew longer as the sun sank.

Dark, rain-laden clouds moved in. She breathed deeply, smelling the moist air. A rumble in the distance sent shivers through her body and she realized how quickly the heat of the afternoon dissipated. She moved to the hearth and nudged the logs, then returned to the window to peer into the gloom.

As if willing him there, the robust figure of Barney astride an ox of a workhorse appeared.

She flung the door open and ran toward her husband, feet scrambling over the ground she and Jay had broken, auburn hair streaming behind her. Her breath seemed to leave her and she wasn't sure if the words she cried would reach his ears.

"Heigh-ho! What is this, Mary? Did you not think I would make it home? I am late, no doubt, and for that I humbly apologize." He grinned at her.

"B—" She grabbed his leg. Why could she not say his name? Why would words not come from her mouth?

He leaned over, encircled her waist, and in one fluid movement swung her high onto the saddle's pommel in front of him.

"What is it? Tell me. What is wrong?" His smile faded and the lines of his brow deepened. "Did something happen to one of the boys? Where are the boys?"

"Barney. Jeremy is here."

He glanced toward the house. "Here? Is he all right?"

"Yes, he is fine, but tired. He went to find Jay and Ben. They are hauling his trunk up to the house."

His arm relaxed around her as he picked up the reins. "Very well, that gives us a moment to share a proper welcome." He urged the workhorse toward the house and rested his chin in the hollow between her neck and shoulder.

Myriad emotions engulfed her, but she

was incapable of acting on any of them. She simply slumped in his embrace and allowed him to take her the short distance home.

As Barney lifted his saddlebags, Jeremy pushed the wheelbarrow into view, with Jay and Ben flanking him. Their eyes met.

She sensed a message was sent between the two, no words needed.

Barney wrapped his arm about her shoulder. "Let us go in and see to the fire. They will join us forthwith."

"It was so hot today, but tonight I feel quite a chill. A storm is coming in. The fire shall feel comforting."

Barney tended the fire while she stirred the pottage and cut crusty chunks of white bread. She laid out cheese and butter, purchased from farmers near the hamlet.

They both turned to the door as Jeremy, Jay, and Ben entered.

Barney helped them lug the trunk to a space beside the far wall and eased it down. He embraced his brother with the Horton clan bear hug and they clapped each other's back. "We began to wonder about you."

Jeremy ran his forearm across his brow. "I'd wanted to come sooner, but it was difficult to leave. Joseph, Benjamin, what say we open the trunk. Your Aunt Lizzie has sent some sweets that I think you will particularly enjoy."

He lifted the heavy lid and dug out a wooden box. He handed it to Ben. "Marbles and tops. I brought books as well."

"Thank you, Uncle Jeremy." Jay opened the box and both boys took the toys out and found a place on the floor.

"The thank-you goes to your Aunt Lizzie."

"So very generous of her." Barney looked at Mary and helped her to return to her chair. "Are you all right, my sweet? Has this been too much?"

She took the seat. "I cannot tell you how I treasure word from home. I have craved it."

Jeremy bent over the trunk once more. "Lizzie sends you a silver sugar box and salt box. And these are sugar shears." He handed them to her. "They were your mother's, Mary."

She closed her eyes against the tears, but one trickled down her nose and she brushed it away.

"Here are French laces and beeswax candles too. Lizzie kept thinking of what she would want if she were in your place." Jeremy continued to pull presents from his trunk. "And I am not without my gift for you — coats, boots, and gloves for everyone."

"And letters? Are there letters, Jeremy?"

His shoulders drooped and he bent over the trunk again. "There is a letter from Lizzie as well." He pulled out a single parchment, folded and sealed with wax.

"And from Papa? Is there nothing from Papa?"

Mary noticed the tender look he gave the boys and steeled her heart for what she knew would come next. She straightened her shoulders and reached for Barney's hand. "Jeremy, you've come with news." She must sound brave.

"Aye, that I have." Jeremy's chest rose with a deep intake of air as he squared his shoulders and faced her. "My years as a shipmaster have given me much practice with delivering difficult news, Mary, but nothing has prepared me for this. 'Tis with much pain in my heart I must tell you of your father's passing —"

"No! No! Oh, please, no." The first no a shriek, the last a hoarse moan. She reached for Barney.

He pulled her into him. They rocked to and fro as Mary sobbed into his shoulder and he stroked her hair.

Jay and Ben dropped the tops and stood.

In two quick strides Jeremy enveloped the boys in their father's characteristic bear hug. "She will be all right. She needs some time to cry. She will need much more time to grieve. Are you both all right? He was a good man, was he not?"

"Yes, Uncle, he was." Jay's square jaw pulsated like his father's did in difficult times.

Ben wept, and after returning his uncle's embrace, he joined Mary and his father as they encircled him in their arms. She knew he did not remember her father much, that his tears were much more a reaction to hers.

She kissed the top of his head and lowered a damp cheek against it, as she let the tears flow. She yearned for Jay to lower the barrier that held him back. "Prithee, come, I must have you near me." Torrents cascaded down her reddened cheeks.

Jay made his way into her arms. He was stiff as she hugged him tightly.

"Thank you," she said in a voice barely audible.

Considerable time passed as the four huddled together. Barney at length pulled chairs near the fire and placed Mary in one, offering Jeremy and his sons the others, while he took his seat next to her.

After long moments, she dragged her eyes from the fire and faced Jeremy once again. "I wrote letters to Papa. He'll never get them."

Jeremy leaned forward, grasping her hands. "Aye, but I told him you fared well in the New World and he was so proud of you and all that you were accomplishing here with Barn."

"Tell me how this happened, Jeremy. How did he die? How long ago?" The last word she spoke cracked, broken.

"Six months ago. The physician said it was his heart." He glanced at Barney and back to Mary. "There was not much warning. When I returned from my last voyage, he was very hale indeed. So hearty that no one, not even Elizabeth, thought he could be ill. Whether he felt pain or not, and did not tell anyone, we will never know. Mary, Elizabeth wants you to know she was with him two days before he passed and he was in good spirits. She wrote you this letter."

He handed her the letter. "I have an apple seedling for you, as well. I will bring it from the ship on the morrow. Elizabeth said he started it from the apple trees in his orchard. He knew you would long for English apples. I believe she sent you some seeds too."

Mary held the letter, smoothing it with her fingertips, then lowered it to her lap. "I shall wait to read this. I fear I need some time before I do. Perhaps on the morrow, when you bring the seedling, I could have a few moments alone."

Barney leaned forward this time, his strong hands reaching out to cover her own. "Take the time you need, Mary. I truly wish I could bear this burden for you, to take the pain and make it my own. I know this is only a small balm for your hurt, but do try to remember Papa is now with your mother and with our Father in heaven. There is much rejoicing, I am certain, amongst the angels that he has come home." His eyes were watery as he kissed her hands.

She stood and surveyed the supper that remained on the table, cold and forgotten. "Thank you, Barney. I beg your forgiveness, but I should like to lie down. Prithee, would you sup without me? 'Tis but a meager meal . . ."

He put his hands on the chair and pushed up. The effort made him look older, as if the past hour had aged him ten years. He took her arm and guided her to their room. "We shall be fine, do not worry about us." He gently helped her to remove the bodice and skirt of her dress, leaving her in her shift, and laid her on the bed, pulling the quilt about her. "I will bring you something to drink, to help you sleep."

But before he returned, her pain gave way to slumber.

21

She slept soundly as Barnabas, Jeremy, and the boys sat at the table, the meal long finished, much of it eaten in silence.

Benjamin played with his crumbs as Joseph stared at his empty plate.

Barnabas leaned close. "Joseph, did you have enough to eat?"

He glanced up. "Yes, Father."

"I want you to know I was proud of you tonight. It was exceedingly kind of you to share in Mary's grief. We have had enough of it ourselves. We know what she is going through, to be sure."

"Yes, Father."

"Sit by the fire with Benjamin and study your schoolwork. I want to discuss something with Uncle Jeremy."

Jeremy nodded toward the trunk. "Fetch the books. Your Grandmother and Grandfather Horton sent them. Find one you like."

"Thank you, Uncle Jeremy." Benjamin opened the trunk.

Barnabas turned to his brother. "I have news from Reverend Youngs and Reverend Davenport. They feel it would serve God better for Reverend Youngs to plant his own church. So many have accompanied Reverend Davenport to Quinnipiac, there are almost more ministers than laymen. Eastern Long Island is not far from New Amsterdam, and they fear the Dutch will inhabit the whole island." He waited for Jeremy's reaction.

"And would you go with him?"

"Aye, I would. My intentions have always been to work with Reverend Youngs in planting a church. If Davenport desires us to go to Long Island, I'm willing. We made great plans, and though they seemingly fell apart once we came to New England, I still believe we will see them to fruition. There have been many difficulties since we arrived, but God has not deserted us."

Jeremy studied Joseph and Benjamin, absorbed in their books. "Does Mary know?"

"About my early talks with Youngs? Aye. But I have just come home with the news of Long Island. I am not sure how she will feel. There is no township there, nothing but wild forests." He lowered his head and rubbed the back of his neck.

"What about property in Quinnipiac? You were to build a house."

"Aye. I cannot plan on that now. Reverend Youngs comes in a fortnight and he should know a little more regarding the plan." He absently traced the *J* scratched on the table. "I do dread telling Mary. Most assuredly she will not like this."

"No doubt I should find somewhere else to be when you do. Mayhap I should take the boys down to *The Swallow* in the morning."

Both boys looked up quickly, eyes bright. Had they heard the discussions about the house? If they had, it didn't show. Mayhap they had learned to take things in stride with their old father. The uneasiness he felt inside spread like a tidal undercurrent. "Very well. Now what say you we call it a night? It has been a trying day. Let us seek God's comfort and wisdom and then go to bed." He picked up his Bible and turned to the blue ribbon. He read a chapter from Ephesians, then led them in prayer. "You boys go climb up to your bed and get your nightshirts on. Wash and rinse your teeth first." He nodded toward the slipware pitcher and bowl.

After seeing the boys to bed, Barnabas helped Jeremy arrange a pallet. "Thank you for being so careful with Mary today. I do appreciate that you waited until I came home before telling her of her father." He scratched at his beard. "I know it was not easy for you."

"I'm sorry to be the one to bring such sadness."

"I know it was difficult. There was something I was going to ask of you, brother. I would have liked to have waited, but now it seems I should take care of this business."

"What is that?"

"She has been through so very much. I should like to demonstrate my regard for her. There is a bed she admires at Mistress Waring's home. 'Tis a very ornate bed from France, with carved posts and rich curtains and tassels. Methinks if you could import one it would make Mary very happy."

"Softening up, eh, Barn?" He wanted to tease him, but he had no heart for it. "I've never thought being drab and stuffy a requirement anyway."

"Aye, I quite agree. Not a requirement, but frivolous finery to call attention to oneself is not pleasing to God. We should desire to be humble. But I know at times she finds me harsh. To see her smile will be worth it."

"Then I will make arrangements. It will take some time, of course."

Barnabas clapped his shoulder and bade him good night. "I'll give you payment for it, and the balance when you bring it, should it not be enough."

His eyes felt wet as he walked to the bedroom. Yes, she worked exceedingly hard and that was all he asked of her. He needed someone to be a helpmeet as he established a safe place for his family to live, worship, and grow. How interesting he'd thought he would teach her a few things about faith, but she was teaching him. Mayhap he was softening, but mayhap that pleased God as well as Mary.

A crash of thunder woke Mary and she lay there remembering the events of the night before. It was too painful to think about what might have been if she had remained in England, close to her father. Too painful to think about much. She listened to the rain pummel the thatched roof and turned to Barney, amazed he still slept. Quietly, she slid to the edge of their bed and got up. Slipping on a robe, she tiptoed to the kitchen and refreshed the embers. She tossed a log into the hearth. She listened intently as the fire caught and wrapped itself around the dry wood, creating a cacophony of snaps and hisses accentuated by pelting rain.

Jeremy walked in with Jay and Ben in tow.

She jumped. "Oh, I didn't hear you."

"We are going down to the ship. We thought we would get an early start. How are you?"

Her dry eyes burned as she closed them, not a drop of moisture left for a tear. "I shall be all right." She looked at the boys and attempted a smile. "God watches over us and I am surrounded by love. That is what I need and desire right now."

Ben gave her a hug.

Jay looked at the ground.

Jeremy leaned against the table.

"Would you like to take a bit of bread and cheese with you?"

He shifted his weight. "Aye, that would be good. I don't know how long we will be."

The meal packed, she tucked it into a sack. She watched the boys, running ahead of their uncle as they headed toward the bay beyond the trees.

I should make a meat pie for our supper. Jeremy would like that. He usually looks forward to good meals whilst he is here. I need to keep busy. Lizzie, oh Lizzie. What shall we do?

Barney entered the kitchen. "I am surprised you are already up. Are you all right?"

"I think so." She looked from him to the window and back. "I don't know. No, Barney. I have missed him so. To think I shall never see him again is something I can hardly bear. Do you think Lizzie and Zeke would bring the children and come live with us? By the time they could be here, our house should be finished." How she longed for her family.

He avoided her eyes.

"Did you hear me, Barney? Are you all right?"

"Aye, I am fine. I'm a bit lost for words because I have something to tell you and it seems you have been through enough for one day."

Her eyes grew large. She looked out at the grayness of the day. "There's more? How can there be more to tell me?"

"Mary, sit by the fire." They both took a chair. "My meetings with Reverend Davenport and Reverend Youngs did not go as I expected."

"Oh?"

"Nay, but we have had some very good discussions regarding what it is that the Lord would have us do."

"What, pray, do you mean?"

"There seems to be good cause to look for another location for our church. We've sent Mr. Hallock across the sound to Long Island to scout the possibilities there. Reverend Davenport's scouts were there previously and had good reports of the area. No one has built anything out on the east end and it seems to be a prime location for a new township, a new church. The Indians that are native to the land are very co-operative, very helpful."

Mary's eyes flitted from her husband to the fire and back. "By your leave, Barney, do you mean we would not be going to Quinnipiac? Not building our house there?" She stood, grasping her sides, and turned her back to him.

"Mary, your disappointment I cannot endure right now." He took her by the shoulders and gently turned her back toward him. "There are many factors we must consider in the placement of our church. It is Governor Eaton himself that has requested Reverend Davenport send planters to Long Island. Connecticut has held conveyances there for a few years, but the danger of the Dutch attempting to take it over is greater than ever. Reverend Youngs and I both feel called by God to plant a church and build a township and we feel led to this place. I cannot tell you how important this is. Can you be patient with me?" He held her shoulders, looking at her, his anxiety clear.

A torrent of tears burst forth. "Nay, Barney, I have no patience left. There are so many things we put off whilst you plan our future. Our home, a family — all this you say to wait on the Lord for. In God's time. How do we know what is God's time anymore? I wanted my family to come live with us and now 'tis too late for Papa. When do we start living our lives? And why would we go to the wilds of Long Island?"

He pulled her to him and held her while she cried. "There now, my sweet, you may cry. Cry all that you need. It is true that we must wait on the Lord and trust in Him. You have been very brave to follow me here, and you have been a strong helpmeet to me. I beg you to remain strong. When Mr. Hallock returns, we will make decisions quickly, God willing, based on his assessment. I promise you. We will make haste, and if it not be a house in Quinnipiac, it will be a house on Long Island. Reverend Davenport tells us the Indian natives call their settlement Yennicott."

She sniffed and cleared her throat, wanting to sound in control. "I do not know why I should believe you. You lied to me at our wedding when Jeremy spoke of coming to New England. All those years you did not once tell me of your desires. When you finally told me we would be coming here, I tried so hard to be strong. I told myself you had been through so much when Ann died. And you put so much blame and guilt on yourself. Wherefore, I do not understand. People get sick and many die. You should not rebuke yourself so."

His arms stiffened, then released her, but still she continued. So much needed to be said. "Barney, I am at the point where I question what I am required to put myself through. I do not understand you. I cannot seem to reach the secret places of your heart. There is a place you hold deep inside, that I cannot touch. I am left so hopeless, so alone." Spent and weary, she sank in her chair.

He reached across and smoothed her hair back from her brow, his eyes kind and forgiving, but wet.

She regretted the words that poured out unchecked. "I am sorry, my husband. I did not mean . . ."

"Nay, you are right to say it. I have not always been open with you and may God forgive me." The trouble with deception was, would you ever be believed again? There was such a fine line between sparing one's feelings and lying. If he told her right now he loved her more than anything else in the world, would she believe him? Nay, but it wouldn't be true either. "You worry God punishes you because we have no child together. Mayhap it is me He punishes. It was hard to deal with Ann's death, Mary, harder than I could ever tell you. Prithee, let that suffice."

His sadness tore at her heart, her being. She brought him into her arms and kissed his tears. "We have been through too much, we two. Say no more. I forgive you as God forgives you."

Jeremy and Jay pushed through the door, a spinning wheel between them and set it in a corner. Ben bounded behind them, a sturdy little apple tree in his arms. She gathered it to her and ran her fingers over the rough fabric that bound the roots. Did Papa ready the seedling for the long voyage or had he been too ill? Yes, it most likely was Lizzie who dug it and wrapped it so carefully. She'd done well. It looked so healthy. The spinning wheel unnoticed, her throat tightened as did her resolve. "I shall not plant my apple tree until we have reached our home, Barney. I pray thee, find it quickly."

Mary, Barney, Jeremy, Jay, and Ben tramped through the thick grass, wet with dew. They paused just short of the lower pasture to watch the sky brighten into eggshell blue with pink-tinged clouds puffing over the treetops.

In reverence, Barnabas's deep baritone broke softly through the still morning, "Sing ye loud unto the Lord, all the earth. Serve the Lord with gladness; come before Him with joyfulness. Know ye that even the Lord is God. He hath made us, and not we ourselves. Amen." Jeremy's tenor and Mary's sweet soprano blended into the amen of the prayer.

"Now look." Jeremy pointed to the lowest part of the slope. "Do you see?"

"See what?" Mary's voice rasped as she spoke, her throat tight from crying. She stood on tiptoe, straining to see.

Barney took her hand to pull her forward. "Let's walk down. It isn't far."

Jeremy nodded and began walking. "I would have told you about this yesterday, Mary, but it seemed you needed time."

As they came close, Jay and Ben ran ahead, but Mary stopped, her breath gone, her heart pounding. There grazed two sturdy English cows that looked amazingly fat after their long journey. Next to them a beautiful black, stout horse, still trying to find his land legs. Jay whistled and the horse lifted his large head, ears pricked forward. A large white star stood out on his forehead.

Mary drew her breath in sharply. "Why, Jeremy, he's beautiful. He's one of Papa's Old English Blacks."

"Aye, he's Northstar. The one a bit older than Starlight. Your father bred him several times and he has an outstanding herd at present. He retired him as a stud and had him gelded. He is thoroughly trained. One of the most comfortable rides you will find anywhere and can work like an ox. For now the laws do not permit mares to be exported, but no worries. Someday that will change and you will have Starlight."

She turned and buried her face in Barney's chest and he held her close, his hand covering her hair. She sobbed as she remembered the day Starlight was born.

Barney rocked her. "Thank you, Jeremy. I cannot tell you how much I appreciate you bringing Northstar to us. We are deeply grateful." He hugged Mary tight. "We've had grave news. This is a blessing."

Jeremy put his hand on his brother's

shoulder. "Aye, this is what John wanted. He wanted Mary to have her horses."

The trio made their way down to join Jay and Ben. As they approached, Northstar nickered gently and Mary threw herself into him, encircling his neck with her arms. He tossed his head and she could just hear Papa. *"Easy now, my girl. Move slowly or you shall spook him."* She dropped her hand to his chin and he nuzzled her fingers. " 'Tis me, Northstar. Everything shall be all right."

Later, Barney helped Mary set out platters of cheese, bread, and thick slices of salt pork. "The food is laid out on the table. Jeremy, I'm so sorry I have not cooked a meal for you."

Jeremy pulled out a chair and pointed to it. "Mary, sit. This is enough. None of us have much appetite. But we should all eat a bite, for our strength."

"Nay, Jeremy, I'm tired. I'm going to lie down. You eat."

Barney stood up and kissed her check. She padded out of the room without a glance back.

Barney followed her much later. "Are you awake?"

"Yes, Barney. Are you coming to bed?"

"Aye." He moved to the bed and sat. "I

know this is a question you do not like to hear, but I must ask. Are you with child?" He held his breath as he waited for her answer.

"Oh, Barney — for the hundredth, nay, thousandth time, no. But you will be the first person I shall tell."

He crawled in and drew her to him. "I'm sorry. I did need to ask. Jeremy said something that made me wonder. Your health is important to me. You will be in God's time. We must work hard and do His will. God is faithful. He will provide."

Quietly he waited for her answer, but only heard her shallow breaths. It probably had sounded like a litany. She was either asleep or she chose not to answer. He lay awake for a long time, the guilt from asking about the babe kept him from sleep.

But the guilt from long ago made him want to keep asking.

22

Mary woke in Barney's arms, her thoughts on the letter from Lizzie, unopened the day before.

He put a finger to her chin and turned her face to his. "Word should come soon about a new settlement, I promise. Do you still desire time alone to read your sister's letter? If you do, I have many things outside that I will occupy Jeremy's time with."

"Yes, thank you. I need this."

They dressed in silence. Mary chose to wear a garden frock of blue muslin. She pulled the brush through her hair and twisted it into a simple bun, securing it with a tortoise shell comb. She glanced at the silver looking glass, but could not look into it. Not today.

Once in the small kitchen, she watched him add fresh logs to the embers. Jeremy and the boys joined them for a meal of porridge.

Barney rose from the table. "Boys, come with me and your uncle. We have enough wood to chop and stack to work half the day."

She sat by the window and watched them file out to the woodpile. The letter poked out of her pocket and she ran a finger around the rough edges, then over the wax seal.

She shifted in her seat and stared at the little apple tree. Once they had a home, she would plant it in Papa's memory. Finally, unable to stall any longer, she turned back to the letter, fingers trembling as she drew it from her pocket and loosened the seal.

My dearest sister,
'Tis with much sadness and a heavy heart that I write to you today. I think of you reading this and I cry at the thought that I am not there to comfort you, to protect you, to hold you. I only pray Barnabas is home and by your side. By now Jeremy has told you our father has joined our mother in Heaven. My hand shakes to even write the words.

He expressed such joy at knowing you survived the voyage well and that you found contentment in setting up a household with so few resources.

Mary, please know that whilst Father was so deeply saddened at your leaving, he did rejoice in knowing you were following your heart. He was so proud of you for being the good mother you are to Joseph and Benjamin. He particularly was pleased to hear of the women's group you have formed and commented that was so like you to want to find a way to nurture.

The little pippin tree is from his orchard. He dug it himself and potted it for its journey to you. The last time I saw him was when he brought it to my house to give to Jeremy. He looked so happy to be able to do that for you. He wanted you to know 'tis hardy stock and will bear much fruit. I know you will treasure it.

I pray thee forgiveness for the brevity of this. 'Tis the most difficult letter to write. Please know that I think of you every day. Ezekiel and the children send their love, as do I.

Your loving sister forever,
Elizabeth

Mary slumped forward until her forehead touched the letter, arms limp in her lap. She shut her eyes as she pictured her father the day they sailed from London, standing there wordless, eyes red. She banished the scene from her mind. She desired to remember Papa from a happier time. A time when they rode in the country, both astride the Great Blacks that were his passion. How he loved the outdoors and taught her to love it too.

The door opened and Jay's head peeked in. "Are you all right?"

"I shall be, Jay. Perhaps not at the moment, but God shall heal the hurt. In time." She looked toward the apple seedling again.

He followed her gaze. "Would you like me to water the tree?"

"I should like that very much. Do you think I could put it in your care until we are ready to plant it?"

"Yes, ma'am. I'll take very good care of it."

"Thank you." She rubbed her eyes and pressed her cheeks. "And Jay, thank you for coming to check on me. 'Twas kind of you."

"I worried a bit. Father said you might like to take a ride with him on Northstar. He's finished with the wood and would take you now if you'd like."

"Yes, that would be good. I have not done anything to prepare our dinner, but perhaps today we could eat some cold meats and cheese once again."

"It's too warm for a hot meal. Cold meats will be fine, I am sure."

She picked up her muslin cap. "Thank you again, Jay." She moved slowly to the door and slipped out.

Mary stood, holding tight to Jay's and Ben's hands as *The Swallow* glided east out of the bay, smaller and smaller until it was a dark blur on the hazy line between sky and ocean. Memories of leaving the London port washed over her, but today she, Barney, and their boys were the ones left on the dock. She waved one last time in the hope Jeremy could see her.

A messenger brought word to expect Reverend Youngs to visit within a fortnight. Peter Hallock returned to Quinnipiac with encouraging news regarding Long Island and the reception he'd received there.

Mary worked hard preparing for the visit. From the garden she harvested turnips, onions, carrots, squash, and melons. The blackberries would be ripe soon, but she picked the strawberries already bursting with sweetness. She cooked the berries with sugar to preserve them, milked the cows, and churned butter.

She checked the supply of cheese, pork, and mutton in the larder. A large, salted pork shoulder and a nice mutton leg would make a fine feast for the reverend. Breads of all kinds were baked. She begged Barney to make the ginger cakes, and he was pleased to oblige.

On the morning the reverend was to arrive, she readied the house, swept the hard-packed earth floor, and spread fresh rush reeds, mixing in some dried mint and sage. She set out the beeswax candles from Lizzie on the oak table and dreamt about having a beautiful, large house with white oak floors and a magnificent hearth like the one in Mowsley. Oh, the cooking and baking she would do, and surely Barney would pass her the tongs. And if Lizzie came, they could cook together with plenty of room for all.

Her thoughts were interrupted by a loud knock on the door. She wiped her hands on a kitchen rag and tucked the errant wisps of hair into the twist at the nape of her neck before opening the door.

"Good morrow, Reverend Youngs." She bowed slightly. He was taller than she remembered him. Perhaps because he was thinner, his shoulders square.

He removed his black felt hat, his sandy blond hair matted from the brim. "A good morrow to you, Mistress Horton."

"If you please, come in. Barnabas should

be on his way from the field. I am certain he shall have heard you arrive." She stood away from the door to allow him to pass. "You have come a long way. May I offer you a chair and something to drink?" She pulled a chair toward him. "You must be hungry after such a long ride. We shall have dinner soon, but may I get you a bite to eat? A piece of cheese?"

"That is very gracious of you, but no, I shall wait for dinner. A drink would be most appreciated." He glanced around their cottage as she poured. "A most comfortable home. Did Barnabas build this?"

"Yes, with the help of our sons."

"Most impressive, indeed."

She was about to tell him of the house he'd built in Mowsley, but before she could begin, the door opened and Barney entered with Jay and Ben close behind. Reverend Youngs rose to his feet and offered his hand.

"John, how now?" Barney clasped his hand. "How was the journey?"

"Long, but that is expected, eh? So good to see you." He turned to Jay. "You did not tell me there was another Barnabas ready to conquer New England."

"Aye, he is that, tall as me and eager to be taller. This is my eldest son, Joseph, and this is Benjamin. And he is eager to be smarter. What is a father to do? And you have met my wife." He crossed the room to where Mary stood and slipped his arm around her shoulders.

"Indeed. She was just telling me about the house. I like what you have done here."

Mary smiled. "Gentlemen, pray pardon, but I need to attend to the fire and our dinner. It shall be ready soon. Reverend Youngs, I trust you have a hearty appetite?"

"Aye, Mistress Horton, that I do."

Barney cleared his throat. "Mary came to our marriage not knowing a whit in the kitchen. She was determined to learn, and much fun to teach. I do believe she now surpasses me in preparing a meal and makes enough to feed the king's army."

As both men shared a laugh, Mary curtseyed and made her way to her hearth.

The roasts of pork and mutton sputtered in the fire and proffered a tantalizing aroma. She opened the lid on the pot to check her made dish and sniffed the delicate scent of the artichokes, almond cream, and rosewater — a recipe her sister had given her. Lizzie said it was French. A stew of root vegetables bubbled over the hot embers.

To ready the table, she brought out her best linens and summoned Jay and Ben to help her set out utensils needed for the meal. As a finishing touch, she picked up Lizzie's candles and touched them to a flame in the hearth. These she placed at the center of the table.

After prayers led by Reverend Youngs, the meal was served. Stories over dinner revolved around the victories and tribulations of coming to New England, each telling a little more magnificent as the afternoon progressed.

A smile played on Mary's lips as she listened to Barney retell the story of the day he went ashore in Massachusetts as if it happened yesterday, and she knew it was most likely not the last time the reverend would hear this tale.

She recounted the day the house was ready and the excitement of unpacking beloved possessions they'd not seen since they left England. It was like Christmastide that day.

Reverend Youngs described the difficulties encountered when he originally tried to leave England with his wife and children. Charged with nonconformity, he was denied permission to leave, but eventually they boarded *The Mary Ann* and arrived in Salem in the summer of 1637.

When Jay spoke of his desire to learn more about astronomy from his uncle and his interest in farming, his words fell over her like dew from the heavens, so encouraged she was to hear him reveal his inner longings.

Ben, not to be overlooked, inquired if the reverend would like to browse his book collection, including a treasured volume his uncle had given him, *The First Folio.*

"Speaking of books, Benjamin, is it not time for you and Joseph to excuse yourselves and settle down to studies?" Barney nodded toward the hearth.

Both boys rose as they were excused.

"Fine lads, Barnabas."

"Thank you, John. Now tell me, what does Hallock have to say? He finds Long Island desirable?"

"That he does, I should say. The Indians call it Matouwac. That is Island of Periwinkle, far as we can tell. But the Dutch call it Long Island and that is far easier. Hallock purchased a tract of land from the Indians whilst he was there. His wife and children are still in England and would not come with him. He is hoping to return to them with news of his purchase and bring them back."

Mary checked the fire and returned with a tray of sweets. She offered her husband and their guest a tart before handing the boys a platter of ginger cakes.

Her husband smiled at her as she sat back down beside him. "Mary is most anxious to be settled. I have promised her once we have the facts, and the decision is made, I will move quickly to establish our home. Tell me of the bay. Would it be amenable to trade? Would a 300- or 400-ton ship be accommodated?"

"Indeed. Peter sailed around the northeastern tip and into a bay that would serve well for all size of vessels. There is a beautiful inlet from the bay and the land to the west of it is well protected from the winter wind by a bluff to the north. It receives warm breezes off the bay in summer. 'Tis there we would place the center of our township. On the east side of the bay, blueberries and cranberries grow wild. Bayberry grows in abundance as well. There are salt meadows to the north."

Mary leaned forward. "He found it acceptable then for your purposes? The Indians were welcoming?"

"Mistress Horton, the Indians are most friendly and ready to help us. They call themselves Corchaug and have several dwellings in the area. There is a fort with a palisade two and three logs thick that they built to defend themselves against the Narragansett tribe. They are logs as thick as Barnabas's thigh and twenty feet tall. They dug trenches and put the logs upright, leaning them crosswise to form a V.

"But they are peace-loving people and look to the English to help defend themselves from the warriors of the north. They are farmers and willing to help us establish our crops. They gave Peter a pipe, which means peace and friendship. He gave the sachem — their chief — a cup. We may settle there with ease, knowing God has blessed us."

Barney cleared his throat. "And the timber? Is there an abundance on this Long Island as we have in Massachusetts?"

"Aye, there is. Our first concern is to build a town meetinghouse, for church services and meetings. We'll need to establish our government, and of course that will take some time. We shall divide up lots for our houses and each man will be responsible for building his own. From the looks of your cottage here, you will manage very well and mayhap could be of service to others in their construction."

"Most assuredly."

"You are also amongst the better educated, and we shall depend much on you as we write our charters and organize our town government. Reverend Davenport and I have made the decision that I will proceed to eastern Long Island and plant the church. May we count on you as well, Horton? You would be an important part of this decision."

Barney took Mary's hand before he answered. "What God has called me to I cannot refuse. Indeed, I am honored to be included as one of the founders. I should like to tell you, Mary is an important part of the decision as well. She has done much here to bring together a group of women, to the end they meet weekly to discuss the growing concerns they have in this part of the world. She tends to understate its importance, but I can assure you that many of the men here agree their wives are faring better than what they expected, and much thanks belongs to her. She would have much to offer the women of Long Island."

The reverend nodded. "You are a courageous woman to have followed your husband to New England, Mistress Horton, and you have joined a brave company of women. A small lot, but very brave. 'Tis a noble thing for you to give of your time to help those who struggle here."

"We are only as brave as our husbands, Reverend." She put conviction in her words and tried to sound courageous. Truly she wanted to be. But in truth, she hardly recognized herself anymore. She had lost herself somewhere along the way. Who was this person going into the wilds of Long Island?

23

September 1638

She wasted no time in preparing for the move. Her fear of going once again to an unknown, wild land was put aside. Regret nagged in her heart that she would leave behind her ladies' group. After Emma's wedding, their bond had deepened, and the support they gave one another remained the backbone of their community. But she knew the firm foundation they'd formed together would fare them well.

The meetings still took place on Wednesdays and many important decisions were made. The moments of levity when they shared a bit of gossip lifted their spirits even during dreary times. She depended on the ladies as much as they depended on her.

The Terrys would be following Reverend Youngs to Long Island too. Embarrassed by her discontent, she kept it to herself. Still, her desire to be settled in their home was great, and dreams of a babe crept into her heart.

'Twas hard to believe Barney suggested he go ahead to build their homestead. "We have gone through much together and I am not afraid to go through it all again. I know what to expect living in a tent, and the troubles of going through a winter without a real house. The boys have grown and can be of help to you. Reverend Youngs tells us the Indians are more than friendly, they are eager to help us. Please do not leave us behind."

"Aye, my sweet, very well. You speak with conviction and 'twould be hard to leave you after that speech. Mayhap but a dozen men will be going with the reverend in this first planting. Some will leave their families behind whilst they build, but a few will bring their wives and children. We go down on a whaling ship, and our belongings come a bit at a time later. It might be well for you to harvest and preserve as much food as you are able before we depart."

"When will that be, Barney?"

"Reverend Youngs will be ready as early as October. I should like to plan accordingly."

"Will the reverend be bringing his family?"

"Aye, he will. His older sons will be of use

to him as we build. Joseph and Benjamin certainly will be, as well."

She set about immediately pulling root vegetables from her garden and packing them in baskets. She picked the herbs and hung them to dry around the hearth. Those that she could, she uprooted to transplant at Yennicott.

Jay and Ben picked plump blackberries and ate their fill in the process, the rest she sugared and dried into a stiff leather. She milked her cows to put up butter and cheese in crocks. The boys helped grind corn and oats from the fields, and she brought in the pumpkin and squash.

The flax harvest was most important. If she could spin most of it before they departed, they would have much linen for cloth. They gathered the seed, brought the reeds down to the river, and set them to soak.

She led Jay and Ben to the river's edge. "If you check these daily for me, I would very much appreciate it. Just be sure they are very soft and the fibers easily separated. We are short of time and I should like to spin this before we leave for Yennicott."

Thank the Lord for days spent learning the art of spinning from the precious ladies of Winnacunnet. No matter now the gossip and complaints she'd listened to. Spinning would be the only way to clothe her family for a time. Who knew when fabric could be imported? And she was not ready to wear only buckskin and fur.

Jay wiped his brow with a sleeve as they surveyed their work. "Yes, ma'am. And I shall haul water for you, if you like, when we come to the river."

"That would be very helpful, Jay. 'Twould be one less thing for me to do whilst I ready for our move. Are you boys excited about this next adventure?"

Ben splashed his face with water. "I am. I liked helping Father build our house here, but he says at Yennicott we get to cut timber and build a wood-framed house with him. He says it'll be very big."

"That means more work, you dunce." Joseph chortled.

"I'm not a dunce. I read more than you do. You're a dreamer."

"Am not!"

"Jay, Ben, enough. I thought you had both outgrown this childishness. You are not behaving like the thirteen- and eleven-year-olds that you are, I must say." She looked sternly at both boys. "To be sure, there is much to be said for hard labor *and* good book learning. You need both to become

upstanding, honorable men of good conse-
quence, like your father. And Jay, there is
nothing wrong with being a dreamer. It was
men's dreams indeed that made them climb
into ships to see what was on the other side
of the water."

Ben hung his head. "I'm sorry, Mama. I
didn't mean to upset you."

"Yes, ma'am. It was my fault." Jay was
quick to accept blame.

"Thank you both for your apologies. We
need to be kind to each other. Our patience
shall be stretched for certain in the next
months. At least we had a township here,
somewhat established. At Yennicott there is
none. 'Tis up to us to build it. We shall need
to depend on one another. Prithee, be kind
to each other."

She did worry about Jay. His main complaint about moving to Yennicott was leaving the special place she'd found for him to
commune with God and remember his
mother. She understood his sorrow.

Inside their tiny house she set about fold-
ing linens. Each piece reminded her of how
she prepared for their last journey. It was
difficult deciding what to bring, what to
leave behind. But the most difficult thing to
leave, of course, had been her family.

The delicate handkerchiefs Lizzie and the

girls had made for her beckoned her, and she held them to her face, eyes closed as she breathed in. The fragrance was but a memory. Lavender came to the top of her list of things to plant. The smiling faces of her nieces danced before her and she could almost hear their laughter. Moisture collected on her lashes and she dabbed with the handkerchief.

She opened her trunk and pulled out the letter from her sister. She sat at the oak table and fingered the envelope. As she considered reading it once again, the troublesome ringlet spilled across her forehead, and as she brushed it aside, memories of her father flooded her. How often would she reach out to smooth his wayward lock of hair? Turn for that last wave goodbye?

There was no escape from the tears now, as they came in a rush. She buried her face in her hands. Her shoulders convulsed and her arms ached to hold her father once again, this time in a joyful welcoming embrace, rather than in the grip of farewell.

She did not hear Barney as he entered. "What is this, my sweet? Why do you cry?"

She allowed him to lift her into his arms. His chin rested on her head as he rocked her gently.

"I thought I would read Lizzie's letter,

but I cannot. The sadness is too much and I think I shall just pack it away in the cask. I do not think I can read it again."

"Aye, it is most likely best to put it away. Mayhap it's time you wrote Elizabeth."

"Yes, I think I should. Perhaps Zeke will decide to bring the family here. What a joy it would be to have those little girls here with me. And Joshua. The boys would enjoy each other's company so very much."

"Do not put too much hope in it. I do hate to see you disappointed. Ezekiel has never expressed interest in coming across the pond. I do not imagine him deciding on something like that." He watched as she shifted her gaze out the window. "Would you like to come out and look after Northstar for me whilst I ready my tools for the journey? I need to fix my wheelbarrow."

She brightened a bit. "Yes, I would like that. Perhaps take a ride, if you do not mind?"

"Nay, I do not. I think it should do you good."

She picked up her riding bonnet and they walked out to the small stable. The big Black's mane was in a tangle and she combed and brushed until he gleamed. She hoisted Papa's saddle to his back and allowed Barney to help her up. She relished the freedom as she urged him into an easy lope toward the trails.

Wind raced past her and the bonnet fell to her back, her hair falling loose and wild. She tilted her chin upward and grinned at the rhythmic pounding of hooves. *Papa, you were right. This is truly an art form and I thank you so much that you taught me. I never feel closer to you than when I run with the wind on Northstar.*

She felt the closeness to her heavenly Father as well. *Lord, I thank Thee for our blessings. And Lord, if I may find favor with You — I'm trying very hard — please bless me with a babe. Amen.*

She gave Northstar his head and watched the hickories' and oaks' fall color fly by in a blur. They entered a low meadow, dotted with an occasional sugar tree with leaves blazing red, where the sun danced in a dappled fashion over the silver sedge and wild rye. She slowed her mount and allowed him to stretch his neck toward the grass for a nibble while she surveyed her surroundings. She noted a long stand of dogwood with wool grass intermingled with chokeberry. Might she find a stream to water Northstar? She clucked and he raised his head and flicked his ears back toward her.

"Come on, boy. Shall we see if there be

water beyond the trees?"

They reached the stream's edge and she slipped off and dropped the reins. Removing her boots, she waded in, skirts drawn high, and giggled as the cold water lapped at her ankles. She settled down on a fallen log and watched her beloved horse drink. Oh, how much fun it would be to ride with Lizzie. To spend an afternoon chatting and sharing their thoughts.

Northstar raised his head from the water and nickered. She looked upstream and toward the meadow, but did not see anything.

With a heavy sigh, she rose and lifted the reins. "All right, are you telling me 'tis time to go home? If you say we must, I shall not tarry."

She pulled on her boots, climbed onto the log, and swung herself into the saddle. She turned her horse toward home, but he stopped. She raised the reins a bit and gave a gentle prod to his side.

He stood rigid, his head up, ears at full alert.

Mary looked about and strained to hear what her trusted horse listened to. "Come on, boy, you are frightening me. Let's go home." She leaned forward, reins up.

Still he stood rigid.

She pressed his side with her small heel and urged him forward, but he began to back. "Northstar, what are you doing? We must go home. Barney might worry. He shall not let me take you for a ride again if you misbehave. Come, now. Let us go."

His head shook and he began to prance sideways, nearing the stream. She looked about wildly, fearing someone might be hiding. She could try to cross the stream but did not know how deep it might be. As Northstar stopped once again, she looked down and there she found the source of his anxiety. A large snake lay stretched out, its broad triangular head the color of copper, swinging to and fro, its tail silently vibrating. The grayish-brown body with red crossbands blended into the leaves and mud.

Mary froze, but her mind raced as she tried to think of what to do. Barney would tell her to pray. He would also advise her God answers prayer "in His time." Oh, mercy. She prayed the Lord would lead Northstar from the danger. *And, Lord, please, if I may ask this one time, please hurry.*

Trusting in God, she relaxed her grip on the reins and gave Northstar his head. He immediately began to back up once more. He backed until they were safe. Finally, he turned and took Mary out into the clearing and headed toward home.

It was only when they were in the yard that she wept as she leaned forward to embrace Northstar's neck. She wrapped her arms around him as far as they would go. He patiently stood, as if he knew she needed that moment, but turned his head as Barney and Jay approached.

"Heigh-ho. What goes on here? Did Northstar give you trouble?" Barney put his hand on the bridle.

Mary raised her head, her cheeks streaked with tears. Words tumbled. "Oh, no, Barney. He saved my life. We found a stream. It was a most lovely spot. I let him drink and then he wanted to go. But when I was back in the saddle, he would not. He knew there was danger and would not let me go near it. It was a big snake, with a copper head. Northstar, you are so brave." She hugged him once again and then fell down into Barney's strong arms.

"It is so unusual to see a snake in these parts. Mayhap you should not ride alone. Thank the Lord He kept you safe and Northstar protected you."

Jay stepped forward and took the reins. "If you would like, I can brush Northstar down and feed him."

"Thank you, I should like that very much.

I do believe I am ready to go inside and see about our supper. Barney, would you come with me?"

"Aye. You still shake. We should sit awhile and not worry so much about our supper. Joseph, ask Benjamin to help you, then the two of you finish your chores."

She accepted Barney's arm and they walked to the cottage. Inside, she looked about at the mess she'd made. "Oh, goodness." Stacks of her kitchen rags and table linens sat beside the crockery and sewing bag. "How did we ever accumulate so much? It seems we did not come here with very much, but look at this — I don't even know how to pack all of it."

"We will take only the essentials with us. Once we have a temporary hut and a place to store things, we will send for the rest of our belongings. It will take time, though. Are you feeling better? You still shake."

"I have never been so frightened. If it were not for Northstar, I don't know what might have happened." She shuddered at the thought of the snake. "I feared I would pray and pray, but God might not listen to me."

"Hush. He listens. You are safe, are you not? It is by God's hand we are safe in this wilderness."

"I pray, Barney, but I become impatient, I

suppose. It was God that guided Northstar and that I do not doubt."

"Aye. He keeps us in the hollow of His hand because this is where He desires us to be, my sweet." His hand fell to her stomach and he caressed it tenderly. "We are taking a step closer to doing what He has set us out to accomplish. To build His church. I believe He will bless us with the child we desire. Our child will be the first Horton born in the wilderness they call Long Island, and 'twill be the link between the old world and the new."

He brought her into his arms and Mary rested there, but not at peace. An old, familiar turmoil began to build within her as she reflected on the years she spent praying and hoping for a babe. In the first years of marriage, she drank a cordial, as instructed by Lizzie, in hopes of conceiving. But the times she believed she carried Barney's child were always followed by such a sorrowful depression, she soon did not like to even consider the possibility.

"I pray so, Barney. I pray that God has protected us for His divine purpose."

Barney picked up his Bible. "In Proverbs it says, 'The hope that is deferred, is the fainting of the heart, but when the desire cometh, it is as a tree of life.' I know how you are saddened when you think of how many years we are without our child. Your eyes still give you away."

She looked away, shaking her head. " 'Tis your constant questioning, Barney."

He fingered the frayed blue ribbon as he closed the Bible. "I know that bothers you. But our joy will be so much greater, because we have endured and depended on our Lord."

"You believe God will answer our prayer. But when, Barney?"

"God knows the desires of our hearts. If we are diligent to do His work, He will take care of us. He knows what we require. He will answer in His own time. That is all I need to know."

She finally melted into his arms. A moment of desire for his love flitted across her mind, but she quickly turned to more practical issues. "Very well, then. 'Tis all I need as well. Let me rouse the fire and tend to our supper. Perhaps after we eat, you and the boys might help me sort through some of these things. I must decide what to take first and what to send for later."

She moved to the table where the letters were strewn. After she stacked them and re-tied the ribbon, she put them in the cask with the linens, next to her handkerchiefs.

She put together some cold meat and cheese and set them on the table, along with cornbread. As she took the crock of butter from the pantry shelf, her eyes fell on the honey pot, so precious to them in this land of no honeybees. Honey was first on the list she had given to Jeremy when he'd visited. She took the pot down and set it on the table. Tonight she would mix Lizzie's remedy.

Perhaps God would bless her twice today.

24

Long Island, October 1638

Close to shore, they anchored the whaling ship. The forty-mile journey across the sound from Connecticut, around the upper point of the Long Island northeast fork, and into the bay seemed uncomplicated and almost pleasant compared to their voyage across the ocean. The men lowered the shallop, and each man, woman, and child climbed over the side into the boat. Only a few of their provisions were lowered down to them.

"Barney, what about Northstar?"

"Once I have you and the boys safely ashore, I will come back to bring him in. But there's time enough to bring everything else."

The shallop rocked as everyone settled and the women and children huddled to protect each other from the blast of an early winter's wind.

After a prayer of thanksgiving and praise, the thirteen men sat backward in the shallop and slowly rowed toward land. The distance between them and the shore seemed small, but the water was icy, the wind cold.

Miss Terry sat with her mother. She would be in Yennicott with them. Had Barney and Miss Terry ever met each other in Boston? She shuddered at the thought. She glanced at Miss Terry and found the young woman looking back, her eyes bleak. Mary turned away. Surely she did not think she would exchange pleasantries with her? But her idea of forming another women's group on Long Island would be complicated if she avoided the Terrys. Compunction nipped at her like the icy wind.

She pulled Ben closer. He seemed so small, though he was growing up. He never seemed to mind when she hovered. Jay surpassed her in height, but she could not refrain from protecting either boy.

Boys. They were practically men. Jay remained awkward with his feelings toward her, but he did show respect and his manners were impeccable. She smiled at him standing there, the apple tree protected in his arms. He went out of his way to be helpful these days. So much like his father.

Ben's breath billowed out onto the air in frozen droplets and Mary pulled his neck cloth up to cover his mouth and nose. Barney remained watchful that the boys were kept from the elements as much as possible and she was vigilant too. "We don't want you sick, Ben. Stay warm. Jay, look at the shore. 'Tis beautiful, is it not?" She longed to find his sweet spot, to know how to reach him.

"It looks like Massachusetts to me, ma'am."

"Yes, I suppose it does. But once we're ashore — look, I see people on the shore. It looks like the Indians that —"

"Oh Mama, it looks like a party." Ben cupped his hands and called, "Father, we have a welcoming party."

"I am certain we do," Barney said. "They promised Mr. Hallock a feast when we returned."

Peter Hallock grunted as he raised the oar. "That they did."

As they neared the shore, Barney and the twelve other men strained to anchor the shallop. Jay quickly stepped up to help and they brought the vessel to rest only a rod from the beach.

Barney clapped his son's shoulder. "Thank you, Joseph. There will be much work to do here — good to have another man around. The water will be cold, and it will be best to roll up your pants. Take off your boots. Benjamin, you too. Mary, I will carry you ashore. Your skirts will get wet if I do not."

She smiled at him. He stood there so tall and brave, and she was proud to be with him. He might not love her, but he made his promise to her father good — he took care of her above all else.

Once again they were on the brink of a new beginning. She closed her eyes. Another chance to win his love.

She clung to Barney's neck, his strong arms wrapped around her, as he slogged through the water. Icy waves whipped about them and she kept her eyes on Ben and Jay as they made their way out front.

"Is that bonfire for us? Are the Indians truly pleased we are coming?"

"Aye, my sweet. The people you see on the shore call themselves Corchaugs or some such thing. They are the ones Reverend Youngs told us about. Do not fear them. They have worked hard and prepared for us quite a bit of land for crops. They've harvested corn and stored much of it for the winter. Corn. It's like our oats, wheat, silver, and gold all in one, is it not?"

He sloshed through the waves receding

from the beach. "We shall need to dry out and warm ourselves. Once we've eaten, we can make our way inland." He set her down.

"Look, Ben, Jay — look at the pretty orange and yellow shells." She bent down and scooped a handful. The delicate shells jingled as she let them fall through her fingers, back to the sand. "What beautiful music."

Ben combed his fingers through the jingle shells and sand. "There's hundreds of them. Look, there's pebbles too."

The beach glittered in the slanting sun with agates, shiny from the water and beautiful in gray, pink, white, and gold. Oyster, clam, and crab shells lay amongst charred wood. Yesterday's supper?

A tall man with a long face approached Peter Hallock. He was dressed in colorful bird feathers with bear grease, tinted black, smeared on his face and arms. His appearance would have been frightening had it not been for his large, friendly black eyes. His skin was a burnished brown and his long hair black as a raven's. He welcomed Mr. Hallock, glad to see him once again, and held out a cup.

Mary was not aware she held her breath until it escaped with a gasp. This was the sachem, the Corchaug chief. The cup was

330

the one they said Mr. Hallock had presented to him during the scouting party.

Mr. Hallock held up the peace pipe the sachem had presented to him on his previous visit. Reverend Youngs approached and the three men exchanged greetings, a mixture of the Corchaugs' native language and English, as they prepared to share the pipe. All fell quiet.

Out of the silence rose Barnabas's beautiful baritone as he quietly led the group in song. "Ye people all with one accord, clap hands and eke rejoice. Be glad and sing unto the Lord with sweet and pleasant voice."

Mary moved closer to him to clap and sing praises. His presence always drew a crowd to him and this day was no exception. He was a pious man who loved his Lord. And people could not help but love him.

A fire, built by the natives, roared on the beach and all moved closer to warm and dry themselves. Clams, oysters, and parched corn wrapped in husks were half buried in the ashes. An elk roasted on a wooden spit alongside rabbits and turkey. Mary remembered their first feast in Massachusetts, and how the men hunted all day and labored to make clearings and build fires before the women and children could come ashore. They had learned from the earlier settlers that the Indians had been helpful to them at one time, but that had changed up north.

To be welcomed on the shore by the Corchaug people, so friendly, so eager to help, gave her hope. She prayed it would always be so. She sat near their fire, hugging her knees. Barney and the boys settled beside her. Contentment draped her like a warm, thick quilt. This truly felt like home.

Three hours later, full from their meal, the party tramped up the narrow path. All carried the few belongings they'd brought with them.

They passed the inlet on the left, with the forest to their right. Tall white oaks stood guard alongside chestnut groves, and the forest was silent, save for the crunch of boots on brittle ground. Tall shrubs with leathery leaves and berries covered in a whitish wax filled in the dense woods.

Relieved the Terrys were far behind, Mary looked around in awe. An early snow had fallen the night before and the mosaic of snow on brown trees and gray rock looked breathtaking, like an art form just waiting to be discovered. "Look, boys. See the pattern in the snow and tree roots? It looks like a fawn."

Ben quickly picked up on the game. "I see rabbits — over there, where the snow is draped over the rocks."

As the sun continued downward, the long shadows cast over the trees, rocks, and snow created myriad animals. Each took a turn pointing in delight. Jay saw a fox, and Barney, his musket in hand, pretended to aim at an elk.

Mary hugged her belongings closer to her. "Do not shoot that pretty picture. I want it to stay just like that in my memory forever."

"Forever is a long time, my sweet. Nothing lasts forever."

"Oh, Barney, you do not mean that." But as soon as the words were out of her mouth, she regretted them. He was thinking of Ann, of course. "I mean, we are fragile beings, of course, but in our hearts and minds memories are for a lifetime. They are a gift from God, I believe. Surely, you would agree?"

"Nay, I don't think they are a gift from God. We have painful ones to deal with as well, and I don't believe God would inflict that upon us. I prefer to forget. That is easier."

Jay regarded his father with a long look. "Well, my memories of Mother make me sad, but I should never want to forget her.

She wouldn't want to be forgotten, Father, would she?"

Ben looked from Jay to his father and waited for the answer.

"Forgive me, boys, please. I shouldn't have said it. Sad, sweet — no difference — memories follow us, that I've seen. Does not matter whether they be happy or not. I suppose you have to pick and choose. For me, they all haunt me. I'd prefer to forget."

Jay glanced at Mary first, and then returned his father's look. "He's not an easy man to live with, is he?"

"Nay, he is not, Jay, I shall give you that."

Barney stopped in front of Jay, his face serious except for a tug of his lips and a wink of his eye. "Heigh-ho, now, son. Are you so grown-up you are now testing me?"

Mary and the boys could not suppress their laughter. He doubled over as well, and she could see he loved the fact his little family was joining in the fun together, even if it was at his own expense.

"Yes, Father, and it will be an arm wrestle tonight."

"You are on, my son. You showed your strength well today and worked like a man. Just remember, I have done this for years." He nodded at Ben and grinned broadly at Mary.

Mary stopped. "Look — the clearing."

The rest of the founders were far behind, many with small children. Some of the Indians had forged ahead to show them the way. As they entered the clearing, the Corchaug men had already stacked the wood for a large fire. Pits had been dug into a small slope, and tree poles, branches, and bark gathered.

Mary eyed a grassy spot and hurried to it. "Here, Barney, may we claim this? 'Tis where we shall call home until you build us our new house."

"Mayhap we should wait until the others are here. We will draw straws, I am sure. I do like that spot, though. It would be perfect."

She put her belongings on the ground where she hoped they could stay. "Of course, that would be fair."

Barney requested the boys help the Indians build the fire. It would be dark soon and would only get colder. With one large central fire continually burning, the family groups would feed their fires off of the main one.

Both the immigrants and the native people worked side by side. The Indians had dug cavelike pits and showed the Englishmen how to cover the opening with sticks, bark, and moss. Sailcloth finished the huts and would help protect throughout Long Island's long, harsh winter. Additional pits, dug deep and lined with branches and reeds, would store and protect their provisions.

All of the women tended the blazing bonfire. The Corchaug women put together corn, squash, and beans into a stew, while the English women speared rabbits and turkeys onto long sticks and arranged them over the flames.

The celebration began, and after sharing the meal, the Corchaugs presented Reverend Youngs and Peter Hallock with deerskins on which they had drawn out a map of the area. They would have lots eighty rods to the west from where they now camped, to build their permanent homes.

Mary savored the meal. "This is one of the most delicious feasts I have ever had, I think." It was beans in what the natives called *samp,* but it tasted like a delicious vegetable stew.

Barney put his arm about her shoulders and drew her close. "What now? And our wedding feast was not? Have you forgotten so quickly?"

"Oh, no, never, Barney. I said one of the most. Nothing could ever compare to our wedding dinner." Her eyes misted. She never would forget. The wedding cake had been the most magnificent she had ever seen or tasted. She pictured the red sugar roses. Forever in her memory.

Forever. That word again. Barney hated it. Funny how fast her thoughts could spiral downward.

One thought led to another. Jeremy had blurted out at their wedding that Barney would be bringing her to the colonies. He tried to deny it at the time, but his intentions became clear over time. Look at them now. Her brow knit in consternation, her lips pursed.

And, what of Miss Patience Terry? Here she was again. The long months in Massachusetts were difficult, to be sure, but the Terrys had gone elsewhere and that had been fine with her. Now they were here on Long Island.

"My sweet, whatever has come over you? This is supposed to be a celebration. We are finally home. Does that not make you happy?"

The Terrys and Wells looked over.

She turned away, peering into the woods. "Nothing, Barney. I'm glad to be here. Home. Finally." She turned back to Barney with a reassuring smile.

25

April 1639

There was much to learn from the native people. Corchaug meant "Ancient Ones." They farmed the fertile land for thousands of years before the English immigrants put their feet on the soil, and they were experts at cultivating. Their knowledge of how to use the land had meant survival for the Hortons' first winter.

The Corchaug men hunted with Barnabas, and the women had taken Mary under their wing and taught her to use flint and stones to scrape the hide, making warm deerskin tunics, breeches, and boots. The native women were amazed at Mary's spinning wheel and were eager to learn to make the smooth fiber that flowed from the wheel. They understood few of each other's words, but friendship grew as they worked together.

Despite heavy rains, the foundations of their town began to form as Barnabas labored with the other men. Joseph and Benjamin worked beside him as paths were widened and lots cleared. A dock was built and the first road ran from the landing site on the bay, northward across the plain to the North Sea. They laid the main road at a right angle to the west.

The highest point on the main road was chosen for the village center, and foundations were laid for the meetinghouse. It would be a place of worship as well as the town's meeting place. Although the new colony remained under the leadership of John Davenport in Quinnipiac, now referred to as New Haven, and the governorship of Connecticut, there was much to do in organizing the new congregation and establishing the laws of the town.

Thirteen men formed the core of the governing body and together parceled the land assignments and decided on the closed-field system for land lot. Barnabas was given a large parcel directly across from the meetinghouse on the main road; his standing in the community and the wealth he brought with him secured his position. Property extending out to the sound, thick with white oak, hickory, birch, and sugar maple and bordered by the road that ran north and south, was assigned to him as well. They called the road between the town center and the bluff over the sound Horton's Lane.

With homes to build and crops to plant, clearing the land was a priority. The cornfields planted by the Corchaugs were their salvation, but the English wanted to plant wheat crops and orchards too. Barnabas would be a leader in establishing the community he'd long envisioned, and indeed, his house would be finished before anyone else's. Of that he was sure.

One brisk spring day, Barnabas rolled up his sleeves and hitched Northstar to the wagon. "Joseph, Benjamin, come, we have much to do out on the bluff." He loaded the sash saw and chip axe into the back. "Gather the chisels and mauls. Get that plane. We'll be downing some timber and squaring it before we bring it back."

The boys put together the collection of tools and climbed up on the board placed across the frame. Barnabas took his seat beside them. "There is much to be done here. There will be no slacking." He grinned as he clicked his tongue to Northstar and urged him forward with the reins.

The wagon bumped along the new road. It would be a short ride, less than 650 rods to the sound side of the island. "We'll need to take care in the trees we choose, sons. The white oak and hickory work well, they are hard. I'll mark the trees we'll cut, but if you have any questions, ask me."

"Yes, Father. Will Joseph and I get to cut the wood?"

"Yes, son, but you must take care. Your mother will not forgive me if you be hurt."

"Father, I can almost beat you at arm wrestling, I think I can saw a few trees." Joseph flexed his arm.

"I grant you that. You're growing into a fine lad. I'm proud of you both. We'll build a meetinghouse that will stand the test of time. Then we'll build our house. I want many generations of Hortons to live in it. We'll build it to last."

Joseph took the harness off Northstar and led him to a small creek to drink, and Benjamin readied their tools. Barnabas surveyed the timber, overwhelmed at the expanse. "Your ancestors in England once had trees such as this. Mayhap not so tall or in such numbers, but still much more than what exists today. Wood to build with is hard to find there now, and heat in London is mostly by dirty coal. Here we have endless forest. But it's a good lesson to keep in mind. Do you understand?"

"Yes, Father."

"Very well, then."

Despite the coolness of the spring day, sweat droplets sprayed freely from Barnabas's forehead each time he swung the axe. Joseph and Benjamin worked equally hard with the sash saw, with their father taking over when they were more than halfway through the trunk.

By the end of the day they had one pile of logs and one of split timber, hewn and squared. As they piled the beams into the back of the wagon, Barnabas noticed a perfect little hickory.

"Sons, come here. I want to show you a good tree for a maul. Do you see the small size of this trunk? It's as strong as iron. Dig it up by the root and throw it in the wagon. Tonight I will show you how to make a maul. And from the crotch of the branches we'll fashion some hooks and from the limbs we'll cut pegs. We'll need many for our house."

"Whoopy!" The two raced for the tree.

"Careful, now." He shook his head. Always in competition they were. But he and Thomas and Jeremy had been the same. Mayhap still were.

As his boys dug the small tree, he stored the tools in a corner of the wagon and fetched Northstar. He arranged the harness, adjusting the collar across the horse's chest. "Good boy."

He stood back to breathe in the fresh, damp air from the sound. A symphony of sorts played in the wind as boughs bobbed in the breeze and the crash of waves from the beach below mixed with the flutelike trill of the wood thrush and the quick tempo of a marsh wren.

Ann would love this spot. He wandered over to the cliff. If there were any way down, he'd like to hike to the beach. "Joseph, Benjamin — over here."

They trotted over to the edge.

"Do you see the path through the barberry? I think deer made it. I want to climb down. The timber and brush are thick, but I think once down past it mayhap we'll see Connecticut across the sound."

The trio climbed down the side, sliding here and there, grasping branches or finding footholds on rocks as they went. At last they landed on the beach, covered in jewellike agates and jingle shells like they found at the landing site on the other side of the fork.

"You see beyond the water? That's Connecticut, whence we came from on the whaling ship. Beyond that would be Massachusetts." He turned to see their reaction.

"Father, methinks I like it here much better." Benjamin glanced up the bluff.

"This will be ours and ours alone. In Winnicunnet it was founded by others, who had
noble beliefs to be sure, but as in Quinnipiac, 'twould be like joining a clan. This is
ours and our fellow founders'. This is the
land God has led us to."

Joseph stuck out his lower lip. "But Father,
what about Mother? Each time we leave a
place, I feel further from her. I don't want
to, but I do. I had a spot in Winnicunnet
where I could go and think about her."

"Joseph, your mother would have loved
this place, that I know. I miss her too. Ask
Mary, she will find you a spot here."

He turned to climb the cliff, back to
home. Yes, this was home. He knew that in
his heart. He would never leave it. Mary
waited and no doubt she'd worked hard all
day. He missed his Ann, but he was thankful God had given him Mary. God was
faithful.

Barney's energy and zeal amazed Mary and
she listened passionately as he described his
accomplishments for the day. He liked to
explain to her how many things from the
old culture they'd brought with them
blended well with the new culture of the

Indians.

She told him how she combined Indian corn with milk from her English cow to create an English version of the Indian's samp.

And when Barney told her the Horton name came from the Latin word *hortus*, which literally meant "garden" and the Indians were ancient gardeners as well, she found it all fascinating.

"Aye, my sweet, we have always been cultivators. Certainly more producers than consumers." He looked pleased with himself.

Mary took delight in her family name and endeavored to live up to it by learning everything she could from the Corchaugs. When she met Wauwineta, a friendship grew as strong as any vine. Her new friend taught her how to draw the sugary syrup from maple trees and where to find the wild cranberries, strawberries, and blueberries. She gave Mary gifts of turtle shell bowls, ladles made from gourds, and baskets of split ash. She taught her to catch herring from a canoe and bury it to fertilize the soil. They planted vast fields of corn, hilling them for support and dropping red beans near each stalk so they could climb. Pumpkins and squash were planted to cover between the rows.

After a month of tilling the soil and planting, Wauwineta stood back from their work.
"We call Three Sisters Garden, the squash,
corn, and beans. They are cycle of life.
Complete. Plant the corn first. When it is
high to your knee, plant the beans so they
climb the stalk. Plant squash so the big
leaves cover the dirt, amongst the corn and
beans. Mary, you do not pull weeds because
they will not grow under the big squash
leaves. In hot summer the leaves hold water
to the dirt and the bugs will be few. Three
crops are ready for harvest together. It is all
anyone would need to live."

Mary gazed at the field they had just
readied. " 'Tis amazing. You know how to
make the land really do most of the work
for you. Wauwineta, may I call you Winnie?"

"Winnie, yes."

"Winnie, where did you learn to speak
English so well?"

"My mother taught me. She lived with
white people when she was a little girl. They
were not mean, but they kept her from family, her Indian family. I learned very well
before she died."

"You did indeed learn well. I am sorry
your mother died. Mine did too, when I was
very young." How much alike they were.
Mary looked forward to spending time with

Winnie to share not only methods of gardening or cooking but of their lives, hopes, and dreams.

She sorely missed the wheat and oats they left behind in England, but learned to depend on the crops that Winnie taught her to grow in order to feed her family. In return, Mary shared her knowledge of cooking on a hearth and milking the cows. She churned butter and produced cheese to the Corchaug woman's amazement. Together they made delicious corn chowders and puddings, corncakes, and breads.

Mary explained to Winnie about the wheat, oats, and honey that were staples of their diet in England and told her Barney's brother, Jeremy, would be bringing beehives and seeds on his next visit. She promised to teach her how to gather the sweet honey and told her, when the wheat and oats were planted, she would bake beautiful white bread.

26

July 1639

The days passed into weeks and summer's humid heat pressed in. Men, women, and children labored from early light to the time they crawled onto their pallets. Mary took pride in her accomplishments, though Barney was too busy to notice. Not that she minded. Everything he did was for her and his children. But his constant concern over whether she was with child or not seemed to have been forgotten for the time being, and she found that a blessing.

One day Winnie appeared from the meadow, Smoke by her side. "*Aquai.* Friend. Your thoughts are lost today." Initially, it was frightening their Indian friends kept wolves as pets, much like they might a dog. But this one, with his thick gray fur and blue eyes, was loyal and protective of Winnie. He seemed to know she welcomed the English immigrants and quickly adopted them as friends.

Mary sat under an ancient chestnut tree, pulling dry corn kernels off the cob. She stretched a hand toward Smoke. "You startled me. Come here, you sweet thing." She looked up at Winnie with a grin. "Yes, my thoughts are lost, I should say. Winnie, you express yourself very eloquently. You meant I am lost in my thoughts, did you not?"

"It is not easy to think two languages. We struggle to understand. Did you not?" She grinned at her friend and squatted, picking up a cob of corn. "Why do you look sad?"

"I am not sad. I'm collecting my thoughts. That means, I'm thinking about my situation — about how things are working out. Where are all of those children of yours?"

"Abigail watches the young ones. She is fourteen, a woman. But your thoughts? Where are they?" Her smile revealed deep indentations in her cheeks. She was a tall woman with thick, raven-colored hair and her eyes were the color of ripe olives.

Mary returned the smile. She treasured the time they spent together and appreciated the help Winnie always gave, often without being asked. More times than not, it was wisdom rather than physical labor that was offered.

"You shall not let me get away with it, shall you? I was thinking of Barney. He is working very hard. He works on our meetinghouse and church most of the day, but he has started to clear the land for our house too, and cut the timber. He works such long days and is so very tired when he comes home. We barely talk."

She paused and studied Winnie. "Perhaps 'tis a good thing, because I was growing weary of him reminding me I am not yet with child. It distresses me so. He wants to have many, many children. I love Jay and Ben, but I want so much to have Barney's child. I think then, he might love me." She leaned back against the tree. "I've worked very hard to be a good wife to him. I've thought more than once he was ready to pass the tongs to me. But nothing has worked." She peered at Winnie. "That was a lot to say. Did you understand me?"

"What tongs do you want?"

Mary laughed. "Of course. 'Tis the kitchen tongs I want. I use them to manage my fire and many other cooking chores. But they are not mine yet. They are Barney's. Usually when a young English girl marries and comes home to her husband's house, she's presented with the tongs. She is then mistress of the house." Her smile fell like the corn from the cob.

"Aye. And I understand more. I watch you. You are not happy." She looked straight at her.

Mary could not hold the gaze. She lowered her eyes so Winnie could not see the tears forming. "I was not happy when Barney first told me we were leaving our home in England. He didn't give me the tongs. I was certain he was unhappy with me. And it was so hard on the ship. I was always sick. I worried that Miss Terry might prove an attraction to him. It was a terrible time for me. I thought Barney wondered why he ever married me."

"Why would that be?" Winnie plucked at the corn.

"He wanted me to have a baby, and it never happened. He still wants that and I've tried so hard to be a good mother to his children — tried to be everything a wife and mother should be. But he keeps asking me if I am with child. I feel like I'm not living up to his expectations. He speaks of how lovely and smart and talented his first wife was. Ann." She turned so Winnie could not see her wet face, her pain. "That part is all right with me. I know he must speak of her so he doesn't forget his dear wife. I wouldn't want that. But he feels so guilty. He holds himself responsible." Gentle sobs racked her as she wrapped her arms over her head and buried her face into her skirts.

Winnie scooted close and put her hands over Mary's. "I understand what you say."

Mary turned her head to the side and peeked at her friend. "I am so sorry, Winnie. I try to be the person women turn to. Now listen to me." She dabbed at her eyes. "You are such a friend to me. I do not know what I would do without you. Do you mean you understand my words or my meaning?"

"Aye." She looked proudly at Mary.

"Oh, Winnie, you make me smile even when I am so sad."

"What do you mean with responsible? What is wrong with Barney?"

"I don't know. He somehow thinks he caused her death. Not really caused it, but if he had taken care of the children when they were ill, she might not have died. I cannot seem to reach him. I do not know why he feels so responsible. He has such sadness in his heart that I do not know how to help him."

"That is so terrible for Barney."

"Yes, it is. My heart aches for him and I do pray for God to ease his pain. I know he loved her very much. It makes my problems seem so small."

Winnie wiped Mary's tears with her fingers. "What are your problems? Is it that you are so far from your land and your people who loved you?"

"You've known me such a short time, yet look how you perceive my heart. Yes, I would say 'tis true. But, if Barney could love me, if I truly believed I met his every desire, I could be content, and I feel God would grant us a child."

Mary looked over the meadow and the tall white birch. "I was not happy when Barney told me we would leave Massachusetts. But to come to this beautiful place and build the home we have talked and talked about, 'tis where we were meant to be, I am sure. Did you know this land looks so much like a beautiful seaside hamlet in England called Southwold? It looks amazingly like it, and Barney felt it was a sign from God that we are doing the right thing to be here."

"It is very beautiful here. We call this Yennicott and the land you build on the Old Village. My father told me it is very important to have your people come here. That you were sent by your God."

"Yes, I believe we were sent by God. I did not like Massachusetts, and the Indians there were not altogether helpful or even very friendly. But, you see, Miss Terry was not there. I could forget about her. But now we are here, and Miss Terry is too. It just does not seem fair, and I can't understand why God would do that to me."

"Why do you think your God would not bring her here? She might seek the beauty that is here, as you do."

"Oh, I would hope it would be the beauty of the land, and not the beauty of Barney." She hiccupped as she tried another smile through her tears. "Of course, she is here because her parents came, and they came for the same reasons as Barney. They are starting a church in which people are allowed to worship as they want."

"Why do you worry of her then?"

"She seems so attracted to him. And she is beautiful and seems to hang on his every word. Of course, Miss Terry has known Barney since she was very young. I just think that if Barney loved me, God might grant us a child and perhaps he would not spend so much time with her. He would value me."

"What do you mean, value?"

"I mean, he would treasure me. Like you treasure Winheytem, and every one of those children the two of you have. Treasure is love and more. Love at its greatest. God gave us that kind of love. I want that kind of love with Barney. He had it once, but I don't know if God grants us that twice."

"Why not? If Barney lost the greatest love God gave him, why would God not give him a greatest love again? But, I think you fear Barney values Miss Terry instead of you. Barney values people. I see that. And he is handsome. I see that. Many women see what you love in him. But Barney chose you. I know he treasures you. But you do not know Miss Terry. I see her watch you at times. She looks like she would like to be your friend, as I am. Do you understand my words?"

Mary squeezed her friend's hand. "Yes, I do, and you are amazing. I have been worried about Miss Terry and I have not even tried to get to know her. Of course she likes my Barney. Who would not? Thank you, Winnie. I think I know what I need to do." She stood, brushing the dried leaves and grass from her skirt. "Winnie, you and God will help me with this."

27

Winnie and Mary found Patience Terry down at the creek, sleeves rolled up, revealing her dainty wrists. Her bonnet hung down her back and she had pulled her straight blonde hair to the side. Clothes were strewn about the rocks, and she scrubbed a shirt with a vengeance, occasionally dipping it in the cold water. She looked up, wiped a droplet of sweat from her brow, and squinted in the sun as they approached. "Good morrow."

"Good morrow, Patience. That actually looks inviting on such a hot day. May we help you?"

Her pale blue eyes widened as she looked first at Mary, then at Winnie. She glanced over their shoulders. "Why would you want to? Has someone sent you to check on me?"

"Why ever would someone do that?" Mary's smile broadened and she tried to look reassuring. Patience would be suspicious of her motives at first, but she had prayed fervently about this as she and Winnie searched for her. It was time to forget about past behavior and to entertain only thoughts about how things were today. She was quite certain this was what God wanted her to do. "Winnie and I were talking. There are so few people here, we should all be friends and help each other. That is all. We do not know each other very well, but do you not think 'tis time we did?"

Winnie stepped closer. "Mary is a very good friend to me. We would like to be your friend too. Friends help friends."

"Patience, you have met my friend, Winnie? She is one of the Corchaug people who live over in the fort."

"Yes, of course. Thank you both for your kind offer. Mary, I'm a little surprised. I thought perhaps you did not like me?" It was a question rather than a statement.

"I truly am sorry if that be how you felt. When we were on *The Swallow,* you tried to avoid me. I thought it might be because of Barney. Prithee, do not take this as an accusation, but you are fond of him, are you not?"

"Oh, yes. Mother and I used to go to his bakeshop, and he would give me a ginger cake. I have always had an infatuation with him. I think you were so lucky to marry him. I truly do hope to meet someone just like Barnabas someday." She paused. "But, of course, Barnabas would never do anything improper. I could not like him, if he did. His morals are part of his appeal, I suppose. He's always been so nice to me, and so patient with my flirtations. Mary, you must know he has never encouraged me, but he would never embarrass me either."

Mary picked up a shawl from the laundry and began to scrub.

Winnie followed suit and started on a table linen. She looked thoughtful, but remained quiet.

Finally, Mary turned to Patience. "No, Barney is too nice to purposely embarrass someone. You do not have to make excuses for him, however. I know he is an incorrigible flirt. You are right, though, the fact that he has such high standards for himself, and yet does not impose them on others, is one of the things that makes me crazy with love for him."

"Mary, I know I was horrid to you on the ship. I have grown up some since then, and I want you to know I understand how wrong I was to behave in such a manner with your husband. Can you forgive me?"

Mary looked into her earnest blue eyes.

"Well, yes. Of course."

Patience stood up, rolling the wet shirt, and faced her. Her words bubbled out. "I hope this means we can be friends. I would like it very much. Someone to talk to would be wonderful. We've made it through the first winter here in Yennicott, but it has been so lonely." She looked to Winnie and extended her hand. "I would be pleased to be your friend too."

Winnie put the linen on a rock and took Patience's hand in hers. "Thank you. To be my friend is to be my sister. From this day, I have two white sisters."

Mary rose up and took their hands. "I like that. Sisters. Our husbands and fathers have founded this land, but we are the Founding Mothers and Sisters. We are important, and we must work together, not apart. Barney likes to say he wants his children and his children's children for all time to know the love, sweat, and dedication the Founding Fathers gave to build this new land. I hope someone remembers it was the Founding Mothers as well. We shall work hard, side by side with our men, providing them with the food, hearth, and love they require."

They stood there, three sisters, arms crossed to hold the other's hand. Their eyes met in unspoken agreement.

Winnie beamed. "It is like I taught you, Mary, three sisters of the land: corn, beans, and the squash. Mary, Patience, and Winnie."

"I love that, Winnie. With each other we are complete. We can do anything."

Barnabas stood on the shell-strewn shore and watched *The Swallow* with its sails at rest in the calm air. He paced as he waited for Jeremy to appear on the deck.

Word came early morning a ship had dropped anchor, and he'd wasted no time getting down to the landing. Hallock's Landing they now called it.

Jeremy was long overdue and concern for his safety was almost a daily conversation with Mary. Hopefully she would not be too upset with him. He should have told her right away *The Swallow* had arrived. But Jeremy should have the bed and that needed to be a surprise. The house wasn't finished yet, and he would need to figure out how to store it until it was.

The crew unloaded cargo from hand to hand. At long last Jeremy appeared up through the scuttle, and Barnabas let his breath ease out.

He met Jeremy halfway up the gangway, and the brothers clasped each other in a bear hug, neither wanting to let go. At length, they pulled back and viewed one another.

"You've got a might more gray there, Barn, eh?" A big Horton grin plastered his face.

"Mary prefers to call it silver. And you have as much, little brother." Barnabas clapped him on the back. "The bed, Jeremy. You brought the bed?"

"Certes. I would not have come back without it."

"Aye. But truly, where have you been? You have had us all worried. Mary, especially. She needs news of her family, of course, but she's been worried your ship had fallen to its fate."

"I've had a few good go-rounds to be sure, but my *Swallow*'s a hardy one and there's not much I cannot outmaneuver. I did wait out a few storms, though, while in England, and it gave me time with Mother and Father and some time in London."

"I thought you were going to tell me you met a lady and were detained." His chuckle caught the attention of the rest of the men.

"Prithee, let me introduce you to my crew. They will help us get the bed to the wagon. And of course, I have a trunk which we'll take to your cottage, filled with trinkets and letters from home. But you will need to tell us how you want to present the bed to Mary. I know it's a surprise."

"The cottage is not much more than a hut at present, but what I'm building is much more than a simple cottage. 'Twill be a house with plenty of room for little Hortons."

"Heigh-ho, Barn, is there finally a poppet running around? Mary must be overjoyed."

"Nay. But someday there will be."

Jeremy began to say something but closed his mouth with a shrug instead.

The men formed a chain once again and handed the goods up to Barnabas and Jeremy, who packed the wagon. When all was loaded, the two brothers climbed aboard and turned Northstar toward the center of town.

Once the bed was hidden beneath shingles behind the new house, Barnabas went on at length about the construction of the timber-framed house. He described how he determined early on to use shingles as weatherboards and shingle the whole house and not just the roof. He showed his brother how he cut the shingles and explained the hand-hewn beams were from only the straightest of white oak. The pegs were carefully squared so once pounded into the round holes he drilled they would wedge in tight. The large house would only be the beginning. He had plans for two more additions as the family grew. After he conducted a tour of both house and grounds, they retreated to the wagon and rode toward the hut.

"We've learned much from the Indians, but their woodwork is the most interesting to me. They know how to take a tree and turn it into almost anything. Sycamore is the tree of choice. I've hollowed out trunks to make storage bins, and I've hewn some smaller ones into buckets and tubs. I've made a long trough to water Northstar. Mary particularly likes the sieve I made her."

They neared the hut and Smoke ran to Barnabas. He jumped from the wagon and knelt to pet him as Jeremy marveled at the wolf dog. Mary sat with Winnie and Patience. The work here was unceasing, with no time for a ladies' group, but he was pleased she could nurture their friendship even as they labored.

Mary jumped up as they approached. "Jeremy! Where have you been? Do you know what worry you have caused us?"

"Aye, your husband has duly informed me. But take heart, little one. I am fine and

I bring much news from a family that misses you." He hurried to get off the wagon and embrace his sister-in-law. "And you. You are fine too?"

"I am now. I am now. Come, you must meet Winnie and Patience." She pulled his hand and flashed a smile at Barnabas as Smoke followed him. "He likes you, my husband."

Jeremy chortled. "Dogs, cats, women, and babies all love Barn."

Barnabas ignored him as he began the introductions. Jeremy was the one Horton who, though he possessed all of the Horton looks and charm, found himself a bit awkward with the ladies. Mayhap not the ones who were unavailable, like his Mary, but give him a sweet young maiden who just might steal his heart and he was all mush.

Fortunately for his brother, he knew Mary would not waste time dragging her brother-in-law and his trunk into the house. True to his prediction, she gave her friends hugs and explained Jeremy would be weary from his journey and she must give him some refreshment and help him unload the trunk.

Barnabas gave the ladies a wink. "Ah, the trunk."

Winnie stood and offered to find Joseph and Benjamin. "Patience, come, they are helping Reverend John." Patience nodded to Jeremy and Barnabas with a blush and reluctantly followed Winnie.

The two men lifted the trunk between them and fell in step behind Mary as she walked toward the hut.

"Do you remember the Terrys, Jeremy? Patience is a sweet girl." Barnabas didn't wait for his brother's reply. "You've made up with her, I see. Yes, Mary?"

"It was really Winnie who convinced me. I'm a little embarrassed I ignored her like I did. You are right, Barney, she is a very sweet girl."

They lowered the trunk to the dirt floor, kept tidy with reeds strewn about, and waited for Joseph and Benjamin. Soon the family bent over the treasure while Jeremy distributed the appropriate gift to each member. There was fabric, pewter, and silver for Mary; tools of iron for Barnabas; and books and writing horns for Joseph and Benjamin. Jars of honey, loaves of sugar, and sweets of all kinds were packed too. But the real treat was the letters from Elizabeth and Grandmother Horton. Mary decided they would save those to be read after supper, before a warm fire.

Jeremy told his sea stories as Mary worked to put together a fine meal. No pottage tonight. Barnabas watched her pull out a salt pork and root vegetables, then glanced at his sons, who listened with rapt attention. It was good to have family surround him.

"Tell me, does Ezekiel see his way here yet? Any chance they will come?" He asked more for Mary than himself, a little surprised she didn't bring it up.

Jeremy looked at her instead of his brother. "I continue to work at him. Elizabeth would come in a moment, to be sure. There are a few things I continue to work to bring to completion."

Barnabas noticed that Mary looked at Jeremy, and his brother gave her a meaningful nod. "Eh? What's that, brother?"

"Our parents, of course. If they gave up the Horton Estate, 'twould be a miracle, but those things do happen."

"Aye. I like that. They would have a room at our house. Certes."

During an evening of stargazing, Jeremy shared his newest telescope with Joseph. As they all moved back in for the night, Mary hung back and asked Jeremy about the blue slate. Her voice was low. "Were you trying to tell me you haven't been able to get the blue slate? Is there trouble getting one?"

"Nay, no trouble. I have purchased it and the words are being engraved. No doubt it is finished by now and waits for me in London."

"So you shall be able to bring it?"

"I will have it for you next trip, I promise. Only so much cargo a ship can hold. I leave on the morrow and will be going directly back to London to do a quick turnaround. My next cargo is the human kind. It continues to be very dangerous in England, as you know. It won't be expected for me to come into port and leave quickly. We'll be gone before suspicions are formed. I'll have your blue slate."

"Do you not have repairs to be done on the ship, provisions to load? Would it be safe to just put people aboard and be off without maintaining your ship?"

"Aye, all that is being prepared for. I spent an extra month in London to work over *The Swallow* before I sailed here. She's more than ready for another go-round. Provisions will be ready to load before we set port, and we'll load during the cover of night. These ventures are planned to the minute detail. They must be. And we have God to guide us, do we not?"

She looked at the infinite heavens, alive with dancing stars, and thought about the people in England gazing at these same stars each evening. The same stars that would guide them across the ocean. God was miraculous. She smiled at Jeremy. "Thank you. 'Tis so very good that you are the ship's master, and God is yours. What should we do otherwise?"

They settled in and Barney took down the Bible. She poked at the fire with the iron. It flamed a bit, warm and inviting. She took up the stack of letters and sat next to Barney. After the lesson this evening she would read them to her family. As he read about the importance of a thankful heart, she truly was thankful. In this wild land she had much. She had family. Could she have his love too?

28

October 1639

Barnabas stood back from the house and admired his work. It was not finished yet, but the chilly nights proclaimed winter would not be far off. He would rather get his little family settled before the weather turned.

Walking across the lane to the church, he found Reverend Youngs. "John, you must come and see the house. I think today I outdid myself and I am ready to bring Mary to see it. We will stay in the house tonight if the boys have not given me away. 'Twill be a surprise for her."

"Barnabas, that's wonderful." He clapped his friend on the back with a thud as they started back across the road.

"I know Mary has felt a bit neglected whilst I've worked on the house. Joseph and Benjamin have worked hard too. But, I am the first of our settlement to finish a home.

I do hope that fills her with gladness."

John chuckled. "I think it will. I think it will delight her, in fact. I noticed she and Miss Terry have become quite good friends. I suppose it was a blessing for her while you were otherwise engaged."

"Aye, that is true. While we built the church she thought me absent too much. But she became acquainted with Wauwineta, and the two apparently decided they would befriend Miss Terry. She is a very sweet-natured girl, once you know her. I'm quite happy they are friends."

"Ah. God is working in her life and I must say Mary's friendship with Wauwineta is such a good thing for our relations with the Corchaugs, do you not agree? Mary is like an ambassador to them. Quite remarkable, she is."

Barnabas nodded. "She is, at that. She has amazed me with her resilience."

They stood in front of the timber-framed house, the first of its kind on the east end of Long Island.

"You've done a magnificent work. I truly am in awe. What a tremendous amount of labor and love. Your wife will be pleased, I know. Shall we bow our head for a blessing?"

"It's not quite done yet, but there's oiled

paper in the windows and the hearth is ready for a fire. Please do come in."

The two men stepped inside and John's voice filled the room. "Our heavenly Father, bless this house to Your good will. May all the meditations within be a joyful noise to Your ears and all that enter seek to serve You. Amen."

"Amen," echoed Barnabas. *And may You bless us with many joyful little noises, amen.* "I'm going to find Mary. I sent the boys down to the harbor just so I could surprise her."

"Aye, so right. You will be at tonight's meeting, I presume?"

"Certainly. I will bring Joseph with me. I know Mary has looked forward to the new house. I shall let Benjamin remain with her and the two can go about getting settled. The boys and I will help her bring up a few things, and then on the morrow we shall move the rest of our belongings."

They shook hands and John went back across the road. Barnabas made his way down the lane. He found Mary, Wauwineta, and Patience huddled together as if in prayer. As he approached, all eyes turned to him.

He smiled broadly to the ladies but went directly to his wife. Kissing the top of her head, he announced to Wauwineta and Patience, "I must interrupt your work here and take Mary away. She might not be back." He liked the mystery his words contained.

"Forever?" Wauwineta looked aghast.

Patience looked at Barnabas with the impish grin she'd bestowed on him since she was a child, then at Wauwineta. "They can't go far. There are no ships in the harbor to journey back to England on, or anywhere else. But pray tell, Mr. Horton, where are you taking Mary?"

Mary looked up at Barnabas with a question on her face. "We were sorting beans. Not my favorite activity, mind you, but we do like doing that chore together. Is this important?"

"Aye, I would not take you away from your companions if it were not. If you wish, you may come back later. But my hope is that you will not." He chuckled as he offered his arm and led her in the direction of what was becoming the center of their township.

"Does anyone else know about this, Barney?"

"Aye, my sweet. Most everyone knows about this. The reverend most recently accompanied me, but you will know why, once you have seen it." He hadn't really thought he could surprise her. She was more than aware of his labors, but he enjoyed this small attempt at intrigue.

As they approached the house, her grip tightened on his arm. "Oh, my goodness, I knew you were spending from sunup to sundown toiling, but I had no idea you were so close to completion. Last Sunday it was but a shell with a roof."

"Aye, I've put the wood-lap siding on and the doors. And do you like the steps?"

Wide, flagstone steps, imported from Boston, led to the front door.

"I love the steps and I have never seen a more beautiful house. You have worked so hard." She turned to him as he enveloped her in his arms.

With one swoop, he lifted her from her feet and carried her over the threshold. His lips sought hers and he kissed her with a passion they had not shared since their wedding night.

"This is the home I promised you." His voice, husky with emotion, broke.

"Barney. Thank you, so much. I'm so choked on my tears . . . I cannot speak."

He kept her in his arms as the tears streamed down her face. He bent to kiss each and every one. His desire to provide for her had been his driving force. His hope and prayers were they now would have the child they prayed for. *Lord, I am determined to be the husband she desires. I am in Your hands.* "I have something more to show you. No one else has seen it, not even John. He came over to bless the house today. But this I have saved just for you."

He carried her to the bedroom and gently laid her down on a sumptuous feather mattress that had been assembled on a beautiful, ornately hand-carved bed.

"How did you do this? 'Tis the most beautiful bed I have ever seen." She ran her hand over the heavy green brocade curtains hung from the four posts, and she fingered the gold tassels that held them.

He sat down next to her. "I asked Jeremy to bring it over with him. I told him to search for the most exquisite bed that was ever built, and I think he did well. I told him I needed it before I finished the house. Joseph and Benjamin will have their own room. I made a third room that I hope someday will sleep our daughters." He kissed her again.

"I don't know if we will ever have any daughters, or sons. 'Tis been a long time that we have tried. I'm sorry, Barney, but I'm afraid I shall let you down once more. I have actually been happy that you have been so occupied with the house. I want to live in it, but 'tis a difficult thing for me as well." She sat up and rubbed the bridge of her nose.

"I didn't mean to hurt you. I promise you, you do not disappoint me. I will not bring up children again, if that makes you happy. I will do anything, my sweet. I just want to see your smile." He tenderly cupped her chin with his hand and pulled her face up toward his.

Her eyes were sad blue, not stormy gray. That was a good thing. He knew what to do with sad. His mouth moved to form the words, but his throat closed. He could not say what he knew she longed to hear. He could not.

She reached out. "Barney?"

He held her tighter. "Just let me hold you." Why did his throat ache so?

"Are you all right?" Her voice was low, expectant. She did not look him directly in the eyes, but bent her ear toward him.

He knew what she wanted, why was this so hard? "Certes . . . in all this earth, you mean the most to me, my sweet."

As he drew her close, joy lit her face and he took pleasure in knowing his words were a gift that meant even more than the gift of the bed. But how could he believe his own words when he knew his true love was Ann?

Before the town meeting, they walked back to their hut to collect a few of their provisions and to bring the table and a few chairs to the big house. Mary sent Jay and Ben in search of dried moss, twigs, and bark for kindling. She planned a warm, welcoming fire in their magnificent hearth. Winnie and Patience offered their help and she gladly accepted, knowing she would have the opportunity to give her first tour of their new home.

She unpacked the tinderbox and quickly hit the striker to the flint. After several attempts, a spark ignited the wiry moss in her hand. She lit a tallow candle with the burning wad and handed it to Barney. With much ceremony, he lit the first fire in the grand hearth, and soon it roared with snaps and crackles, its bright flames captivating.

"This is wonderful. I could not ask for more." She looked at the saltbox and the pantry shelves filled with iron and clay pots. Paraphernalia of all kinds were in the kitchen closet. A peel, a rake, and a newly hewn moulding board stood ready next to the grand oven built into the bricks. Her butter churn and spinning wheel stood side by side, with more room than she ever dreamt of. "Barney, this truly overwhelms me. I do wish Lizzie could see this."

"There will be more, of course. I will add rooms and I'm already working on the cellars. We will have an ice house and a stable. All in good time, of course. There are other families that need my help now."

He read from the family Bible before their simple supper of leftovers from the noon dinner. Winnie and Patience joined them.

"I promise you, tomorrow Barney and I will cook you a feast from our new hearth. Winnie, you must bring your husband and children, and Patience, I pray thee, bring your parents." As they started to protest, Mary insisted. "We shall do much entertaining in this house, and I intend to start on the morrow." There. They could not say no.

Barney nodded in agreement. "Yes, it will indeed be our pleasure to have your families join us. And Miss Terry, you must tell your father that now I have our house almost complete, I will be turning my attention to help him finish yours. We must get everyone into their homes before winter."

After the meal, Barney and Jay walked across the road to the meetinghouse. Barney carried his musket in one hand and the family Bible in the other. Winnie departed to the fort and Ben escorted Patience back to her hut.

Mary looked about her, in awe of the grand house her husband had built. She sat at the old table and drew her finger around the two hearts. One with the *J,* the other with the *B.*

The door burst open and Ben bounced in. "You look happy, Mama."

"That I am, Ben. I was just thinking how blessed we are. Your father worked so hard to build us this beautiful house. He is amazing, is he not?"

"Yes, he is."

"You and Jay worked so very hard too. Your father and I are both very proud, Ben."

He smiled at her compliment.

"I wish your aunt Lizzie could be here. And I miss the children and Uncle Zeke. It makes me sad when I think my father will never see this house." Did Barnabas have the same sad thought about Ann?

"You do miss them, don't you, Mama? Are you all right?"

"Oh, yes, I am fine. I'm very happy and content tonight. We had a good visit with Uncle Jeremy, did we not?"

"Yes. Father says he will bring the other horse with him next time he comes."

"Starlight. England is changing the law

for exporting mares. I shall have my horse and what fun to be able to ride to Winnie's hut."

"Father would not approve of your riding by yourself, but I would be happy to go with you."

"Why thank you, Ben. I should like that very much."

"Father worries when you ride. You mustn't upset him by going off on your own."

Voices came from across the road as the church meeting dispersed.

Soon Barney and Jay walked in. After a family time of prayers and reading the Bible, everyone retreated to their new bedrooms.

"Tell me of the meeting, Barney. What did you discuss?" Mary patted a spot next to her on their bed.

"Oh, many things. We talked about the structure of the church — how we shall organize it. And about our township, our government, the laws we shall need." His scratched his jaw.

"There is so much to accomplish, is there not?"

"Aye, and it is not an easy thing. We talked about laws to govern us, Mary, and I found one or two of them quite repulsive. It seems most of the men were inclined to allow a man to hit his wife, as long as the stick were no bigger than his thumb." He held up his calloused thumb and frowned.

She pulled his face around, gently forcing him to look at her. " 'Tis terrible, Barney, what did you say to them?"

"I said I had never hit Ann, and I had never hit you. I told them I did not believe God would take a rib from man and make a helpmeet for him and then allow him to hit her. I have never believed it to be right. Never."

Mary kissed her husband's cheek. "You are an honorable man, Barnabas Horton. I admire how you stand up for what you believe."

He sighed and rubbed his eyes with the back of his hand. "It did no good. Only one other person would agree with me."

"You were still right to say what you believe."

"The thing that pains me, though, is I might one day have to be the one who rules in court on these very issues. There was talk of making me a magistrate, which I would accept as my duty. But this I can promise you. I shall never hit you. You are safe with me." He looked deeply into her eyes.

"I believe you. I have never feared you. I

have always felt safe." She studied his face as she weighed her words carefully. "I do not mean to cause you hurt, but I do struggle with trusting you. 'Tis still a problem at times. But I have seen a change in you, Barney — just since we arrived here at Yennicott. That means a lot to me. 'Tis my choice to trust you. The alternative is to be miserable and I do not want that. I pray that I am right."

The night air was warm and heavy, but he pulled the curtains around them. "I do not wish to hurt you, not with a stick, nor with my actions, nor with my words." He wrapped her in his arms and tenderly kissed her.

29

The next morning she woke to the sun already shining through the window. Barney had surely been up for hours. Why had he not called the family for morning prayers? She pulled on her muslin frock, brushed through her hair, and piled it high on her head, securing it with pins.

Barney had left oak and cherry logs, split and stacked on end, next to the hearth. She tied her apron around her waist and stirred the embers she'd banked the night before. She stacked several of the logs in triangle fashion, making sure there was a channel between each for air to reach the flames. Dried moss and pieces of bark tucked between the logs ignited as air swooshed from the bellows. The flames leapt upward toward the logs. It would take almost an hour for the wood to burn down to the hot, orange coals.

As the fire grew, she hauled water in from

the rain barrel to fill the large, black iron pot that hung to the side of the fire. She kept it filled daily to ladle hot water for cooking, washing dishes, and bathing.

After poking the fire here and there to encourage the flames, Mary donned her cap and walked down the lane to the storage pit where their cold food remained until Barney finished the cellar for the house.

Mistress Terry was working in her garden as Mary passed. "Good morrow, Mistress Horton. Patience tells me you request our presence for dinner this day." She smiled broadly, a yes on her face.

"Yes, my husband and I would be grateful if you would come and share a meal with us."

"Indeed. We would be honored to join you. Patience tells me that your home is lovely and I would enjoy seeing it. Mr. Terry and I have been admiring the construction."

"I shall look forward to giving you a tour." She grinned and bid her good day. She stooped at the herb garden she kept near the storage pit to pluck bunches of sage, mint, lemon verbena, and thyme and stuffed them into her apron pocket. She removed the deerskin from the top of the pit and lifted the turkey she had plucked the morning before. Carrying it carefully in her arms, and humming a soft tune, she breathed the cool morning fragrance of bayberry bushes and honeysuckle in bloom.

She entered her kitchen, arms full, singing her "mares eat oats" song.

Jay stood up from the table to help her. "I have a surprise for you."

"A surprise? For me?" Hmmm, from whence did this come — certainly he'd never surprised her before.

"Aye. No need to worry, I do think you will like it."

Ben walked out from the bedroom, boots in hand. "A surprise?"

"Not for you, for . . . for . . ."

"For me, Ben. He has a surprise for me."

He looked at his brother. "For Mother? Why can you not say it?"

"Ben," Mary said quietly. " 'Tis all right. Jay, I would truly like to see your surprise."

Jay looked relieved and started for the door. "Follow me. You too, Ben."

They followed him out and around to the back of the lot. There, standing straight, its branches reaching out and waving in the wind, stood the English apple tree, almost as tall as Ben.

"Jay. I cannot speak." Tears wet her lashes and her lip trembled. She walked forward and knelt on the ground, her fingers lightly caressing the leaves. "Thank you. You have taken such good care of my little tree and a better spot could not be found." She looked around at Jay, dabbing her cheeks with her apron. "You touch my heart with your kind spirit."

"I'm glad you like it. I'll keep it watered for you. In a year or two mayhap it will bear apples." He looked back at the tree, his cheeks ruddy.

"Pippins, sweet English pippins. Now, shall we go in and have a bit of cheese before I start my dinner preparations? After we eat, the two of you should go find your father. Perhaps he is across the lane with Reverend Youngs. I have plenty to do here." She loved the fact she had a house to tend. "And, prithee, would you ask your father to invite the reverend and his family to dinner?"

They broke their fast, and the boys went off to find their father. Mary continued her preparations. She poked a skewer through the fat turkey and propped it above her fire. She timidly put her hand between the flame and the turkey breast, testing the heat. It met with her approval and she made a mental note to check it often. She added a rabbit stew to another trammel.

She went out once more to gather the rest

of the meal. She picked a beautiful pumpkin that would go together with the beans she had soaking, nestled in the embers on one end of the hearth, and the corn she had ground with Patience and Winnie. Simmered with some salt pork, it would become samp porridge, a favorite of Winnie and her people.

Back inside with her treasures from the field, she turned the turkey a quarter turn and measured the heat once more with her hand. She threw another log into the fire with a thwack. The shower of sparks she created drew a smile. She gave a series of little kicks to the log until she was satisfied with its position.

After the seeds were scraped from the pumpkin, she set them aside to dry and cut the pumpkin into chunks. She gave the turkey another twist, pleased with the appearance of the rich, golden skin.

She took her heavy iron pot from the shelf and wiped it with her rag. Barney had brought it home as a gift after one of his travels to New Amsterdam. Setting it down on the hearth, she studied her coals. The glow was captivating and only after she felt the heat radiate on her face did she realize she was staring, transfixed.

She gathered the ingredients she needed

to prepare her bread batter. Today she used the basic recipe Winnie taught her when they arrived, but would add molasses, eggs, and cow's milk. Butter, churned the morning before, would be melted in the bottom of the flat-iron pan. Although she and Barney favored the yeast breads, the johnnycakes baked in the fire would save time.

A knock interrupted as she wiped the mug she used to measure ingredients. She moved to the door. "Patience, good morrow. 'Tis a delight to see you. I've passed your mother twice this morning."

"I thought you might need some help. I have brought you a basket of cranberries that I picked. Mother told me you were back and forth to your cold storage. Is there anything else you need? Anything I might get for you?"

Mary gave her a warm hug. "Nay, I think I have everything on hand now, but I do appreciate you coming to help. Thank you for the cranberries. I'm going to mix a johnnycake and put the samp together. I think the berries would be delicious in the johnnycake, do you agree?"

"Ohhhh, yes — let me put it together for you."

They worked together, chatting about how wonderful it would be when everybody had their homes built. It would be a true neighborhood and they would once again be a part of the society they had left so long ago. Winnie arrived early, ahead of her husband and children, to offer her help. She brought with her potatoes and what Mary called Indian turnips, the tuberous root of the jack-in-the-pulpit plant. The three prepared a feast that could feed the whole township, with flavors and foods that blended the two cultures.

When Barney and the boys returned with the reverend in tow, Mary sent Jay and Ben out with baskets to pick strawberries. The crowning dessert would be a fruit and cheese tart. Someday, she promised herself, she would make a lovely apple pie, brimming with the luscious English variety of the fruit and carefully tucked into a light and golden crust.

Joan, the wife of the reverend, entered with their six children. The boys' excitement could not be contained and they all traipsed out to the yard where a game of race quickly became one of chase.

"I could smell the turkey from the church," Joan said as she entered the kitchen. "What may I do to help?"

Mr. and Mistress Terry arrived and Mary gave them a tour as they expressed amazement at what Barney had achieved. Mr. Terry ran his hand along a window casement, admiring the workmanship.

Soon Winheytem and his six children appeared with armloads of wildflowers.

"They are beautiful and perfect for our table. Thank you." Mary made a curtsey as she accepted the bundle and tucked a bunch into her red slipware jug.

Abigail offered to take her brothers and sisters out to the yard and soon all fourteen children chased each other like fireflies. Mary's eyes misted. If she could but have just one of her own.

Barney and John took Winheytem to the yard and they watched the children play while they conferred on the best spot for an orchard. Perhaps where the little English apple tree stood would be the best location after all. Mary caught Barney watching her through the open window, as she bustled about. His look said it all. He was not only proud of the fine house he'd built, he was proud of her as well.

She and the ladies soon had the table laden with bowls, tureens, and platters of steaming soups, sauces, vegetables, and meats. As the men entered, Mary placed a platter of cheese and preserved fruits at the end of the table. The children were called, and after a blessing led by Reverend Youngs, everyone piled their plates, helping the children first.

Mary rang a silver bell. "Children, Jay and Ben will take you outside and show you their favorite spot to have dinner on the ground. Abigail, can you help them too?" She scooted all but the littlest out and turned to Barney.

He stood with a plate heaped for her, and another of his own, and together they sat down with their guests. The conversation was relaxed and warm, and Mary smiled as she watched her guests enjoy themselves.

Everyone helped in cleaning the dishes and putting away the food, most of it packed for guests to take home. As guests began to depart, Jay and Ben excused themselves and retreated to their room for the night.

As Winnie prepared to leave, she took Mary aside. "Thank you for the good feast. We have learned much from each other, but there is much more to learn. In a new year, when you have your bees and field of oats, we will have much work to do."

Patience joined them and Mary smiled contentedly at her two friends. "Yes, Winnie, we shall. Jeremy will return soon with my beehive and seeds. We can help each other plant and cultivate it." She rubbed her belly. "My, I feel like I shall not eat for another week, I ate so much today." She tried to stifle a yawn, but her friends did not miss it.

Patience took her hand. " 'Tis been a long day and you are very tired. We should go now and let you rest. Thank you for including us, this was very special."

Winnie offered her hand as well. The three stacked their hands together and said their farewells.

Barney stood at the door with Mary as the last of their guests departed. He wrapped her in his arms. "This was magnificent, Mary. I am astounded by your ability at preparing a meal. My sweet, you have officially outdone even my finest meal." He kissed her soundly.

It took her a moment to catch her breath. "Thank you, but you err. I will never outdo our wedding feast. Never, no matter how hard I try."

He smiled. "You remember the feast with your emotions, and it makes the memory all the sweeter. No, you handled your duties with grace and I am pleased with all you have done today to entertain our friends." He led her to the hearth and picked up the large iron tongs. With a bow he offered them to her. "I officially hand you the tongs, my sweet."

A quiver pricked her heart and she brought the tongs to her chest as she stepped close to him. "I am overcome. I — I do not know what to say." She looked up into his face as if she could search his deep, moss-green eyes and see to his soul. Would the words she longed to hear be written there?

He kissed the top of her head. "Now shall we retreat to bed? I do believe the boys have."

"Yes, Barney, you go ahead. I shall be right in." She took a step back but held tightly to the tongs.

"Is there something I can help you with?"

"Nay, I shall not be long."

He left the room and she carefully set the tongs on the shelf above the hearth. She poked at the last embers and covered them with the ash. Slowly she sank into the chair by the fire. Head bent, she covered her eyes with her hands. The day had been full, the food abundant, and the shared friendship to be treasured. Barney had been so sweet and attentive.

Why did she feel so sad? Was this not a day she dreamt about? The tongs, he'd given her the tongs. But what of his love?

She looked toward the bedroom where he

waited. She took a breath and with determination decided to be brave. Perhaps he waited to tell her the words she longed to hear.

He must love her. The days ahead would be so sweet. She pushed the bedroom door open and walked to the bed. He clutched his Bible, open to the page with the frayed blue ribbon. The sadness in his eyes could not be missed.

"Barney, what is wrong?" She lowered herself beside him.

"Nothing, nothing, my sweet."

"Nay, I know something bothers you."

He laid his head on the pillow and turned away. "It was a good day. Truly. But once I sat back here, I could not help but think how Ann would have loved all of this. That is selfish of me, I fear."

She climbed into bed beside him and a biting coldness crept into her soul. Had he not told her he loved her just by giving her the tongs? Perhaps not in words, but was that not what he meant? She put her hand gently on his shoulder, but he did not turn toward her. "I am sorry, my love. I am here beside you, whenever you want to turn to me."

There was silence as she settled beside his back and quiet tears slid down her cheeks.

30

January 1640

Christmastide came and went quietly, but by the first of January, winter's cold blast hit Long Island with a roar. Mary and Barney recovered from that horrid night when they had slept side by side, yet so very far apart. Once their winter stores were full, their days had been consumed with helping the rest of the township build homes, and nights became their refuge.

She pulled the green and gold quilt up to her cheeks with a shiver. A ray of pale winter light bathed her face, and her lashes fluttered as she woke. She opened her eyes to Barney's wide smile.

"You are so beautiful when you wake up. 'Tis one of my favorite times of day."

She smiled back. "You always watch me when I sleep. Sometimes I feel you must lie awake all night just watching me. Not that I mind that, my husband."

"Sometimes I wake up long before dawn, long before our prayer time, and start my own prayers." He drew her near to him. "But when the light starts to fall on your face, I have to pause and appreciate what God has provided me."

They lay together a long while in silence. Finally she turned her face to his, but he was lost to a place far away. Was it an ocean away? Which memories did he think of now? How quickly he could change.

She drew a breath and opened her mouth to ask, but a gentle tap on their door drew their attention. She welcomed the interruption.

"Mama, it snowed. It snowed! Come look."

Barney sat up and pushed off the bed. "Now, Benjamin, it will not melt so quickly. Give Mother a chance to don her robe. You don't want her to freeze."

"Hurry." Ben trotted back to the parlor. "It's starting again!"

Barney drew on his breeches and handed Mary her robe. He pulled on his boots. "I should gather some wood before it gets too wet."

She followed him to the parlor and found the boys peering out the window. The diamond panes of glass that replaced the oil paper before winter's grip still brought a smile each time she gazed outside. Huge flakes floated down, much like the papery white doilies her mother used to crochet. Angel tears. Angel tears of joy. She loved the snow and the imagery her mother made up about the snow held a special place in her heart.

She put her arms around Jay and Ben and hugged them close. " 'Tis beautiful. I think after our prayers, we should have some porridge and then bundle up and go out to play. I know your father objects, but we've all worked so very hard for so very long. 'Tis time to play, do you not think so?"

Jay squirmed out of her reach. "Mother wouldn't allow us to play in the snow. Too cold — and wet. She said we would get sick. She knew about those things."

Ben looked first at his brother, then at Mary, his face falling.

Her throat squeezed tight. Had they not shared some very sweet moments? Why must Jay be like this? No matter how many times he turned on her, it still took her aback. "Your mother would be right. You could become very ill, if you overchill and do not take care to properly warm yourself when you come in. But I have played in the snow all of my life. I shall be sure to help you all dry out and warm yourselves. Come help me set the food on the table, and when your father comes in, we shall discuss with him playing outside."

Ben grinned. "We could have a snowball fight, Joseph."

Mary tousled his curls. "Oh, yes. Or perhaps make snow angels. I shall teach you."

She stirred the embers. Jay got up and with a sullen face put out bowls for the porridge. He needed something to cheer him up. Perhaps once outside he could let himself go and have fun.

"Could you please get out a knife as well as the spoons? I think this morning we shall have last night's bread with our porridge, and butter and cheese too. It will do well to have a hearty breakfast before we venture out to the snow."

"I thought we would ask Father first, before deciding if we will go out?"

"Certainly, Jay, I just want to be prepared. I think your father will find it a grand idea."

With an enormous thud, the door swung open, hitting the wall. A cold swirl of air filled the room as Barnabas entered with logs askew in his arms. He stamped his feet to loosen the snow that clung to his boots.

Cold emanated from him as his presence filled the room. "It is so bitterly cold out there. Not fit for man nor beast."

Joseph smiled and looked at Mary, victory written on his face. Benjamin's face fell for the second time that morning. She turned to her husband and straightened. "Why, Barney, you surprise me. But then, look at you. You are but in your robe. What were you thinking? Come put the wood down and stand by the fire. We'll have some warm porridge after our prayers. Once you are warm, I have a question for you." She winked at Benjamin.

Barnabas put the wood down near the hearth, stacking it on end to let it dry. He put his hands out to warm near the flames.

Mary set the porridge and bread on the table. She brought out two crocks, one of butter and one of strawberries preserved in sugar. Thick slices of cheese and dried venison completed the feast.

Barnabas raised a brow and nodded toward the large repast. "Are we to eat all of that food this morning? Is there a celebration you have not told me about?" He eyed her belly.

Mary blushed. "Yes, 'tis a special occasion. My mother always said the angels among us were crying happy tears when it snowed, and we always went out to rejoice with them. Of course, we need to fill our stomachs well and dress warmly. We wouldn't want to get sick. Do you agree, Barney? May we go out and play?"

"I don't know. It is exceedingly cold."

"Every winter since we've been in New England, be it Massachusetts or here in Yennicott, we have been working too hard to enjoy ourselves. Our work is far from done, but at least we have our beautiful house over our heads, and enough food stored to well keep us through even the longest of winters." Her lip trembled.

He nodded and looked at Benjamin's expectant face and then at Joseph. He could see his eldest son had reservations and he knew whence they came. "What do you think, Joseph? Do you think we should play with the angels?"

Joseph glanced at Mary. "I don't know, Father. We could get sick. Mother always worried about that."

"Joseph, aye, you are concerned for what your mother would do and that is noble. But, today it is Mary who makes the decisions in caring for our household. Shall we give the snow play a go of it?"

Warmed by the fire, Barnabas picked up the old Horton Bible for their Scripture reading, ending it with prayer. His private prayer was for discernment. He always tried to do what was right, but depended on God to fill the cracks. This was a difficult thing, this family thing, giving honor and love to Ann's memory and honor and love to Mary. It was so very hard to support Mary when he knew Ann would handle it differently, but he knew he must.

They sat down to their porridge, each one silent. Barnabas blessed their food and looked up. Mary rubbed his hand and gave him a smile.

After the meal, Benjamin jumped up, eager to run out to the snow.

Barnabas laughed. "Where are your manners? Please sit back down and ask to be excused properly."

His son quickly sat down, got the formality out of the way, and shot back up as soon as he received a nod.

Mary called after him, "Remember I said we need to bundle up. We need coats, hats, and gloves on your hands. Do not forget your neck cloth."

Joseph asked to be excused and quickly joined his brother. Barnabas chuckled. He knew his elder son would not be left behind by the younger, no matter what.

The boys ran out of the house, into the

snow ahead of Mary.

She held Barnabas's hand as they watched them plow into a snowdrift. They came up out of the drift with handfuls of snow and immediately started throwing it at each other and then at their father.

He put his arm around his wife and squeezed. "Are you sure they will be all right? 'Tis one thing to have to go out to work in the snow, and work a sweat. But burying yourself in it? I do worry. Will they be all right?"

She smiled and snuggled her head against his chest. "Of course. They are big, strong boys now. Do not worry. I played in the snow all of my life. 'Tis great fun. They shall be fine and they shall sleep well tonight. Now, I must show them the snow angels." And with that she threw herself into the snowdrift. As she came up she heard the laughter and applause of her husband and children.

Benjamin dove in first to join her, with Joseph only a moment behind. Barnabas took a deep breath. A snowflake landed on his cheek.

31

February 1640

Three days later Joseph woke before dawn, the labored breathing of Benjamin hot and dry in his ear. "Benjamin, what's the matter? Are you ill?"

Benjamin stared back with dry, red eyes, his mouth slack, and labored breath. Joseph touched his brother's forehead with his fingers and jerked back from the intense heat. As he flew from the bed, a series of deep, rumbling coughs erupted from deep within Benjamin's chest.

Joseph raced into his parents' bedroom. He found his father already in his morning prayers and stumbled as he grabbed his arm.

"Heigh-ho, what is this, Joseph? Pray, what is the matter?"

Joseph's eyes grew large, his mouth opened, but no sound came out. He pulled desperately on his father's arm. Finally his father followed.

"Joseph, you must tell me what is wrong. What has happened? Are you ill?"

He looked back, his mouth still gaping, as he tried to form words. All he could manage was to shake his head in a slow "No."

As they entered the bedroom, heat radiated from the bed. The rattle of Benjamin's breath told him just how sick he was.

"Father, I don't know what happened. He was fine last night at prayers, was he not, Father? I didn't know he was sick until he tried to wake me. I didn't know what to do." The words finally tumbled from Joseph in a string.

"You did the right thing, son, you fetched me. Now, go tend the fire. Make a large blaze. We need to keep the house very warm. I shall go to the kitchen to get remedies for the fever. We must relieve it quickly."

He hurried from the room, crashing into Mary. "Barney, what is wrong?"

He glared at her. "Benjamin is ill. I knew they should not be out in that bitter cold. Wife, what were you thinking?"

Brushing him aside, she rushed to Benjamin, passing Joseph, whose glare matched his father's.

Barnabas continued to the kitchen, trying

to recall the herbs and spices that Ann had used for the boys. He searched the shelves, gathering rosemary, feverfew, mustard, and calamint, all grown in the kitchen garden for just such an event. He started back toward the bedroom, but hesitated.

The red sheets. Where were they? He'd wrapped Ann in them to bring down her fever. And a physician, he needed a physician. If he'd only had a physician to bleed Ann, she might still be here. Retreating to the storeroom, he pried open one of the casks that served them so well on their voyage from Old England.

Arms full of red sheets and cloths, dried herbs and spices, he hurried back to the sickroom. He entered quietly and leaned over his son, wrapping the cloth and sheets about him.

"Barnabas, what are you doing? Does he not need some cooling cloths?"

He turned on Mary. "Pray thee, go out and check the fire with Joseph." He handed her some of the rosemary sprigs. "And put these into the fire." He turned back to Benjamin, preparing to apply the mustard seed paste to his chest. "We have no physician here. No one who can bleed him."

Mary did as requested and found Joseph

sitting by the roaring fire, crying. She touched his shoulder. "I am so sorry Ben is sick."

He brushed her hand off and ignored her.

She went about poking the fire and added the rosemary. "I wish your father would allow me to help. I think Ben needs cooling cloths. Perhaps that is what I should do, prepare some cooling cloths."

"Why don't you keep out of it? You have done enough. Father knows what to do." He turned back to the fire, his face hot and wet with tears.

She came closer and laid her hand on his shoulder. "I am so sorry, Jay. I truly did not think our play in the snow would make anyone sick. I love you and Ben so much. I would never want anything to happen to you."

He shrugged her hand aside, a little more vehemently this time. "Leave. Me. Alone."

Mary closed her eyes. She prayed Barney did not intend to bleed Ben himself. It was dangerous enough when a physician did it. Her lips trembled. She must help Ben.

Quickly she went to gather as many kitchen cloths as she could hold. She doused the cloths in the water pail and ran outside with them. A shiver ran through her as she buried them in the cold, then pulled each out and stuffed them with a little snow. She packed more snow into the bottom of the pail, then put the folded cloths in a stack, neatly inside the bucket, and covered them again with snow. Picking up the pail with both hands, she hauled the whole thing back inside and into Ben's room.

Barney looked up at the commotion. "What are you doing? Is that snow?"

"Yes, and cold cloths for Ben's fever. We must cool him." She set about pulling the first cloth from the pail, carefully tucking a bit more snow into its folds.

His face turned an angry crimson. "Take that out of here now. I want you to leave this room. I will take care of my son. Do not come near him. He needs to be kept warm, away from the elements. And what do you do? You bring the elements to him — the very ones that made him ill in the first place. Leave! Now!"

She could feel the blood drain from her face and left the bucket in her hurry to retreat but decided not to go back. She entered their bedroom and gazed sadly at their bed. So beautiful with its ornate carvings. So sweet of Barney to have cared enough to ask Jeremy to bring it as a surprise. The memory brought a sharp pang to her chest and she crumbled upon the bed.

Deep, sad moans surged from within, erupting into wails that could be heard throughout the house. She cried not just for herself and the love lost, but for Benjamin, the young boy who had been her constant friend and loved her like a mother. *Lord, make him well, I pray.* He was such a good boy. And Barney could not go through another loss.

The hours crept by and as night fell, all remained quiet in the house. She did not dare go to Ben's room. Finally, her sobs gave way to a fitful sleep. When she woke to the morning's meager light, she sat bolt upright, fingering her clothes from the day before. Her mind, as stiff as her fingers, took a few minutes for the reality of the previous day to dawn on her.

She swung her feet off the bed and moved toward her door. Barnabas might be angry still, but she would risk that. She had to find out if Ben was all right. She crept to his door and leaned a shoulder against it, pushing, and peeked in.

Still wrapped in red sheets, Ben lay next to his sleeping father. That Barnabas was asleep at this hour told her he had not slept much at all through the night, and his haggard face confirmed it. Ben's breathing was still labored, but at least he was breathing. The cold cloths remained in the bucket, now filled with the melted snow.

As she moved to close the door, Barnabas woke up. He raised his head and nearly growled at her. In a hoarse, hushed voice he said, "I — told — you — to — stay — out."

Mary quickly shut the door and fled back to her room. In desperation, she looked around and tried to plan what she should do. She remembered the day on the dock when her sweet family, who loved her so much, had courageously said goodbye to her. How she missed them. She'd thought she could leave her family. She'd wanted to do it for Barney. She loved him so and wanted to be the one to take care of him and help him through his pain. But he would not let her. Oh, why would he not let her? Why could she not touch his heart? What was she to do? Give up her whole being? What about her dreams? It felt so selfish asking this, but when would she be loved? She'd left the only ones who'd truly loved her. Except for Ben. He loved her and now he was dying. Why must she be punished this way? She prayed the Lord would forgive her, but she wanted to go home.

It hurt to know she would never have Barney's love. She had to go. She would not be able to take much, only what she could carry. One change of clothing. Her everyday dress would be enough. She could only bring a bit of cheese and bread. She supposed she would have to beg or work for her food on the voyage back to England.

Not much of a plan, but it would have to do. There must be a ship in port, Lord, there must be. She gathered her clothes, silver mirror, brush, and doll, wrapped them in a sheet, and stole to the kitchen to pack her few provisions.

She bundled a loaf of bread and a slab of cheese. With her cloak about her shoulders, she walked over to the hearth. The kitchen tongs perched on the shelf above. Giving her the tongs had not meant the same thing to Barney that day. He hadn't told her he loved her. He could not.

Jay still sat in the chair by the blazing fire. It was evident he'd kept it burning all night. He eyed her cloak, muff, and small bundle. "Where are you going?"

"I need to go away for a time. Your father is angry with me, and I will be of no use to Ben. I do not expect you to understand, but I beg of you, do not tell your father. Let me just leave." She looked imploringly at Jay.

"I could care less what you do. I will not breathe a word to Father, nor do we really care where you are off to." He looked back to the fire, as if he had not stopped staring into it from the night before.

Mary stood there for a long moment. She'd tried over the years to reach out to him, to be the friend he needed, or the mother he might want, but it would never happen. He would always be in her prayers. She prayed he would find peace.

She let herself quietly out the side door and heard a neigh. Northstar? It would do no good to take him. She set her wide-brimmed hat securely on her head and pulled it close to her brow as she turned down the lane. She turned once to look at the beautiful house Barnabas had built for her and his boys. No one would wave to her. No one would care.

But she would never forget it, nor would she forget the man who built it with his own hands, the man who had stolen her heart for all time. And Ann. Oh, Ann. She'd tried so hard for Ann. She felt like she'd let her down too. But Barney would be happier, and better off without her, she was certain.

She followed the snow-laden road, the same path the founding party had first walked, to the inlet. Cold, tired, and thoroughly dismayed when she realized there was not a ship in port, she dropped on the beach and knelt, not noticing the pretty jingle shells that now cut into her knees, or the hundreds of agates glinting beneath patches of snow. She covered her face with her hands. Where could she go? She couldn't go to Patience or Winnie. They would say she should go back to her home, to Barnabas.

Hours passed. The wind swept her hat to the water's edge, but she was oblivious to anything but the storm in her heart.

A cold damp nose nuzzled her cheek and Mary wrapped her arms around a wet furry body. She buried her face in his neck. "Oh, Smokey."

Someone tucked a heavy blanket about her and she looked up into Winnie's comforting face. "How did you know I was here?"

"Barnabas sent Joseph to the fort to ask for a medicine man. He told us Benjamin is very ill and might die. I asked Joseph about you and he told me you had left. I asked him when, and if his father knew this. He told me Barnabas did not know, and that you asked Joseph not to tell him. Mary, Joseph looked frightened. He thinks he is about to lose everyone. Do you not think you should go home?"

"No, Winnie, I cannot. I know you shall not understand, but I cannot. You and I have talked much about how I try to honor Ann's memory. About how I love Barney with all of my heart, and I do. But the truth is, I shall never fill all of the expectations he has of a wife, because Ann filled them so perfectly. No matter how I try, I cannot reach his heart. I want to be loved by him. But in truth he hates me. Joseph does too."

"But Mary, you have told me you knew when you married him that he did not love you in that way. He needed a mother to take care of his children, and to give him more children. You told me all of those things. How has it changed?"

"It has not. I thought it had when he gave me the tongs, but it has not. And now Ben. I — I cannot speak of Ben. My heart will break. I pray God will let him live. Did the medicine man go to the house? Will Ben be all right?"

Winnie kicked at the snow, scattering shells underneath. "I do not know that. There is more, though. Tell me."

"Jay hates me. He wishes he would never see me again. There have been times when I truly thought we were becoming friends. He is so much like his father, it would be very hard for me to not love him, and I have prayed fervently that God would heal his hurts. Winnie, I know how terrible this

412

sounds, but God does not listen to my prayers."

Winnie scanned the skies and offered her hand. "Come, I will take you to my home. You are welcome, my friend, to stay as long as you need to. But let us move quickly, the storm is coming in. There is snow in the clouds."

Mary took her dear friend's hand. Each cold muscle and frozen joint protested as she stood. The rough muslin of her wet garden frock clung to her ankles. Grateful for Winnie, she allowed her friend to lead her to the Corchaug trails, through Calves Neck, toward the hut, with Smoke by their side.

Winnie turned to her. "It will be noisy inside with children. We will eat a meal, and then after they are asleep, we will talk again."

She nodded, but looked away. "I do not really want to talk."

"We must, but later."

The children were excited to see her, but knew of her sorrow and allowed her to sit while Abigail helped Winnie prepare a samp. With plenty of cornbread to round out the meal, everyone ate heartily. As Winheytem and Abigail put the younger children to bed, Mary and Winnie settled down next to the open hearth, smoke spiraling upward to the opening in the thatched roof.

"You were not finished talking when the storm came in. You must tell me all that bothers you, Mary. I know you love Barnabas and his sons. I need to know why you cannot go home. It is not Joseph and Benjamin. Tell me."

Smoke curled at her feet and she absently stretched her hand to rub his ear. "Barney blames me that Ben is ill. He is afraid Ben will die like Ann did. And he might. Barnabas hates me. He would not let me help with Ben. He really does not want to see me again. He has always wanted me to have many, many children, and I think he has come to resent that we have none. The sad thing is, when we moved into our house, he gave me the tongs. I thought he loved me then. I so wanted to believe it, but 'tisn't true. Truly, I suppose I never know what to believe with him."

"He told you he resents you are not with child?"

"Nay, but I see him looking at me in that way. He is looking at my stomach. I know what he is thinking. He is disgusted with me. Disgusted that he ever married me. If I go back to England, perhaps he could take a wife that shall give him children."

"He has been looking at you in a strange way?"

"Yes, but then he is always wondering when I will have his child."

Winnie studied her friend's stomach. "Mary, I see your waist thicken. I see the flush about your face. I know what Barnabas sees. Do you not know you are with child?"

She followed Winnie's gaze and ran her fingers across her gown. "I wish I were. I used to pray about it all the time, but it was too painful to keep hoping. 'Tis been some time since my monthlies, but you know that happened on the ship too. I believed I would have a babe, but I was wrong. 'Twas nothing. It made me feel so sad."

"On the ship, things were hard and you were very sick. But, Mary, I look at you and this time I think you have a child. Let me feel your stomach. I know these things well." She ran her hands over Mary's stomach.

"You — you think I am with child? How could that be, after all of those years?"

Winnie smiled at her friend with understanding and patience. "You say you don't believe God hears your prayers, but you forget what Barnabas has taught. God answers prayer, but in His own time."

" 'Tis true that Barney speaks of God doing things in His own time. But Barney hates me now, and I have left Jay and Ben when they need me the most. How could this possibly be God's time?" She tenderly rubbed her stomach. "Winnie, this is not good. I do not know what to do. This would be awful timing." Mary cradled her stomach. Smoke laid his chin in her lap.

"A baby is never awful, my friend, and I do feel one in your belly." She placed her hands over Mary's. "God knows what you should do. I will tell you, Joseph was so lost when he came to me for the medicine man. He needs you to be there for him, while Barnabas is taking care of Benjamin. He needs you more than he has ever needed someone. They all need you. God brought you together for a reason."

"But what if Ben dies?"

"You must not give up hope."

"Barnabas is so angry with me. I do not think he cares to even know my whereabouts. Joseph told me he does not. Winnie, I want to go home to England, to my sister. I want to go now!"

32

Joseph and the medicine man rode quickly back to the large house on main street. Barnabas greeted them at the door with urgency.

"Father? Is Benjamin all right?"

"He is very strong, Joseph. He fights a good battle. But I do not know if he will survive." He turned to the medicine man. "I have done all I can do. I have left him in God's hands. I pray He will favor me and give me my son back. I find I have lost one person today. I pray I shall not lose another. You are a man of medicine and faith. He needs to be bled. I could not do it, but you can help him. Let me take you to my son."

As the three entered the hot, stuffy room, Benjamin's racking cough shook the whole bed. Barnabas, no longer able to endure his son in such pain, walked to the front hall once more to check on the fire.

He finally settled in the chair by the

hearth and stared at the empty chair opposite him as the room grew dark. He was too tired to think of anything, save his son. He could hear the racking cough and the murmurs of the medicine man. He slowly drifted to a fitful sleep.

The following morning a familiar sound awakened him with a start.

"Heigh-ho!" Jeremy's voice boomed as he beat on the front door.

Barnabas jumped and ran to the door. He threw the door open, and the two brothers embraced in a fierce hug, pounding each other's back. "Jeremy, I am so thankful you are here. How did you know?"

"Know what? I told you six months ago I would return."

"Benjamin is very ill. I don't know if he will make it. I have done everything I can." His head hung low. "The Corchaug medicine man has been in the room with him all night. We have no physician."

"Barn — it cannot be. Benjamin? Where is Joseph? And Mary?"

"Joseph is in with him now. I do not know where Mary is."

Jeremy swung around to face his brother. "What, pray tell, do you mean, you do not know where she is?"

"We argued. It is her fault my boy is sick.

She insisted we go out to play in the snow, of all things. She insisted everyone would be fine, it would be healthy for us. Certes! She hauled in snow to put over him when the fever came on. She would kill him. I told her to stay out. I am sorry for that, but my concern has to be for Benjamin."

"How could you treat her like that? And I've come with great news for her. On my next voyage here, I will be bringing Elizabeth and Ezekiel with the children. I have a letter from Elizabeth for Mary." He took it from his pocket and pushed it toward his brother.

Barnabas eyed it, but didn't take it. "She has dreamt of that day. I think she never really believed they would come." He suddenly grabbed his brother's shoulders, his fingers shaking. "Jeremy, I think she may be with child. She has not told me. She favors the loose garden frocks, so I had not noticed before. But as of late, I think she has a bit of a belly. Surely she's noticed. Why did she not tell me?"

Jeremy carefully replaced the envelope in his pocket. "I would not know. Mayhap, she wants to be certain. You constantly harass her about having a baby and mayhap she did not want your hopes to be dashed. I do think she tries to put having a child far from her thoughts."

"Aye, but I have tried of late not to do that."

"She knows you want children. It haunts her. But I have something to show you. Come outside. It was to be a surprise for you, something Mary arranged for, but I think you need to see it."

"What, pray tell?"

"I think under the circumstances, she would not mind that I show you. You have to know, Barn, she loves you dearly. I would have to say she adores you, brother. And, Lord forgive me, but it does leave me envious. You are a cad not to see the adoration she holds for you."

Barnabas looked toward Benjamin's door. The hacking cough could still be heard. "Let us go look then. It tears my heart to listen to his pain, but I do no good for him in there."

The two walked side by side to the road. A sleek, black horse, hitched to a long wagon, turned toward them and nickered a soft greeting, steam pillowing out from her flared nostrils, a faint star visible on her forehead.

He stopped. Starlight. "You brought her."

"Aye, I said I would. But here, look." Jeremy pulled the heavy sailcloth back from the cargo.

Barnabas grabbed the wagon board for support and looked over the side. "Gracious, what is this?" The slab of blue slate, the one he had wanted to bring with him on their first journey to the colonies, lay before him, complete with his own epitaph. The memory of Mary at the cemetery, reading his words, crying at their meaning, rushed in.

The salty tears that had been shed so many times for Ann now flowed freely once again. What was this he felt? His heart surged with love for Mary, something he thought would be impossible. Could God do this for him? He knew God was a merciful God, but would God bless him a second time with such a great love as he'd had for his dear Ann? But had he not just lost that love?

He dropped to the harsh cold of the snowy ground, and on his knees began a prayer. "Lord, my Father, I have been so wrong to not see what You have given me. Forgive me for driving her away. I pray, Lord, that You will give my Mary, my love, back to me. I ask Your forgiveness of my sins and, Lord, I also pray that in Your infinite mercy, You will heal Benjamin. Amen."

Jeremy, kneeling beside him, added his hearty "amen" and clutched Barnabas's shoulders. "We will find her. We must go see about Benjamin. After that, we will make our plans."

He helped Barnabas to his feet and the two trudged solemnly up the walk to the house.

Before they could enter, Joseph rushed to meet them at the door. "Father, it's Benjamin. His eyes are open, he speaks!"

"Thanks be to the Lord." He broke away from Jeremy and bounded to Benjamin's room. Joy grabbed Barnabas's heart as he looked at his son, propped up on a pillow, sipping water offered by the medicine man.

Benjamin shivered, and coughs sputtered from his chest as his father gave him a massive hug. Gently, he pulled the red sheets up about his son's shoulders and eyed the wet cloth that lay askew on his forehead.

Joseph stepped forward. "The medicine man saw the cloths in the pail. They weren't cold anymore, but he said they were cool enough. He said to bathe Benjamin's body with them. He said we must cool him — just like Mary said. I thought since nothing else was making him better, we should try. His fever is gone."

Pain gripped his heart at the memory of

his rage toward Mary and her cold cloths. His son would survive. He knew what he must do. "Aye, I see. Benjamin, you had me so worried. I could not think straight. Are you now cold? Should we get you into dry bedclothes? Do not try to answer. Save your strength." He turned to Jeremy. "Go and make a broth for Benjamin. None of us has eaten for two days, I believe. We shall all have the broth and bread."

"Aye, Barn." He moved toward Benjamin. "You frightened us all. Thanks be to God you are all right."

"Joseph, I'll fetch some dry bedclothes. You stay here with your brother." He turned to the medicine man. "You were sent by God and have healed my son. I owe you my life, but I will pay you with food from my pantry and other gifts as you desire. Please, come with me to the kitchen."

Joseph followed his father to the door. In a low voice he said, "What about Mary? Does she not need to know Benjamin will get well?" The concern in his voice touched Barnabas.

"Aye, she does. Jeremy and I will do what we can. I hope to bring her home. God has been good to us. I hope He will be once more." He gave his son a clap on the shoulder and Joseph went back to the bedside.

He took a last look at his two sons together. His chest swelled, and he seemed to breathe for the first time since the ordeal began. He was humbled he had found God's favor. If he could but find it once more.

Jeremy stood over the fire, tending a large pot filled with vegetables and salt pork. Their eyes met but words were not needed. Barnabas turned to the medicine man and, with praise and thanksgiving, loaded a sled with coats and provisions to keep his family through the winter months, and sent him on his way.

"I thank God that Benjamin will be well."

"There is much to be thankful for there." Jeremy ladled the broth into a crock.

Barnabas took the bowl, but remained before his brother. Moisture collected in the corners of his eyes. "I must find Mary."

"I know." He took the crock once again and set it on the table. He rubbed the wrinkles on his forehead. "She knew I would be arriving soon. I know she was excited about the blue slate. Mayhap she is down at the bay now."

"Do you think she wants to return to England?"

"She has never quit missing her family. I know she tries to make all seem well, but if she has given up on you, I think it is where she would go. There are not many ships that come to our harbor. Mine is the only one at dock. If she sought passage on *The Swallow,* she would know that I would advise her Yennicott is where God wants her to be. But still, she might decide to seek my help."

"As soon as I am sure Benjamin is going to be all right, I want to go to the ship. I have to find her. I cannot stop until I do."

"Barn, we are not thinking this through. Methinks we ought to ask Mary's friends first. Truly she will want to go back to England, but do you think she would go to the harbor first?"

"You're right, of course. I'll send Joseph to the Terrys'. Most likely we'll find her there."

33

Joseph returned with the unhappy news that Mary had not been seen. Benjamin, nourished by the soup, sat up for the first time in two days. He joked with his father, uncle, and brother, but panicked when he found no one knew the whereabouts of Mary. "Father, you must find her. I love her. We can't lose her. You and Joseph both want her back too, do you not? You love her, do you not?"

"Certes. Benjamin, I do. But you must rest. Uncle Jeremy and I are ready to go and search, but I needed to know you would be all right."

He left his sons and went out to ready Northstar. He rode circles as Jeremy unhitched Starlight. He'd rather go alone, but his brother wouldn't hear of it. Mary might have fled to the Corchaug fort and Winnie, but inspection of the trampled snow in the front yard didn't yield a clue. Jeremy swung up on Starlight and they urged the Old English Blacks down the lane.

Snow shimmered like diamonds in the clear sunlight, and they studied every nuance in the crystals.

"Look, Barn — see the footsteps? They're small like Mary's boots, and they head for the harbor."

"Let's go. You were right — she wants to go home." They rode hard down the tree-lined road and images of Mary, smiling as she pointed to snowcapped roots on their first day here, haunted his thoughts. This was home now. Her home. He must find her.

They reined in the horses and left them huddled together by the dock. Barnabas could not contain himself and hurried up the plank to the ship. He paused at the top and was joined by the first officer. Jeremy gave the order for all crew to search the ship. He wasn't convinced Mary didn't slip aboard unnoticed.

Barnabas charged ahead to the great cabin, the one he and Mary had shared with the boys. He looked back at Jeremy. "I know you want to lead the search, but I must look here first. Methinks this is where she would come." He burst through the door but found it empty.

A thorough search from stern to bow, upper deck, lower deck, and 'tween deck revealed no clues of Mary's whereabouts. With sagging shoulders he followed Jeremy reluctantly down the plank. The creaking and groaning of the ship as it rocked in the water seemed to emphasize the emptiness he felt.

Billows of smoke rose in the west. As Barnabas swung heavily onto his horse, he caught his breath.

Jeremy followed his gaze. "Is something burning?"

"Aye — it's a signal from the sachem. He told me if he ever required assistance from me, he would send the signal. Do you see the pattern? One smoke, a pause, three. In a few minutes he will repeat that same pattern. Let us not tarry. It's a message meant only for me." He dug his heels into his horse and Jeremy followed suit.

They urged their horses to a gallop, hooves barely touching the slippery snow. The smoke signal could not be ignored. He'd made a solemn vow to the sachem and would not break the trust. Besides, what if Mary was there? She wasn't on the ship, and footprints were obliterated on the shore. She could be anywhere.

He urged Northstar yet again, and Jeremy

kept pace with him, Starlight's sea legs hitting firm with each stride.

Their horses' sides heaved and steam blew from their flared nostrils as they rode through the log palisade and finally arrived at the center of the fort. The men rode directly to the waiting sachem. He looked deeply troubled, but there was not a threat apparent. "I saw your signal and we came with haste. I pray you are well, and your people are safe?"

"Treasured friend. I am well. But my people have heavy hearts. Today we learned your son will live. That gives us great gladness. But we have one amongst us who brings with her a sorrow we all share. You, treasured friend, are the only one who can bring joy to this fort again."

"Mary! Is Mary here?"

Jeremy put out a hand to steady his brother.

The sachem stretched out his hands as well. "Wauwineta found her by the bay and brought her here. She was distraught and looking for a ship. She made Wauwineta promise not to tell anyone. After a night's sleep, Wauwineta has requested I find you. She wants to talk to you." The great sachem looked at Jeremy. "Alone."

"Of course." Jeremy turned to mount

Mary's horse.

The sachem stopped him. "You are brother to my friend. I have a pipe to share with you." He nodded toward his dwelling.

Jeremy bowed. "I would be honored." He glanced at Barnabas, who stood staring at Wauwineta's home. "God is with you, Barn." He followed the sachem inside.

Barnabas closed the distance between him and the hut. The door opened before he could reach for it and Wauwineta appeared.

"Mr. Horton, I am glad you are here," she said softly. "We must stay outside. You have spoken to our sachem?"

"Aye. He tells me Mary is here. Let me go to her, I beg you. Now. I cannot wait." He started to brush past her, but she held her ground and took his arm to gently steer him away from the entrance.

"We must speak. There is much for you to know about Mary. She will need to tell you, but I must tell you things first. She hurts —"

"Aye, I know. I have caused her to hurt. It is my fault. I know that. I accept all blame."

"Let me finish my words with you before you speak."

He looked down at his feet, knowing he would do anything he had to, anything God required of him, to have Mary back.

"She is in much pain and she wanted to go back to her people. Her people in England. She hoped it would be best for you and someday you might love again. She wanted that for you because she loves you so."

He looked up quickly into Wauwineta's dark eyes. His voice hoarse with emotion, his words a plea. "I do love her. With all of my heart. She is my life now and I cannot go on without her. I have asked God's forgiveness. I must tell her, she needs to know."

"I will go and speak to Mary. If she says yes, she will come to you to speak. She must be the one who decides."

"Tell her I love her. Tell her Benjamin is getting well and Joseph is so very worried about her. Please."

Wauwineta slipped inside the hut, Smoke at her heels.

Peace washed over him, knowing the outcome was in God's hands. He looked up to the sky and thanked his Father that Mary was safe. Dark clouds drifted in once again, bringing the possibility of more snow. He took a deep breath. The snow had caused so many troubles, but he would keep the peace that passed all understanding. He would put his trust in God.

Winnie sat down next to Mary, by the fire. "I am still learning about your God. There is much to learn. But, Mary, there is something He has taught me long ago, even before I knew His name. And that is His gift of love. He has blessed us with it. Do you not believe your Barnabas could love you after he had such a love with Ann? Let me tell you.

"When Abigail was born, I loved her so much my heart ached. I found quickly I was with child again. I watched my little Abigail grow while my belly did too. And I despaired. How could I love another child? How could I love it with the same deep, abiding love I felt for my first child? It was a love I would die for. And then Wren was born and God had blessed me twice with the overwhelming love that is a mother's. I have six children now, and He has never forsaken me. Do you think He would do less for you?"

Mary never doubted the deep love Winnie had for her children. God's love for His children was like that, wasn't it?

Winnie continued. "How great is our God! He did not leave Barnabas when Ann died. No, instead He led him to you. He blessed him twice with a great and wonderful love. Barnabas knows this now. We have spoken and I see his heart. Do not run away. Be strong. Do this for Barnabas and the child in your belly. Do this for you and your Lord."

Tears welled as Mary looked at Winnie. "Did you tell him we shall have a child?" Her voice trembled.

"No, my friend, he does not know. He does not know and yet he is desperate to find you. He is desperate to tell you of his love. He does not need a child to make him love you. I look at him, and I think he has always loved you. But he was afraid if he loved you, he would be saying goodbye to Ann. I see that."

"Winnie, I tried so hard to win Barney's love. I forgot to ask God to guide me."

"But God has not forgotten you." Winnie took Mary's hand. "Are you ready to talk with your Barney? He waits outside. I thought he would not listen and come right in, but he is respectful of you and does not want to lose you." She walked to the door and turned back to her friend. "Are you still his?"

"Yes, Winnie. I have always been his." She closed her eyes. "Lord, thank You for answered prayer. Forgive my impatience. Amen." She walked through the door.

Barney wandered to the inlet bordering the fort as the sun slowly sank from the sky, casting a shimmering stream of liquid gold on the water. As the last bit of light disappeared, he bowed his head. "Lord my Father, I pray Thee, do not take my Mary from me. Do not let her disappear from my life." As the full moon rose and the clouds closed in, he turned in agony.

There stood Mary. Her beautiful face turned to his, her eyes glistening with tears. He wished he could see their color, to know the source of her tears. "Mary . . ." was all he could manage.

"Barney, there is much to say, so much to tell you." Her body quivered as she spoke.

His heart lurched in fear that she would tell him she wanted to go back to England. That she no longer loved him. "Hush, my sweet, hush." He leaned toward her and tenderly lifted her chin with his finger. His lips pressed hers with a tentative kiss. He wanted to take her in his arms and hold her forever, but did she want the same?

"Barney —" She began again.

"Aye, there is so much to say. I only pray we have a lifetime to say it. Mary, my Mary.

Do you not know? You are the love of my life. There is no one else on this earth that I could love more. Ann was the love of my life the moment I met her. I loved her with all of my heart, with every breath I took. If God had indeed allowed me to take her place the day she died, I would have gladly — I loved her so. To love someone again in that way was beyond my comprehension. But God is the author of miracles. Only He can take a man as empty as I and fill me to capacity. It does not mean I love Ann any less. Indeed, that is the miracle. God has shown me that."

She collapsed into his arms. He drank in the sweetness of her scent as his lips gently kissed the top of her head and traced their way down to her eager lips. They kissed, sharing all of the joy two hearts could hold.

Mary stepped back and took his hands in hers. "There is more to think about than just you and me, Barney." She took a breath and continued. "First there is Jay. He is so unhappy with me and I know not what to —"

"You know how much Joseph is like me. He hurt so much when he lost his mother. Mayhap he was afraid of letting her go. Or mayhap he didn't want to love and lose again. I don't know. But I do know that he realized how much he cares for you when he thought he'd lost you."

Finally he drew back. "Mary . . ." He struggled to continue. "Something happened the day Ann died . . ."

"I know, Barney. Lizzie said it would take time. She —"

"Nay, my sweet, that is not what I need to tell you. I have struggled so much with this."

"What, Barney? What happened?"

"There was a babe. A sweet little girl. We did not know Ann was with child, though I thought she might be. I had noticed a thickening of her waist. I waited for her to tell me. Mary, I fear I was wrong to wait. I should have asked her. If I had known she was with child, I would never have let her tend Joseph and Benjamin. They were so sick, it would not have been good for Ann in such a condition."

"Do you think she knew?"

"I know not, but most certainly if she'd felt a quickening she would have told me. She became very ill. I wrapped her in the red sheets, built the fire. I wanted to call the physician, but she said nay, she did not want to be bled. The next morning she miscarried and then died. I was so stricken with horror at what had happened. There was no time to call a physician or a midwife.

My beautiful wife and baby girl were both gone.

"I knew they would not bury our little girl. No church burial for such an early birth. I named her Anne, after her mother, and wrapped her in a blanket to bury her myself. I would have liked to have buried her with her mother, but people would have thought me mad. Instead, I put her in a little grave, under the cherry grove." His chest convulsed in a silent sob.

"I am so sorry — I . . ."

He breathed deeply, determined to tell her everything. She needed to know. He needed to finally allow her into those hidden places of his heart, those places he had tried so hard to keep from everyone. "I had just lost my love, and to bury our sweet babe was more than I thought I could endure. I never told a soul. I sent young Joseph, with Benjamin in hand, down the lane to fetch the reverend, and I wrapped Ann in her robe. Her funeral was a nightmare for me and the guilt I felt was overwhelming. I set the blue slate over her grave and promised her I would never forget her, or our love."

"Oh, Barney, the pain —"

"Pain, aye. The deepest pain anyone could imagine. I thought I could leave the pain in England, but it followed me here. I could not see that I let my pain hurt you, Mary. It was not until you left that I handed the pain to God and put it in His hands. When I saw the blue slate, I knew you not only loved me, but understood me in such a perfect way. It could only be from God. I fell to my knees and prayed that He would give you back to me. God waited patiently for me to surrender my all to Him, and then He led me to you."

He searched her face, looked deeply into her misty eyes. "I know you have disliked this question in the past . . . but, Mary, are you . . . ?" He placed his hand on her belly. "I must know this, my love. I must take care of you, protect you."

Her radiance reminded him of the day they were married. "Yes, we shall have a babe. Winnie has told me I am with child. She knows these things. She tells me the babe will come after the summer." A blush spread across her cheeks, and her eyes, the color of brilliant emeralds, shone as the dark clouds played hide-and-seek with the sugar-cake moon.

Barnabas thought of Ann, their two beautiful boys, and the little girl they never knew. His heart beat wildly, but with joy. He tenderly pulled Mary close, his thoughts of the child they would have, the love they would share. "You make me the man God intended me to be. I love you, my sweet."

A single, moonlit flake of snow drifted down to land perfectly on his cheek. Mary traced it with her finger and smiled. "Look, Barney, angel tears. An angel cries tears of joy tonight."

ACKNOWLEDGMENTS

Writing a novel seems like such a solitary endeavor, and indeed it is as the creative juices flow and the author puts words on paper. But publication is never a solitary venture, for it takes the proverbial village to produce a book. But not just any village.

I've been incredibly blessed by the people God has put in my path. I would like to begin by thanking God, my Father, for His tender care, mercy, and grace.

My mother was the inspiration for this book, and my dad gave me the foundation: a love of family, a love of books, and a voracious appetite to read. When I began writing my novel, he gave me encouragement. Thank you, Dad, for believing in me. My three sweet daughters, Jennifer, Lisa, and Kelly, thank you for showing me what family truly is!

An enormous thank-you to my editor, Vicki Crumpton. You have a keen insight and attention to detail, wrapped in humor and kindness, and I know how lucky I am! I am so blessed to be able to work with you and the whole Revell team! Lindsay, Erin, Michele, Jen, Claudia, Barb, Cheryl, and Twila are all fantastic to work with. I love you all!

Thank you to my tenth-grade lit teacher, Mr. Muldoon, for reinforcing my love of story.

I am grateful to Geoffrey Fleming, director of the Southold Historical Society, for his assistance and expertise on the early years of Southold. He regaled the three sisters from Oregon with his tales of buried silver spoons and impressed on us what it means to know your family's story. I'm also grateful to Melissa Andruski and Dan McCarthy, both of the Southold Free Library's Whitaker Collection. Their knowledge and willingness to help me track down elusive information enriched my story and made research a delight. Dan also works in the archives at the Southold Historical Society and has been invaluable in assisting me on my trips to Southold. He continues to send me links and tidbits important to my work. Melissa has been incredible in her enthusiasm and gracious support. Her willingness to assist me in accessing material went beyond the Whitaker Collection. She knew my desire to see (and touch!) the actual oak cask that Barnabas and Mary brought with them on *The Swallow* and met me early on a Saturday morning with the key to the Historical Society's Pine Neck Barn. The loft also housed a diorama of Barnabas and Mary's kitchen. What a thrill — and I was able to use my snapshots of the cask and kitchen for my novel descriptions!

I had the amazing opportunity to study seventeenth-century cooking with the wonderful Alice Ross at her studio in Smithtown, Long Island, and spent the day learning how to bake bread like Barnabas did. We cooked a complete hearth meal — including splitting our own wood — with only the fare and implements that would have been available to the colonists. Thank you, Alice, for your generous hospitality and the chance to relive what my ninth great-grandmother lived every day!

In 2008, I answered a tiny ad in the local paper that read "Tell Me What You Read" and found myself the office manager for one of the top literary agents in the country! Thank you, Natasha Kern, for teaching me not only what it takes to be an office manager but for mentoring me in the world of publishing.

Not many authors have the opportunity to thank two agents for one book, but I am so honored to have met and signed with Barbara Scott, of the WordServe Literary Agency, and agent extraordinaire! Thank you, Barbara, for your belief in my novel, your friendship, and your hard work. I have such heartfelt gratitude for you!

In 2009, I was fortunate to meet one of my favorite authors, Jane Kirkpatrick, at her book signing in Hood River, Oregon. She would be teaching at Bob Welch's Beachside Writers Weekend Conference in Yachats, Oregon, and they still had an opening. I jumped at the chance to attend and have gone almost every year since. She is truly an inspiring author and speaker. Thank you, Jane, for validating me as a writer and for the wonderful friend and mentor you are!

I'm thankful for the incredible opportunity to learn and be mentored by the industry professionals of the American Christian Fiction Writers, the Romance Writers of America, and Bob Welch and Jane Kirkpatrick's Beachside Writers.

A big thank-you to author and freelance editor Christina Berry Tarabochia — a mentor and friend — for her support and advice.

Through all of this, Tom has been with

me. He is my first reader, my friend, and my one true love. Thank you, sweet husband!

For more information about Rebecca DeMarino and her books, please visit www.rebeccademarino.com. You may contact Rebecca on Facebook at www.facebook.com/AuthorRebecca DeMarino, Twitter @rebeccademarino, pinterest.com/rebeccademarino and google.com/+RebeccaDeMarino

My mother, Helen Jean Horton Worley, grew up listening to stories about her ancestor Barnabas Horton, and how he'd come across from England on a ship called *The Swallow*. But the details were obscure, and it wasn't until my brother became interested in genealogy and traced our links back to Barnabas that we discovered our history in Southold, Long Island.

In 1999, I found Horton Point on a map and asked Mom if she'd like to fly out and visit the lighthouse named after her eighth great-grandfather. We flew first to Boston to visit her sister, then drove down through Connecticut and took the ferry from New London to Orient Point. Little did we know we followed almost the same path as the Hortons did in the 1600s!

We were amazed at the information about Barnabas that the Southold Historical Society possessed and marveled at the Horton Point Lighthouse, commissioned in 1790 by George Washington. It was built in 1857 on the land originally owned by Barnabas Horton.

We discovered Barnabas was considered one of the founding fathers of Southold and had built the first timber-framed house on eastern Long Island. He was a widower with two young sons when he married Mary and then sailed to New England. There seemed to be much information about Barnabas, but little about the woman who was my ninth great-grandmother.

My mother passed away in 2005, and since then I've made many trips back to Southold, always wondering about Mary. A large slab of blue slate, with a legible epitaph he is said to have written himself, still marks Barnabas's grave in the Old Burying Ground of Southold. I've never found Mary's grave.

I wondered about Mary's motivations and hopes and desires. Why did she marry this man with two young boys and follow him across an ocean, leaving family behind? And so, in the fall of 2008, I began writing my novel.

In my research I found few original documents to base my story on. It is believed that Barnabas and Mary Horton came over on *The Swallow* somewhere between 1633 and 1638. There are no ship passenger records to prove that and no records for *The Swallow.* There are no diaries or journals that remain from the first English families to settle Southold — or Yennicott, as it was called in the early 1600s. Indeed, they may have been too busy surviving to record the events as they happened.

The earliest of the Southold Town Records, from possibly 1639 or 1640 to 1651, have been lost for generations. Rev. Epher Whitaker, historian and pastor of The First Church of Southold, wrote in 1881: "In their absence it seems impossible to determine how early in 1640, or it may be in 1639, the first English settlers were living within the bounds of this Town, which has long been noted as the oldest town on Long Island." He also notes in his book, *History of Southold, L.I.,* that most likely the early settlers were there many months, perhaps two years, before the official organization of the church on October 21, 1640.

The dates I have chosen for my story are based on the likelihood that the immigrants were in Yennicott a year or two before the township and church were established and because Barnabas and Mary's first child, Caleb, was born there in 1640.

The exact date Barnabas built their house is not known, but the plaque on the corner of Horton Lane and Main Street states early 1640s. It was a grand house and six generations of Hortons lived in it before it was torn down in the 1870s. Barnabas's occupation on one document is listed as a baker, though his family were wealthy land and mill owners in England (another paradox), and for story purposes, I have him build a large house for Mary, with an amazing hearth and oven. Most likely, the original house was small and added on to as their family grew.

The spelling of places and towns was another difficulty, as spelling among even the well-educated Englishmen was subject to phonics and words were spelled the way they sounded. Thus, I found Barnabas and Mary's hometown of Mowsley, England, spelled four different ways, including "Mousely" on the blue slate gravestone. Yennicott is also found as Yennicock, and Long Island could be found spelled with an "e" among other spellings. My editor suggested going with the modern-day spellings, and in the end I'm glad I did!

In addition to definite historical differences, I also had family lore to honor in my story. For example, it's been passed down through generations that Barnabas brought his blue slate with him when he sailed on *The Swallow.* Historians of the 1800s say that was highly unlikely, due to the weight restrictions on the small ships and the fact the cargo was actually people with few of their possessions. I was intrigued and decided to write that controversy right into my story.

Epher Whitaker wrote in *History of Southold, L.I.,* "A goodly number of women — faithful daughters, wives and mothers — who have no written record here (Southold), doubtless surpassed in patience, industry, virtue and piety many sons, husbands and fathers whose names are thus known. They shall in a future day and henceforth and forever have their proper and honorable meed when the names, written in the Book of Life, become known to all mankind."

Indeed, their names shall be known in God's Book of Life. For today, it is my humble desire to give a voice to those courageous women who followed their men across a tempestuous sea to a wild, mostly unknown land.

As I wrote *A Place in His Heart,* I took the sometimes confusing facts, added in some fun family lore, and laced it with imagination. I hope you enjoyed reading the story as much as I enjoyed writing it!

ABOUT THE AUTHOR

Rebecca DeMarino is a member of American Christian Fiction Writers, Romance Writers of America, and The Southold Long Island Historical Society. Rebecca is retired from a major airline and lives in the Pacific Northwest with her husband, Tom. This is her debut novel. Learn more at www .rebeccademarino.com.

The employees of Thorndike Press hope you have enjoyed this Large Print book. All our Thorndike, Wheeler, and Kennebec Large Print titles are designed for easy reading, and all our books are made to last. Other Thorndike Press Large Print books are available at your library, through selected bookstores, or directly from us.

For information about titles, please call:
  (800) 223-1244

or visit our Web site at:
  http://gale.cengage.com/thorndike

To share your comments, please write:
Publisher
Thorndike Press
10 Water St., Suite 310
Waterville, ME 04901